FIELDS OF LIGHT

Fields of Light

Based on the true story of
Brian Grover and Ileana Petrovna

JIM RICKARDS

BLAKE

Published by Blake Publishing Ltd,
3 Bramber Court, 2 Bramber Road, London W14 9PB, England

First published in Great Britain in 1995

ISBN 1 85782 077 0

British Library Cataloguing-in-Publication Data:
A catalogue record for this book is available
from the British Library.

Typeset by Pearl Graphics, Hemel Hempstead

Printed in Finland by WSOY

1 3 5 7 9 10 8 6 4 2

Fields of Light is entirely based on a true story.
However, certain characters and events have been
fictionalised by the author for dramatic purposes.

My thanks:

to Helen Trickett who helped me with all things Russian, underwent painstaking research for me and never lost patience;

to mum, dad, Katie and Sue, for telling it like it was (or wasn't) depending upon how fragile I felt at the time;

to John, for waiting for two years;

to Bernard Millar, (wherever you are) for getting me started again;

to Nicki, for keeping me going;

to Jacky Jackson, for making me finish;

And finally, to Helen Willey – I told you I would.

In loving memory of
Justin Hathaway.
We'll all miss you.

Over lakes, over ravines
Mountains, forests, clouds, seas
Beyond the sun, beyond the ether
Beyond the limits of the galaxies.

My soul, you move with agility
And like a good swimmer who collapses in the water
You furrow the deep expanse
With an unspeakable male delight.

Fly far away from these fetid marshes,
Purify yourself in the upper air
And drink like some pure divine liqueur
The clear fire that fills the limpid spaces.

Beyond the boredom and the endless cures
Which burden our fogged existence with their weight
Happy is the man who can, with vigorous wing,
Fly up to the fields of light and serenity,

The man whose thoughts like larks
Make free flight towards morning skies
– Who hovers over life, and understands effortlessly
The language of flowers and voiceless things!

Charles Baudelaire – 'Elevation' from *Les Fleurs du Mal*

SOUTH AFRICA
1991

Here I am now, an old man in a dry month, staring at a land cracked at the seams. The air holds a pressure against my face. There is no wind, but the calm is thick with unease. You would not think so, Lena, if you were sitting here with me on this *stoep*. You would take my cold hands and squeeze them, rubbing the loose skin that clings desperately to bone, until they felt life again. You would turn my head in your palms, kiss me, and say, 'It will be fine'.

I live on the farm alone now and I feel the empty spaces around me. Where there used to be children fighting over a catapult there is a still room; where there used to be the clattering of pans and bubbling of boiling water there is a clean, cold kitchen.

Yet there is advantage in every disadvantage – you just take the negative away. It is peaceful here. The quiet helps bring to order thoughts that clatter around my skull, memories untamed by the strictures of time. They jostle for position, overlap. The spaces between events expand or contract until I am no longer sure what went where or who was who. I should not be surprised – life does not run from A to B. It is constantly pulled back or propelled forward. The present is shaped by the past and the past, through recollection, transformed by the present.

Now, however, as a wisp of cirrus hovers over the Soutpansberg mountains, I listen to the regular tick of the grandfather clock in the hall behind me and I have a sense of perspective. I place events with every swing of the pendulum and while the cloud disperses over the mountains, the view grows clear.

To my left is the track that winds through the farm, down a gentle hill then onto a flat plain where it meets tarmacked road. It runs straight for miles to the nearest village. Sometimes I come out here just to follow the road with my eyes. It is enclosed on either side by a wire fence with regular wooden poles, a regular six feet apart. And sometimes when I need a walk I go down the track and stand in the middle of the road facing the direction of the village. The fence posts close to me are unique. One has a knot that sticks out like Vesuvius, another a small inscription, TOBY LOVES ELLIE, cut into the bark. But further away they become black sticks, all the same. The spaces between them get smaller and smaller until finally they merge into one.

The edges of the road are different. They point towards each other but never meet. Perspective, like age, can be a great deceiver.

My hearing is still good. I can tell a cricket from a cicada, a whisper from a whimper. And though, when the sun sinks rapidly as it is now, blacked out by the bush on the horizon, my eyes strain for the definition, for the detail I might once have recognised, my sight isn't as bad as it might be. I can still read my books. Without glasses I might add. And the bones may creak when I roll out of bed in the morning, but, after a few warm rays to oil the joints, I can ride into town on my bike, pop into the local store, say my hellos. My heart beats fainter than it once did but the blood still gets round. My skin is like leather, weather-beaten, eroded by time, but the flies no longer bite (no juice) and the sun no longer burns (you can't tan leather twice). There are indeed advantages to age.

The chair creaks as I rock to and fro, wood on wood, flexing my toes against the evening. It is comfortable, and should be. It has moulded into my shape over the years. The intricately woven cord has loosened round the frame and stretched in the middle. It has complied willingly with the requirements of a body that needs to sit most of the time. It has taken on my impression and the thought is comforting. When I get up, I am still there in the seat.

That's what people really want. To leave their indelible mark on the world. To be able to say, before finally crossing the line, 'I did this. I caused that smile.' Even a small mark like a scratch on a tree in a forest. One instance would be enough, so I've been lucky. When I go, I will go contented. For nothing physical is indelible in the end. The bark grows over its scars, the tide smooths the footprint in the sand – even the smile fades. Time erodes material things. Only memories can be preserved. True, they might grow blurred at the edges as you get older, but you can catch them, a moment in time, put words on paper, pass on tales from parent to child. The details may change in the retelling, the locations more exotic, the characters somehow not as you originally intended, but the essence remains the same.

I am ninety. That's 2,838,240,000 seconds, give or take a million. And each one was a unique moment in time. These moments, together, make up my life. My story.

THE MANOR HOUSE
1909

Until I was nine years old, I didn't go to school. I was educated by a governess called Miss Roberts. She looked after me and I loved her. She was the opposite of everything my parents had taught me to be – lively, warm, open-minded. She showed me how to perceive things, how to scratch the surface of the world and peer inside at the uncompromising core.

It was sharp and windy the morning we went to see the pond. The sort of day where you think you can bite a chunk out of the air. Miss Roberts took my hand and we walked through the apple orchard and into the grove where the light was thin, the air damp and smelling of moss. The ground was spongy underfoot. We were intruders in an enchanted land.

Miss Roberts talked to me in her soft voice, words bouncing against the trees in rhythm with our steps. 'This is an oak, and that is a sycamore, and there is a birch with its silver bark.' Along the way, she told me how to work out the age of a tree that had been felled by counting the rings on the stump. We stooped over one, an oak chopped clean through, and I reached one hundred and twelve before stopping, out of breath but proud that I had counted so far.

'Do trees die of old age?' I asked, amazed that anything could live so long.

'Eventually. Everything does, Brian.'

'Did this one?'

'No, no. It was cut down by Alex.'

Alex was a farmhand who sometimes helped father at weekends. He was a big, burly man with a hairy back. I remembered him from the previous summer heaving great rocks into our stream so that we could step across when we went for a walk. I remembered him glistening with sweat and grunting against the weight.

'Why did he do that?'

'So that you could be warm in winter.'

I couldn't make the connection. Miss Roberts noticed my frown and chuckled.

'How do we keep warm?' she asked me, hands on hips like a school mistress, which I suppose in a way she was.

'In front of the fires.'

'And what do we put in the fires?'

'Coal in the stove. And wood by the hearth.'

'And where does wood come from?'

I waited a few seconds before answering, seeing the sense of it. 'From trees.'

'There you are. You'll make a professor yet.'

I stared at the stump and at the empty space where the oak once was. I pictured what it would have been like all those years, bending in storms, catching rain in cupped leaves, standing cold as stone in winter.

Miss Roberts stroked my head, patted me on the back. She sensed something wrong. She always could. 'Don't worry. There are lots more.'

'But not this one.'

'No,' she sighed, 'not this one.'

We left the stump, let it disappear behind us. Ahead, there was an opening of light. I picked up a twig and swished at it. I walked head down, kicking my feet with angry stabs through piles of rotting leaves.

Though kind, though understanding, Miss Roberts did not tolerate any degree of subversiveness. She whirled me round, a hand on each shoulder. 'Master Brian, I will not have you sulking on a fine morning like this. I came out here before breakfast because you said you wanted to come. I didn't have to, it's not expected. You have a choice. We turn back now or you try, hard as it might seem, to put some semblance of a smile on your face.'

'But it's not fair Miss Roberts.'

'What isn't?'

'Alex is a murderer!' I blurted it out and I immediately wished I hadn't.

Miss Roberts' face changed then. It creased down the middle, eyebrows darted inwards and her nose contracted narrow and pointy. It happened in no time but I saw it all, each bit separately. I saw her hand swing out, tried to duck, but it slapped against my ear. I yelped like a puppy, but couldn't hear my own cry for the ringing in my head.

'Don't you ever say that again!' Miss Roberts cried and her mouth was a dark cave. 'Or I'll tell your father and he will put the belt to you so hard you won't be able to walk for a week. Do you understand?'

I nodded through tears.

'Right, now we shall go to the pond. If only to take your mind off such disgusting notions.'

We walked in silence through the tunnel of trees. After my sobs softened to an occasional sniff, Miss Roberts quietly slipped her hand into mine.

'You must understand,' she said, 'that young gentlemen

do not say things like that. Alex is . . . Alex is a kind man, a good *gentle* man. He helped us all through the winter.' She seemed to emphasise the 'all' and there was a faraway look in her eyes which I didn't understand. 'He keeps the estate in order,' she went on. 'Sometimes that means chopping down trees and pulling up weeds. And yes, it is killing, but there is good reason behind it. So it's not murder. Besides, that tree hasn't disappeared, it has simply changed. When it's put on the fire, it burns into soot which goes up the chimney and into the air.'

We reached the clearing where the pond was. She pointed at the sky where a small puff of cloud skidded past.

'Some of it is probably up in that cloud. Think of it like this: when leaves fall off the trees in autumn, they don't just go away, they transform. The leaf feeds the soil, the soil feeds the tree, the tree feeds the leaf – all in a big circle. That's how the world works.' She swung her arm in a great arc. Despite myself, I smiled. It sounded like a fine notion.

The surface of the pond was opaque white, but when I got close I could see the bottom. Gravel and slimy pebbles, swathes of weed like hairy monsters, and tadpoles. Great sweeps of them, scatting in every direction when I dipped my hand in the water. They were all head and no body, just little wiggling tails. Miss Roberts called me over to the other side of the pond where she was peering over a bank of bullrushes.

I joined her, nestling my head under her arm. I could hear her breaths short and shallow. She pointed to a white mass just beneath the surface. Thousands and thousands of eggs. Tiny, translucent spheres encasing specks of black. I peered closer. One of the eggs was moving, the black speck pushing hard against the walls of its prison. Suddenly, it broke through.

'How did it know. How did it know to do that?' I cried out looking up.

'Now that *is* a question,' Miss Roberts replied. 'If you discovered the answer to that one, you'd be a God.'

When I looked back the speck had gone. A gust of wind swept over the pond and the surface buckled in a million places. I thought of the bits of life lost in their enormous sea and I knew, with a certainty that shook me, that one day I would leave my parents' world of sparkling silver and carpet lawns behind me.

Part One

DANCE

SARAWAK, BORNEO
1930

The Rejang river was deep and cool and smelt of late summer. It drifted slowly, with nowhere to go except the next bend. Our raft hung in midstream, held by a rope-and-stone anchor. I tightened the last thread of vine around the last cane pole and sighed.

'That's it,' I said. 'All done. Not bad eh?' Frank sat with his legs dangled over the side, nursing a bottle of the beer that was specially imported to keep all the riggers happy. He grunted.

The sun dipped finally behind a bank of cloud and on either side of us the forest closed in. Century-old roots clawed at the banks. I watched them turn from silver to grey as the light faded. Then I lay back and stared at the sky. There was little of it left. The trees curled over the river like a tunnel of hands clasped in prayer.

'It's over, you know,' Frank said.

'What is?'

'Everything.'

I kicked the water. Spray scattered into the evening air, landed on the surface with a string of pops.

'You've had too many beers Frank.'

'I never drink on the job.'

'What are these then?' I rattled the empty bottles beside me.

Frank nodded slowly. 'Doesn't count – there's no job anymore.'

He pulled a bunch of bottles from the water and untied one with a practised hand. 'You got a bit of catching up to do. Here.'

I caught it, cracked it open with my teeth. A feat I had learnt from Frank years ago. 'How do you know?'

'Because I listen. I take in what's going on around me. Unlike some.'

'What's that supposed to mean?'

He chuckled grimly. 'The intellectual with his head in the clouds. The prof who knows a little of everything but really knows nothing.'

I didn't rise. He would have his say, apologise later. I was used to it.

'You haven't even heard the rumours Brian. I was told today, confirmed by Lord God Almighty himself.'

'Butterworth?'

He nodded. '"End of the month," he said. "I'm awfully sorry, but I'm afraid wah going to heff to let you chaps go."'

'Sounds as though he was heartbroken.'

'Sure.'

We sat silently for a while, the raft bobbing gently beneath us, then Frank said, 'Hope the bitches dry up soon as we're gone. Hope they drill through to the other side of the earth and find nothing but shit.'

'Steady on.'

Frank wheeled on me and the raft lurched precariously.

'All you can say is *steady on*. They've screwed us, man. Where are we going to find work now? Mars?'

Sarawak, Borneo 1930

'We're all in the same boat,' I said quietly. 'Things'll look up.'

Frank was not a violent man but he was big, and when he was angry he was very big. I had seen him like this a few times, always when he felt helpless and the only way to bring him around was to speak soft, coaxing words as though he were a baby. Perhaps he had a right to be angry. He'd been working the wells for twenty years from Texas to the Middle East, seen every kind of hardship there was, erected derricks in heat so fierce you could fry an egg on the steel slabs. I remembered him on the first well we built together, hanging from platforms a hundred feet up, swinging along the girders like a baboon. He had layers of dead skin on the underside of his fingers where blisters had popped and healed over a hundred times. His massive shoulders emanated raw power, his forearms were flecked with ingrained tar and scarred by blasts of scalding steam. His body was designed for this life, it had absorbed all the knocks and even at forty was still capable of more. But now it seemed there was to be no more.

I had met Frank here in Sarawak six years ago. I was fresh out of Cambridge, a naive college boy with an engineering degree and the wrong accent. No-one – least of all my parents – understood why I wanted to dirty my hands. A man with your background they said! They couldn't see that it was my background I was trying to escape from. I had been moulded all my life by them and naturally, I would join the army, I was good officer material, the right blood and all that. Why else would one educate one's child at Charterhouse? My father expected to be, if not proud, then at least justified in his narrow hopes for me.

I left Cambridge at the age of twenty-one with a nagging doubt in my heart. It had wriggled into me slowly without my realising it, a little snake that one day hissed, 'You don't *have* to do what is expected, you know.' The words, clear in my mind for the first time, shocked me. But what shocked me more was that I had not considered it earlier. It was so easy.

A week after graduation I deliberately missed the long-planned interview with the army recruitment officer and spent the day at Shell headquarters in London instead. My father blustered, my mother sighed but I would not be swayed. Sarawak. I rolled the syllables round in my mouth. They tasted exotic. The day I left, my father handed me a little Hindi-English dictionary. 'It's all they speak out there. Learn this, you'll have them eating out of your hand in no time.' His understanding of the world, defined in an out-of-date pocket-book.

The first few months in Sarawak were hard, littered with mistakes and failed friendships. My background made me an outsider and, without Frank's arrival on the scene, I might have thrown the whole business in and returned to England to become the Sandhurst prodigal son that my father dreamed of. Frank Brown, a great lumbering driller from Texas, just turned up one day all smiles and backslaps and hearty handshakes. A man who commanded instant respect. To my surprise, he singled me out for his attention. I was grateful but puzzled. When I knew him well enough, I asked him why and he said simply, 'You looked like you needed help.'

I had. I was green to the business and unripe to the heat. We teamed up together and he showed me how to keep on the right side of the right people while not becoming a stooge. I learned my trade through him. He taught me the practice, I taught him the theory. By the end of the year we were overseeing a successful team and were responsible for the main well on the field.

It occurred to me now, as I cracked the top off another beer, that perhaps I had initially been just another of his pet projects, a challenge. What had happened, quite by chance, however, was that we'd formed the foundation of a long-lasting friendship. Frank never feared danger, that was clear in the way he set about his work, but he did fear vacuums. Maybe I'd been chosen to fill a space.

I patted him on the back. 'At least we got the raft finished.'

He had become quite still, staring out across the water.

'Yeah, least we did that,' he mumbled.

We had been working on it for weeks after each shift's end, going down to the village on market days and buying the cane from the locals who served us with bemused grins. The rest of the men thought we were mad, tiring ourselves out for no obvious gain. But it had cemented our friend- ship again, given us time to talk, away from the non-stop banter on the rigs. The sort of thing two boys might have done during a school holiday. Maybe for Frank that's what it was, a means of regressing. For me it was an oppor- tunity to concentrate my thoughts. There was a lot to think about.

As the day died completely, Frank lit our lamp and placed it between us. It cast a soft glow across the water. Moths danced on our shadows.

Of course, deep down even I had realised it was coming. It had been in the air for weeks. After news of the Crash had reached us there were uneasy grumblings from the men. Nobody throwing themselves off the derricks, perhaps, but a sense that things were ending. Out here on the raft, though, with the water lapping at our feet, it didn't seem to matter. We had completed our project. I wanted to enjoy the moment.

Frank had seen more into my reaction to his news than I would care to admit. Never one to mince his words he said, 'How's the dragon lady?'

'Still breathing fire across the oceans.'

He shook his head slowly. 'Should never have accepted the transfer, you know.'

'Hindsight.'

'Common sense.'

If I'd had any it would never have happened. In '26, against Frank's advice, I left Sarawak for a job on a rig off Long Beach. It was a move I lived to regret. Her name was Madeleine. I met her on the boat over to New York. She seemed fun. She'd been over to Europe, done the obligatory tour and confided, after a few drinks, that 'Mother wants me to settle down.' That appeared unlikely. She could never stop moving, spent most of her time at the tables of the ship's casino. She hunted them for opportunity, eyes flitting from table to table, establishing the best chance. I fell for her. The sophisticated lady who scoffed at tradition, the wild lady with a passion for living the moment. By the end of the voyage, I would wake in the morning, immediately planning our first meeting of the day. I dreamed of an exciting future together. I got a future with her, but it wasn't the one I had anticipated. And now it wasn't even together.

'Where now then?' Frank said. It wasn't really a question. More an expression of resignation. Sarawak had become his home over the years. In his own way, he was settled. I don't think he could ever accept that events completely out of his hands should affect his life. He simply wanted to stay put. If the world crumbled around him then let it. He would get drunk with his mates in drinking dens, wake up in some unfamiliar bed and go back to work the next day as though nothing had happened.

I, on the other hand, relished the prospect of change. The longer you stayed in a place the further your feet sank in the mud. There were a million places to go. Getting there would be half the fun.

So I said to him, 'Wherever you want. I'll probably go to

London first, see what happens. Something's bound to turn up.'

'It always does, the way you look at it.'

'You should come with me.'

But all Frank said was, 'Maybe.'

The alcohol was beginning to bite, forming shadows and lights in my mind. I was determined the shadows would lose.

'You can't run away forever, you know,' Frank said.

I could. If Madeleine was involved, I could run for as long as I wanted.

'Who says? Frank the wordly sage?'

'Frank the realist. She'll come after you one day and screw up your life.'

'She's done that once already. I won't let it happen again. Not her, not anyone.'

Frank roared a long, long laugh. When it died down I asked, 'Would you like to share it with me?'

He smiled, this time warmly. 'Brian, Brian what am I going to do with you? Whatever you'd like others to think, I know you're not the single type. You plunge in headfirst, leap before you look. So you've been bitten, but you're sure as hell not shy. For the last few months you've been a regular playboy,' he slapped me on the back, 'a regular one of the guys. Me, I know better. It's just a reaction. It's not really you.'

'And how come you're an expert suddenly on the inner recesses of my character?' I hiccupped and for a second the sound seemed to fill the silence around us.

'*The inner recesses!* The academic strides forth, the impulsive cowers. Brian, listen to me. I know you.' He grabbed my cheek and gave it a friendly shake that made me wince. 'You're a romantic. You're just too damned English to admit it!'

'Here we go. The English academic. You'll never let it drop will you?'

'No sir, I shall do my utmost to keep it going.'

'Anyway, I'm *not* a romantic.'

Frank gulped down the last of his bottle and automatically reached for another. 'Yes you are my friend. One day you'll meet a woman who'll melt your bones when you see her. You'll want to be with her every moment of the day, you'll want to know every thing about her, touch every part of her body. And when it happens you won't be able to stop yourself, no matter what's happened in your past. You'll be a jelly-legged swooner.'

'You know your problem, Frankie boy. You display all the traits of an uneducated commoner. You talk without thinking, whereas I think without talking. More constructive. At least I was taught that before you draw conclusions, you need proof.'

'OK, I'll make a bet with you.' Frank held out his hand. 'You'll prove to me by your own actions that I'm right.'

'Never in a million years!'

'I'll give you five. Five years and you'll be glued. Tempted?'

'Certainly.' I'd won already. I'd just have to wait a while to collect. 'What's the forfeit?'

There was a moment's silence as he considered the options, then he declared, 'Luncheon at Simpsons in the Strand and enough bubbly to fill a bathtub, all expenses paid.'

'And if you lose?'

'I won't. But I'll do the same for you.'

'Done.'

We shook hands on it in the dark. It was a good bet. One I had no intention of losing. Wherever we went from now, I knew I would not change.

Somewhere in the distance a voice called. It might have been my name but the words were lost in the trees. It was getting late so we went in anyway, paddling the raft to shore with planks of wood then dragging it up the muddy bank to the little hut we had used as a workshop. The voice called again, this time clearer. 'Grover, Brown! You're wanted.'

'Not for much longer,' Frank muttered. He turned to me and there was a quiet sadness in his movement. 'Still, we had some good times didn't we?'

'That we did,' I said, 'and there'll be many more ahead.'

Frank did not seem to hear me. He started the slow trudge back to the complex. I waited a while, watching him as he followed the curve of the path and disappeared.

LONDON
January 1931

I have never believed in fate. Things happen to you and you react, or you make things happen and the world around you reacts. But sometimes I wonder about the side streets, the small diversions that lead to undiscovered destinations. An overheard snippet of conversation that sparked off a thought, a letter from a friend I hadn't seen in years . . . saying yes when I should have said no. The avenue I walked down was always branching, every second of every day, and yet it is impossible to form a clear picture of anything other than the one I took. The permutations are too great. A map charting the route emerges only after many years and it is always incomplete – a single jagged line cut through a maze of ghost streets that fade into nothing. I can point at a sharp bend and say, 'There, that's where it all started', point at another earlier on, later on, and say 'But what if . . .' The fatalist might say, 'Look at the pattern, here and here – it was meant to be'. So I do, but I see only a series of decisions and external events, some which seemed unimportant at the time, others which caused much soul-searching and I come back to the same conclusion. Nothing is pre-ordained, there is no great hand of fate.

The Crash of '29 affected everyone, and though it meant upheaval to me then, perversely I am grateful for it now. If there is one defining kink in the route then that is where it must be. For without it, I might have stayed in Sarawak a few more years, grown weary and trudged down-hearted back into the arms of Madeleine and lived out her dreams of reaching the coveted title of Bank Manager before middle-age took its toll. Without it, I would never have met Lena. And without Lena my life could not have been the same. The great events shape the general direction of one's life, the choice of which side street to take is what fine tunes it.

The decision to move on from Sarawak was made easy by the sackings. I felt I was still young, still had a lot to offer. To me the world was not a fearful place. It seemed natural to just get up and go. But where? London was the obvious choice but I hadn't seen my parents for six years. We wrote to each other, two or three letters between Christmasses. A few dry words on crumpled paper. If I returned, all the old sores would break out again. I knew that but, partly out of a sense of duty and partly because it would seem like a new experience all over again, I resolved to return. When I told Frank, he grinned. 'Run home to Mumsy, there's a good boy,' he said. But I wasn't running home to anything, I was still running away. And it was my running away, along with the combination of events that followed my return to England, that led me to Ileana. Not by design, by chance.

In the end, I lasted only a few days. Mother and Father bickered at me constantly for 'the mess I had made of my life,' and the more they did so, the more they hardened my resolve to keep living the way I had. What possible sense was there in emulating the lives of these people?

We were aliens, but there were two of their species, only one of mine.

We came from a moneyed line, had the society credentials, the 'modest' mansion in the home counties. We had reputations to live up to. Now that I had come to my senses and returned to the fold, they expected me to join the West End pack – the fading glitterati who descended on theatreland in their chauffeured Bentleys and lavished their wealth on the shows as though it were some kind of charitable act. Without us, my dear, they would *all* be closed.

Mother prayed for my respectability again. Perhaps if I mingled with the suitables I might find a decent lady with whom to idle away the rest of my days. I had failed, in my parents' eyes, not only myself, but the family name. And that was hard for them to understand, and near impossible to forgive. The only advice Father had ever given me I had ignored by shunning the military. The only advice my mother had ever given me was 'never marry a woman without money' – an unbreakable law, drummed into me from birth. What did I do? I made lifelong vows with Madeleine and had lived to regret it. Money, however, was never really the problem. Our separation was probably the only thing in my life that *was* pre-destined. The closer we became, the more she mutated from the woman I had met on the boat. She desperately wanted to settle down, I desperately didn't.

I spent the week before Christmas enduring a 'told-you-so' atmosphere. They were vindicated because my life had come to naught. Father, precision-sculpted to the last detail, carved the goose on Christmas day, exhaling creakily with each thrust of the knife. *You* slice *would* slice *not* slice *listen*.

On Boxing Day, when a dusty old family friend joined us for a luncheon chat, events came to a head. Over dinner

Mother chatted politely about the great deeds being done for the poor through the Rotary Club. Father blustered that the beggars were never grateful whatever one did and I contemplated quietly the places I might be come the New Year. Coffee was served and the conversation turned to what I had been doing all these years away. I was about to answer when Mother said through thin lips 'Brian's been exploring, an expedition in Sarawak.' I cleared my throat, ready to correct her when I saw Father. His hair clung to his scalp with smooth perfection, his Kitchener whiskers twitched furiously. His eyes said, 'No.'

Finally, I understood. It wasn't just disappointment, it wasn't just shame, it was embarrassment. Their son could not be who he was. He could only be what he *should* be, or accept being nothing at all. I was a name and a life spat out in conversation only after prompting.

I let a suitable interval pass, in which Mother rapidly changed the subject, before making my excuses. Quietly, I went to my room and gathered my belongings. To admit to a son of theirs being an oil man would conjure images of coarse roustabouts with grubby hands. To admit to a son of theirs even mixing with such types simply would not do. I suspected Father had not heard of 'I am what I am,' and if he had, he would probably have thought it an unnecessary repetition.

They were a dying breed and, if I'd had any doubts before, I was convinced then that I didn't want to die with them. Yes I'd made mistakes, including thinking I could come back and be greeted with open arms, and I would continue to make mistakes but at least they would be mine.

I left a note on my dressing table explaining my sudden departure. I was sorry they felt the way they did. I would keep in touch. Perhaps the next time we met up we would be able to accept our differences. They were not to worry about me. I could look after myself. I always had.

London, January 1931

Smarting, but revelling childishly at my last line, I left the country house with its carpet lawns and sparkling silver. Two bags banged against my shoulders and in my wallet was a list of addresses where I might get work, given to me by Thomson the family lawyer. A failed marriage, three months' severance pay and parents who shrank from my inclinations. Not much to boast about after six years working around the world, but I still believed in a Happy New Year. It was one of the few resolutions I'd always been able to keep.

Early morning Charing Cross bustled with men in hats and three-button suits in different shades of grey; some rushed to work, others made the well-trodden journey to the labour exchange, a few just wandered, window-shopping for items they could no longer afford. It seemed to me they walked without thinking, passing boarded up shops, tramps curled tight in the doorways greeting oblivion with a bottle, and taxis in rank waiting idly for the next elusive customer. On the surface there was life, collectively there was movement but, when I picked out a particular face, the hopelessness hammered at me with a terrible resonance. Those lucky enough to have jobs lived with the constant fear of losing them, and would do anything – take pay cuts, tolerate miserable working conditions – to keep them.

I knew I couldn't stay here much longer. After a month of bed and breakfast and a demoralizing tour of every engineering firm in London, I was heading for my final address. Stephen Talbot, 104e The Strand. Beside it, Thomson had written, 'If all else fails, try this one. He normally has something up his sleeve. Just beware of what type of something it might be.'

Didn't sound too promising. But today was not a day

17

to be downhearted, for joining me in my last ditch effort to utilise my skills was Frank. Bleary-eyed, five o'clock shadowed and more than a little disgruntled, he had met me at Victoria Station after travelling straight up from Southampton docks on the overnight. I'd telegrammed him immediately after leaving my parents, putting a little more gloss on my situation than was honest. To be exact, I wrote: COME OVER NOW. OPPORTUNITIES GALORE. To which he replied: LIAR. SEE YOU 28TH. VICTORIA 7.30AM.

Frank jostled beside me against the tide, stabbing each passer-by with a mortal look. 'So this is the centre of the great Empire?' he called as a briefcase shoved him forward. 'No wonder it's crumbling.'

Sour grapes. Nothing approaching opportunity was to be found in the land of plenty. My telegram had caught him just as disillusionment was setting in. The moment I met him, however, it became clear that his trip here was the last of a long list of last resorts.

We made our way down St Martin's Lane, then onto the Strand coming eventually to a cubbyhole entrance that bore the name *Talbot, Enterprise Unlimited*. The T had slipped upside down and it was obvious that the sign hadn't been washed since it was erected. Newspapers were strewn across the ground and the ripe smell of old urine hung in the air. We peered through the door window. A dusty staircase and a dark landing. No lights, no sign of life.

Frank looked at me unbelieving. 'I spent weeks churning my guts out across the Atlantic for this?' It was pleasing to know that, man of the world though he was, his constitution was fallible.

I shrugged. 'This is the place. Who knows. . .'

'Yeah, yeah. Scrubbing pans, washing table tops, perhaps a bit of road-sweeping.'

'And they said the English were snobs.' As I grabbed his arm to pull him in, a gust of wind caught us full in the face. Frank yanked away from me, turned his collar up and squashed his hat firmly into his head. 'I must be mad,' he cried. 'I could be on vacation in Florida now watching the 'gators snapping the ass of my Ma. I could be in Borneo with a beer in one hand and a girl in the other. Hell, I could be *anywhere* but I'm not. I'm here, with you, following some half-assed scheme to get us a shitty job. I mean, *look* at this place.'

He had understandable reservations. I had not passed on the warnings about Talbot, fearing Frank would abandon the whole thing.

'Come on. If you don't like him, all you have to do is say no.'

'Well I'm saying no now. I'm gonna spend a few days in the country then book the next boat home.' He took a few steps down the street before I caught him.

'That's ridiculous! You've tried all your contacts, I've applied to every company in the directory. Nobody's hiring. If we leave empty-handed, go and have a holiday, make your journey worthwhile. But this Talbot fellow might have something great for us. Where's the harm in trying, at least?'

Frank faced me slowly. 'You know your problem, Brian?' I didn't, but Frank always seemed to. 'You're an optimist.'

'And what's wrong with that?'

'Life deals you an eight-high and you go "There might be possibilities here. Maybe everyone else in on seven." '

'Actually, I do know what my problem is. I'm standing on a pavement on a freezing January morning arguing with a Texan who possesses the brain power of the only Dodo that was kicked out of its nest at birth for being too stupid.'

While we stood there getting older and colder, a woman approached us. I hardly noticed her at first, I was too busy trading insults. But as she got closer, I could not help staring. She was old, no more than five feet tall with eyes sunk deep into a face of criss-crossed lines. She wore a head-scarf tied so tight around her chin that her skin rolled over the knot in a little sack. She came right up to us with inching steps. Frank hadn't seen her and was still in mid-flow when she tugged at his coat. He looked down bewildered.

'Scuse me sir, something for your button-hole sir?' She said in a tiny voice, swiftly producing a tiny sprig of heather. Frank shuffled uneasily while she reached up and popped it in his lapel. Then she did the same for me. I rummaged in my pocket for some change but she shook her head and laughed. 'Free,' she said. 'You good-lookin' gents deserve the very best.' Then she shuffled off, mutter-ing to herself or the street, whichever cared to listen.

It was a simple thing really. A fine-tuning of which I could not have understood the significance at the time.

I'd been on the verge of giving up. Frank had been adamant. He simply would not entertain the idea of being interviewed by some 'double-dealing sweatshop merchant.' But the old woman had put some perspective on our situation. She was much worse off than us, probably spent most of her days going from soup kitchen to night shelter and yet she had given us something for nothing. We, on the other hand, were about to spurn an interview that millions out there would die for simply because Frank didn't like the look of the place.

Frank smiled sheepishly. 'She's got us dressed for the occasion. I guess it would be rude not to go in,' he said.

So we did, and since that day I have silently thanked the woman who passed us on the Strand for changing the course of my life forever.

He was round as an air-balloon with lacquered hair slicked in a side parting. He wore trousers a little too tight for ample stomach. As if to compensate, his weight was securely held in by a rather garish paisley waistcoat. There were laughter lines around his eyes but whether they were a result of good humour or stress I could not tell.

He greeted me warmly, pulling the door open and me inside with what seemed a genuinely excited, 'Grover, my good fellow, thanks for the letter. Good to see you.' He looked over my shoulder to Frank who was hovering in the doorway, probably half thinking of making a quiet exit. 'And this is?' Frank nodded uneasily when I introduced him, offering his hand after an embarrassing pause.

'Here, sit down, sit down.'

There were boxes and files everywhere, paper scattered on the carpet, charts on the wall, books dusty and unread on a sloping shelf behind the desk. He cleared an in-tray off a chair for me then looked about the room in a vain search for another.

'I don't mind standing,' Frank said.

'Nonsense,' Talbot took his arm and Frank stiffened slightly at the touch. 'Here, rest your seat on this.' He dragged an upturned tea-chest across the carpet. 'Mind the edges, they're sharp.' Frank perched on a corner and gave me the raised eyebrow.

'Sorry about the mess. I seem to have let things slip a little,' Talbot said.

He eased into his chair and clasped his fingers together around his belly.

'These are terrible times,' he began portentiously, 'and they breed terrible measures. You are just two of the millions of casualties, thrown on the scrap heap because the multi-nationals' profits are down. But your resumés are impressive – intelligent men with quite a bit of experience behind you. There's always a demand for people like you, it's just a question of finding it. Find the gap and fill it. That's been my philosophy from the womb to the present day and it's served me well indeed.'

Frank leaned forward at this. 'And what gaps are there, if you don't mind me asking? My friend here has tried every firm in London.'

Talbot's eyes beamed. 'Well you should have tried me first. Know what my satisfied customers say about me? Where there's a Talbot, there's a way.'

Frank coughed to hide a laugh. Smiling at our interviewer as though my face had been glued that way, I kicked my friend hard on the leg. He coughed again, this time I hoped in pain.

'You should do something about that cold of yours,' Talbot said. His hand disappeared into a drawer. 'Must be the climate, new to it I suppose.' Frank muttered a 'Yes'. 'I know I've got some Friars' in here somewhere.'

While he was looking, Frank shook his head at me, slicing a hand across his throat. I smiled, nodded silently and gave him the thumbs up, pretending not to understand.

Talbot gave up his search. 'No luck, which is a pity because you might need it if you accept what I think I'm going to offer you.'

Already? The man moved quickly. I'd grant him that.

'Which is?' said Frank.

'All in good time, all in good time. If we're to do business, we need to know each other a little more,' he said and started to tell us what amounted to his life story. How he vowed never to work for anyone else but himself, how sticking religiously to that belief was the secret of his success. Initially, he had set himself up as a tea merchant, selling into major Russian cities before the Revolution scuppered his 'rather handsome earner'. He told his tales with a zeal that concealed the fact that they must have been told countless times before. Every money-making deal he mentioned brought a spark to his eyes. Words flowed from his mouth like syrup. (Life was easy, if you knew how. Don't find objections, find solutions.) He was a natural persuader. About halfway through his speech I suddenly realised where he got it from. Underneath the self-made-man-affecting-a-gentleman's accent was an Irish lilt, all but smothered, there nonetheless. He brought us into his conversation, drew us in as though we were co-conspirators. He sounded as though he were confiding in friends he'd known for years. And then he ended abruptly, turning to me and saying, 'So, you know about me now,' and though, in fact, I knew nothing, I felt I could like him. In a strange way I even admired him. At least he had drive.

'Tell me,' he said, 'are you good with languages?'

'I can get by in a few. French, German, Spanish.'

'And Mr Brown?'

Frank shrugged. 'Me, I get problems trying to understand my friend here.'

'Ah, right . . . . What would you consider to be your special talents?'

'Could you rephrase the question please?'

Talbot hesitated, gave me a questioning look. 'OK, what are you good at?'

'Look at my work history.'

'Would you say you're a good communicator.'

'Depends who I'm communicating with.'

Talbot sighed at this. 'Evidently.'

Frank stood up. 'Where's the john, I'm busting.'

We both stared at him. Talbot puzzled, me fuming. I wanted to strangle him.

'Out the door, first on the right.'

Frank clattered out of the room.

'He needs to work on his interview technique,' Talbot said as the door closed.

'Sorry. He doesn't always give a good first impression.'

'Unfortunately they last,' Talbot said pointedly. He

began to shuffle his papers together, then held out his hand in a way which I knew from experience meant 'Goodbye and good luck'. I couldn't believe it. This man was about to offer us a job and Frank had blown it, deliberately.

'He's only just got off the boat from New York,' I tried desperately. 'He's not like this normally. He's just tired.'

Talbot shook his head. 'I'll be straight with you. I'm doing some business in Moscow for a few months. I need a couple of people with your kind of knowledge to give me a hand. You, I can deal with, but your friend there . . . .'

'We'll take it. Whatever it is.'

'He doesn't exactly seem keen.'

'We won't disappoint you, I promise.'

'Look, I'm a fair man. Why don't you both come back in a couple of days when he's had a rest and we'll see what we can do.'

I knew what that meant too. We'd return and the position would be filled. So, with nothing to lose, I said 'No.'

Talbot looked surprised at first, then a smile crept across his face. 'OK, OK. I like a man who says "No" for an answer but won't take it. Go on, get your friend back in and we'll discuss details.'

I nearly ran out the room. Russia. I hadn't even considered it. It didn't matter what we'd be doing. We'd be away from here.

He was on the street smoking, waiting nonchalantly for something to happen in his life.

'What the hell are you playing at?'

Frank drew on his cigarette with a little popping sound. 'He's no good.'

'The feeling's mutual.'

'He's a con-merchant.'

'He's just offered us a job in Russia.'

'You what?'

'You know, where you do things and people pay you for doing them.'

'In Russia? What the hell do we wanna go there for?'

I had images of sparkling gold-roofed palaces, plains of ice that stretched to the horizon, vodka frenzies in firelit taverns, almond-eyed women hidden behind furs. It seemed obvious to me. 'It'll be an adventure!' I cried.

'It'll be cold.'

'It'll be beautiful.'

'It'll be wet all year round.'

'But Frank. Moscow. Think about it. Who d'you know who's been there?'

'No-one. That's exactly my point. No-one would want to.'

'It's the opportunity of a lifetime.'

'It'll be full of stinking Bolshies.'

'At least they've got people working. I don't see many round here with that luxury, do you?'

'I'm telling you Brian, I don't trust him.'

'Why? He seems OK to me.'

'So did Madeleine.'

There was a silence. Then quietly I said, 'Thanks,' and turned to go back up the stairs. He might have travelled thousands of miles to share in my misery but I wasn't going to turn this down. What did he know? Bolshies, indeed. They couldn't have made much more of a mess than the West. I wasn't a political animal, never had been, but from what I'd read Comrade Stalin was getting things moving. And what was wrong with spreading out the spoils a bit?

'Hey,' he called but I ignored him. He caught up with me. 'Hey, I'm sorry.'

I kept walking, staring straight ahead.

It worked. He followed me right back into the office and when Talbot offered us the job, he couldn't really refuse. Guilt is such a wonderful weapon. Believe me, I know.

What we'd be doing wasn't exactly clear. Talbot explained his set-up in vague terms. He regularly went to Russia to forge deals between British firms and Soviet government agencies. We'd be runners, gofers, 'vital links in the machinery of high-level business negotiations' according to Talbot, 'pack horses,' according to Frank.

Despite the warnings, I accepted the man for what he was. A salesman. It was in his blood. He'd probably sell the benefits of a Christmas present before giving it to his kid. The way he talked, the way he bragged, was all part of the deal. He showed us a string of membership cards of every conceivable club; they concertinaed out of his wallet, a testament to his ego and a convincing front of social acceptability.

'Know people,' he told us. 'The fundamental secret of success. These are the habitats of the men of influence. So they talk about wine as though they've just scoured the dictionary for adjectives, who cares? People of influence know other people of influence. And soon you have a list. Each name at any given moment is a potential goldmine. Talbot's Law.

'You see, not everyone lost their fortune in '29. Some got out in time, then bought up cheap. These people are rolling in it personally. It's their businesses that are having a hard time. They can keep going, but they want to be ahead of the competition when the good times come again. That's where I come in. Commission in advance and I'll get them links in the Soviet Union. It's an untapped market and mutually beneficial to all parties. The Bolshies get the expertise, we get the coin.'

'I still don't understand what's in it for you,' Frank said.

'You pay for our fares over, give us free accommodation, set us up with new jobs. Where's the catch?'

'Believe me, once you get to know old Talbot, you'll realise there isn't one. The deals I'm setting up are for tractor cranks, winches, trolley wheels – any mechanical widget our boys make, they need, because theirs have a habit of falling apart or arriving at their destination without wheels. My reputation rests on good investments. For that I need good advice. You have expert engineering knowledge – QED you'll be my advisors. In return, I can join you up with a few of the trade ministers, the head of *Soyuz*, something like that. They're desperate for people with your skills. And, I don't mind saying, I have a bit of clout with them. Simple really.'

I knew little about Russia, but enough to realise that their oil fields were the largest in the world. Once we got in, our contracts would run and run.

'Sounds good to me. Frank?'

He nodded but said nothing. He knew there was nothing else, and though he had an instinctive dislike for the man, the package was very agreeable.

We sealed the arrangement over lunch in a little wine bar off Villiers Street, kindly paid for by Frank at Talbot's request. Our new boss reasoned that that since my friend was so sceptical he should foot the bill – that way he would be reassured he wasn't getting something for nothing.

It took a day by train to Berlin, a day to the Russian frontier and another day to get to Moscow. We had a compartment to ourselves, a clear view out of the window and stories to exchange. Whatever Frank's reservations, Talbot was an extraordinary man. Within a few hours I felt he was a close friend. He had that ability to connect. There was an engine inside him that gave him life. His face lit up at a new joke, he listened with interest if you had something to say, would reply intelligently and originally. He looked at things in a different way. Always obliquely so that just when I thought I had figured him out he would surprise me again.

We were a couple of hours from Berlin, and the conversation had lulled into that particular silence which only occurs when travelling. For a while, most subjects seem exhausted, the constant motion dulls your senses and you curl up in your own shell of thoughts. Frank was clumped against the window, mouth sagging open and snoring. Talbot was reading his *Telegraph*. So I started to learn the hundred-long list of Russian phrases he had given me. At first it was torturous, but once I got the feel of the language it grabbed me. I'd learnt Greek and Latin at school, revelled in the different sounds and subtleties of meaning, and now they stood me in good stead. With perseverance all languages are the same. Once you have grasped the mechanics, it all clicks together.

Talbot said suddenly, 'Look at that, just look at that.'

Outside, the winter sky was darkening, pale yellow on the horizon. We were crossing the Elbe. Little rowing boats moored to the banks rocked on the water. About a mile away someone was fly-fishing, swishing a line in graceful loops. Along the left side of the river ran a crooked row of cottages, windows shuttered up for the cold night coming. It looked like the scene had been washed in sepia.

Talbot had his head resting on his hands. 'You could pass here tomorrow night and it wouldn't be the same. I could take a photograph now, but it wouldn't capture it. It would just be a picture postcard, pretty but that's all.'

I nodded. I knew what he meant. The train crawling over the bridge, wheels creaking on the rails and us in a closed off travelling room looking out. Separately these things meant nothing, together the experience became something memorable.

'I love trains,' he said. 'You press your nose against the window and watch the fields flash by. Villages you don't know the name of close around you for a few seconds then are gone. And people live in them, with their own little lives, their own little problems and you know you will never meet them. And you realise that if you got off, went to a bar and sat down for a few drinks, you could strike up a conversation. All those potential friendships that will never happen.'

I chuckled. 'You have more friends than you can handle, Stephen. You can't know everyone in the world. You'd forget their names.'

'In my business, you don't make friends, you make lists.' The corners of his mouth turned up briefly and slid back into a flat line. 'I don't know. Stupid really.' He got out his *Financial Times* and flicked to the stock index. A wry smile creased his face. 'Vickers is up three points. I've got a thousand in them.'

When the train stopped in Berlin for refuelling, Talbot disappeared for a few hours saying, 'Business to attend to boys. Don't let it go without me.'

Frank was still sleeping. He'd hardly stirred since the morning. He was already warming to the idea. At least he was out of London, at least we were in work. Yesterday he'd even had a conversation with Talbot that included full sentences. Things were looking up.

I stared at my reflection in the window. A tall man with a narrow face and deep-set eyes stared back. Not so young, but not so old either. My eyes were still blue, my hair was still thick. Friends said I was handsome in a craggy sort of way, whatever that meant.

Tomorrow I'd be over the border. Nobody could touch me there. Not my mother, not my father. Not even Madeleine.

MOSCOW
February – April 1931

I

In Russian, Moscow is a feminine word. *Moskva*. The mother of the people, the city that cradles its arms around its inhabitants, pampers them and tells them not to worry. It is the heart of the biggest nation on earth. For centuries, people travelled there for change, to seek solace from the torpor of their lives and Moscow welcomed. It was the everything city, Talbot told me. Everything is illegal, but everything is also possible. It was just a question of *blat*. If you had influence and knew how to play the rules, it was the most wonderful place in the world. Talbot had so much *blat*, he could have broken it up into little pieces, sold it on the black market and still have enough left over for him to make his deals with high powered ministers.

It was also a city of extremes. Talbot warned us that we'd be there at the fiercest time of year but nothing could prepare us for the shock of the Moscow winter. We stepped off the train and our eyelashes stuck together. We stood gathering our luggage on the platform and when we tried to move we had to prise our feet from the ground. Within minutes of leaving the station Frank was pleading

31

for the next train back to civilization. This was a city under siege, (its inhabitants bumbled along the streets under a mountain of clothes, all skin hidden from the slicing wind, because whoever you were, no amount of *blat* could influence the weather) but I fell instantly in love with it. It was so beautiful I almost forgot that my fingers were chapping and my face was flaking away. We arrived early morning and the sun was creeping above the skyline. We were surrounded by palaces of ice and crystal. Rainbows bounced off slabs of hard-packed snow, churches shone in intricate detail so that each brick, each tower was defined in razor-sharp lines; dark passageways veered off main avenues, smoky and mysterious, frozen mist lingering in the pale glow of street lamps; parks with skeleton trees appeared from nowhere between massive office blocks; signs of life were few. This, finally, was a city of opposites, of extrovert statements and hidden things.

Talbot ordered us a cab for the Metropol. We crossed the river. A couple of children had braved the early morning cold and were skating around the stanchions of the bridge. When we reached the north bank, Talbot pointed out a massive fortress with sheer walls fifty feet high.

'The Kremlin. Nearly a mile wide in all. That's where all the money is. That's where all the deals are.'

'Sod the money,' Frank grumbled, 'just get us somewhere warm.'

'All buildings in Russia are warm, heating is the one thing they're experts in. Besides, you're staying at the best hotel in Moscow. It's got the best views, the best food and it's close to my office. I'll pick you up tomorrow and show you around.'

'If it's so good, how come you won't be with us?'

'I have a flat of my own. And we may be friends, Frank, but we're not yet close enough to live together.'

I ignored them both. We passed Red Square, a vast white plain at the moment, dotted with occasional moving specks, humans engulfed by the enormity of what their ancestors had built.

The Metropol bore out Talbot's descriptions. The opulence of the building was staggering. Marble staircases sprang from massive hallways covered in wall paintings and mosaics, priceless Persian rugs stretched from wall to wall in the dining room. It was a relic of the past built by an eccentric millionaire, the manager informed us, then taken over by Lenin during the revolution. In a way, it was like a Victorian folly. A giant mismatch of styles and influences from baroque to modern. Dust had gathered on the gold chandeliers, the mosaics in the restaurant were fading and, in the lobby, there was a huge stuffed bear on the podium, reared up on its hind legs and looking ready to pounce on anyone stupid enough to pass its way. The Metropol, we soon realised, was an institution slowly going to seed.

When we arrived, the manager hovered around us as though we were VIPs. 'We don't have so many foreign visitors these days,' he explained in English, 'and this is a quiet time of year.' He showed us our rooms, cavernous chambers with four poster beds and balconies overlooking Prospeckt Marksa and Red Square.

'If you require anything,' he informed us, 'pull the bell handle by the wardrobe, we'll attend as soon as we can.' We tried it later that evening. 'As soon as we can' meant an hour and 'attend' meant the arrival of a sullen and distracted waiter in a crumpled suit. He looked old enough to be my grandfather's grandfather.

Talbot met us the following morning after we'd gorged ourselves on a breakfast of black bread and sour cream cheese. He was laden with shopping bags. 'Presents from your new boss,' he boomed and produced an array of fur hats, woollen coats, fisherman's jumpers and boots that looked like they'd been chopped off the legs of a yeti. We tried them on there and then in the dining room. The few residents still eating ignored us. Nothing was unusual in Moscow it seemed, and if it was, it was best not to complain.

'What do you think?' he asked us eagerly.

'I feel like a bear,' I said.

'Better watch the old boy in reception then. He gets a bit frisky come spring.'

Frank walked around the room, testing out the new attire. 'What *are* these things?' He wiggled a leg, as though trying to shake off a persistent dog.

'They're *sapagi*,' Talbot said proudly. 'The best that dollars can buy.'

'Why can't they call 'em boots like everyone else.'

Talbot sighed. It was starting again. 'Because you're in Russia, and everyone else surprisingly happens to use a Russian word. You'd do well to follow suit.' He delved into another bag and brought out some books. 'Here, this might help.' We each received an English-Russian dictionary and step-by-step language course. 'Russian for simpletons. You'll get the hang of it.'

It took a while, but we did. I spent most evenings working through the lessons while Frank propped up the hotel bar where he picked up a few useful phrases of his own. 'Another vodka please, another brandy please,' – the variations on the theme were endless and he never tired of explaining to me how useful the word 'another' was. Talbot, to his credit, let us settle in gently. He showed us his office, a few blocks away on the Bulvar, then left us while he set up his contacts. For the first few weeks we had free afternoons. Often it was too cold to spend much time outside but we took in the main sights. I soon realised that my first impressions had been false. We'd arrived early morning before the madness started. By day, the streets were a chaos of frenzied determination. Posters everywhere screamed THE FIVE YEAR PLAN IN FOUR. Roads were being ripped up and relaid for heavy vehicles, old buildings pulled down and in their place severe blocks of flats erected to house the workers. Convoys of trucks raced up and down the main streets and wherever one cared to look there were piles of rubble, constantly being created and constantly being cleared.

Frank tagged along behind during these excursions, not exactly intrigued by the amazing collection at the Pushkin museum or the five golden domes of the Cathedral of Assumption or, stretching along the banks of the Moskva, Novodevichy Convent where Chekov found his final resting place. I tried to introduce him to the concept of 'culture', but even the concept of 'concept' carved deep frowns on his ruddy face. Moscow was a means to an end, an Arctic aberration in the otherwise tropical course of his life. It was necessary. It was to be endured. Did I have to try and make him enjoy it?

Soon, his problems were answered. The free time bestowed so generously by Talbot evaporated at the end of February and the real work started in earnest.

II

Talbot's smiles grew wider by the day. We would tumble into his office about eight in the morning, and every morning without fail he'd beam at us saying, 'Money in the bank, but there's more to be made.' He'd hand us a personalised list of tasks for the day. Deliver this package to that address. Pick up contracts from address A and hand to C. In the drawer of my unstable desk was the related list of addresses and names. An infuriating rigmarole challenged by both of us on our first day of the new regime.

'What's all this?' Frank had asked.

'A system to make life easier,' Talbot told us.

'For who?' I said. 'It's crazy. Why don't you just address the packages?'

'You ever tried writing in Cyrillic? Takes all day. This way I get them all down once and never have to do it again.'

Frank snorted.

'We can take the lists with us,' I said to him, 'it's not so bad.'

''Fraid not chaps. The lists stay here.'

'You what?' Frank exploded. 'We got to memorise these things?'

Talbot leaned back in his chair, lord of his little empire. 'They're too valuable. You lose them and I have to redo the lot.'

'But it'll take hours!' I said.

'You'll get used to it,' he replied. 'Cabbies get the knack, you can too. Besides, it's a working introduction to the most wonderful language in the world. You can put those lessons to good use. The piles are over there. One says Frank, one says Brian. Think you can work that out?'

'What happened to the Grover-Brown advisory service?' Frank protested. 'You said we'd be meeting important people.'

'You're not ready yet.'

'When will we be?' I asked.

Talbot shifted uncomfortably in his seat. 'Look, you have to serve out your apprenticeship, before you take on the big boys.'

'Apprenticeship! A-ppren-tice-ship?' Frank grabbed the edges of Talbot's desk and leaned over him menacingly. 'You talk to us like we're damp-eared babies.'

'All I'm saying is, for the moment, leave the contacts to me. You don't know how easy it is to mess things up.' Cowering, he looked to me for support and received none. 'I've spent years with my connections, a few choice words from you could ruin me. Everything you say might be a treble *entendre*.'

'OK Frank.' I stepped in. He was beginning to look dangerous. 'Let's leave it for now.'

Seeing an ally, Talbot became bolder. 'I got your visas, got you shacked up in a lovely hotel, gave you three weeks easy ride. I'm only asking for a bit of graft in return.'

'You''ll get it Stephen, don't worry. C'mon Frank.' I took his arm but he shook it away from me.

'There's one more thing I want to discuss, civilly, with our employer. You promised us a link with the oil companies. Any progress yet?'

'I'm working on it,' Talbot mumbled.

'How long?'

'You do your bit and I'll do mine. I promise you.' There was an edge to his voice I hadn't heard before which I didn't like.

We left him to sort out our workload. When we were at the door, he said to us. 'By the way, when you get stopped, and you will, show your cards, smile and be stupid.' He turned to Frank, 'That shouldn't be too difficult now should it?'

'Welcome to the world of full employment,' Frank muttered as we staggered into the street under the weight of our deliveries. 'You think he's ever heard of a union?'

'You ever heard of tact? The rate you're going we'll lose our jobs before we've started.'

He ignored me. 'Pack Horses Anonymous has a ring to it don't you think?' he said.

We crossed the city many times, learning the streets and the names and the landmarks to guide us. Every day before setting off, we were stopped by the uniforms who checked our permits (city and suburbs only) with an officiousness which in time drew from us only weary amusement. We explained where we were going and what we were doing by rote. Then we produced Talbot's authorizations from his ministerial contacts and we were immediately left alone. Once, a young guard, seeing my credentials, offered a lift to my destination. Bearing in mind Talbot's words of warning I declined.

And over the weeks while we slogged, Talbot dangled carrots to keep us going. February became March and there was still no sign of the promised contacts. One evening, after a particularly arduous round, he summoned us back into his office.

'I've a surprise for you,' he declared and we both thought he'd finally come up with the goods. 'Tonight, you drop all your plans, you don your classiest evening attire and you come with me. We're going to the most famous theatre in the world.' He pulled a pair of tickets out of his jacket, 'One for you, and one for you,' then stood back like a magician. There was no reaction. Frank was too tired to moan, and we both felt too let down to express our disappointment.

'Come on men, I want to see some smiles!'

'Find us a new job, you might get one then,' Frank mumbled.

'This is a way of thanking you for everything you've done so far.' I think he genuinely thought we'd be happy with his gift. He looked a bit hurt so I tried to express interest.

'What time does it start?'

'You'll be picked up at the Metropol seven sharp. I've laid on the works, horse drawn cab, there and back.'

'It's very kind of you. Thank you.'

'Don't mention it,' he said, flipping back to his usual

brash self, 'A boss should always keep his workers happy, that's my motto.'

On the way back to the hotel, I wondered just how many mottos this man had.

Moscow at night was wonderful. The dark descended like a balm. The streets were quiet, the lights came on illuminating snow flakes as they fell on the hats of passers-by. The collective spirit was held off for a while and men and women, if they had the means, dressed up to go out. At six o'clock, the city lurched into pre-revolution mode, smiling at its excesses, blinking at its severity.

With full evening dress under thick furs we tramped up the drive to the Bolshoi. It was my first sight of the building. It stood on the edge of Sverdlova Square like a palace, glistening in the blue light from a string of lamps placed at the feet of eight huge stone columns which supported the grand entrance. To our right was an ornate fountain pond, completely frozen over. 'They don't build them like this anymore,' I said to Frank but he made no comment. He'd agreed to come reluctantly and only after a deal of persuasion. I felt the frustration too but argued that working with Talbot rather than against him was the best way of ensuring he met his part of the deal. Anyway, it was a night out, on our boss. It was the free drinks that swayed it.

In the lobby, Moscow's elite gathered to make small talk before the performance. It was *The Rite of Spring*, a special privilege. Champagne flowed and Party cards flashed. There was no room for the peasant worker on a night like this. They were usually treated to such delights as modern operas extolling the virtues of concrete and two-hour pastorals to the glorious tractor.

Talbot was in his element, circulating among the people

of influence. When he saw us he ushered us straight up to our box, careful to avoid any unnecessary introductions. Noticing our glares, he told us, 'Your time will come soon.' We let the matter drop and settled into our seats, binoculars in hand.

The box was decked in plush red velvet, our bodies treated to soft leather chairs. Crystal chandeliers flashed over the heads of the Party faithful. Everybody was in evening dress, the required proletarian uniform for the occasion. From the general murmur in the hall, I could imagine individuals saying to each other, 'We Communists can enjoy ourselves too.'

Talbot pointed out important faces in the crowd that he recognised. 'Minister of the Interior, known him way back, even he can't get a box.' I sometimes wondered how, with so little tact, he managed to make a success of himself at all.

As the lights went down and a hush descended over the audience I realised there were two empty seats beside me, yet everywhere else was packed.

I leant over to Talbot. 'Were you expecting friends?'

'Nope. Got these tickets last minute. They're like gold dust.' He peered past me. 'Whoever squandered theirs doesn't know what they're missing.'

The vast orchestra finally groaned its way into tune and an expectant silence filled the hall. The curtains swung to the sides, the conductor raised his baton and behind us the door to the box opened. A women entered then hesitated. She tutted to herself and unwrapped a fur cape from her shoulders. She wore a simple red dress printed with black flowers. It was nothing extravagant, but on her I thought it hung like a ball gown. Frank and Talbot shuffled to their feet, pushing their chairs back. She smiled, murmuring *Izvinitye, izvinitye* as she squeezed along the aisle. I stood up to let her by. She looked at me in passing. I saw the sleek line of her chin, and a single dark hair that fell across her cheek. There was a smell of rose water in the air. I glanced at her as she arranged herself tidily in one of the empty seats and wondered who her lucky partner was.

The performance began and, dutifully, I tried to concentrate on it. Talbot leaned forward giving himself to the show. I tried to focus on the ballerinas but they seemed silly leaping pompously around the stage. My head turned again. My brain said keep your eyes to yourself, but like unruly troops the muscles in my neck wouldn't follow orders.

I watched her through the gloom. She clutched a small pouch tightly on her lap, her fingers playing with the strap. She was looking down at them, but her eyes weren't following their movement. A muscle tensed in her cheek and held. Whoever was meant to appear had decided against it. Irrationally, I felt angry at this absent friend. How could he stand her up like this?

I dared not stare too long for fear she would turn around, but the more I looked the harder it was to stop. She blinked, and the moment caught in my mind. I imagined her asleep. I saw the light through my bedroom window falling on her face in the morning. I saw her yawning, arms outstretched, her hands in fists, hair unpegged and spread like a fan on the pillow and I wondered what the hell was happening to me.

Watch the show. But the show meant nothing, the show was beside me.

Talbot was wrapped up in the ballet. Frank eyed the proceedings with an expression of profound confusion – everybody was looking the same way except me.

She opened her pouch and pulled out a programme. It shook in her hand so she tried to steady it with the other, gave up and flattened it on her knees, feigning interest in the cast list. Then suddenly she looked directly at me. There was defiance in her eyes, then indecision, then fear. She stood up, stuffing the programme back in her pouch and rushed for the door. I sat for a moment taking it in, my face flushing cold. I'd offended her. The least I could do was apologise, yet even as I scrambled after her, ignoring Frank and Talbot's questioning looks, I knew that the urge to follow was more than that.

The stairways were empty. I tapped down them, hoping to catch her in the entrance hall. Nothing. I went to reception.

'Did a young woman come past here a few minutes ago?'

The man behind the counter cast me a surly glance, saying nothing.

'She was quite small, brown hair, wearing a red dress.'

He tutted, rearranged some tickets on his desk. 'There are many women in Moscow.'

Bribe time again. I slipped him a pound note. 'Please, it's very important.'

'She left.'

'Which way?'

Shoulders shrugged. Another note. 'There is only one exit.'

Hugging my jacket, I ran outside, through the huge portico entrance and onto Ploshad Sverdlova. Except for a solitary car making slow progress through the snow, it was deserted. Almost immediately, I started to shiver and my breath froze about my face. I scanned the darkness. Behind me, music filtered tinnily through the thick walls.

This was madness.

I was about to go in when I caught a movement out by the fountain pond. I crossed the heavy stone slabs, acutely aware of the crunching of my shoes in the silence. Between the columns of the grand façade I peered again. Snow flurried horizontally in the blue light and I had to squint.

Moscow, February – April 1931

There was a figure standing at the edge of the water, completely still. I caught a glimpse of red.

She didn't see me coming so I called, not wanting to shock her again. She turned at the sound and started to walk away.

'Wait a minute!'

Her steps faltered and I ran up to her. She was shivering violently.

'Here.' I wriggled out of my jacket and wrapped it round her shoulders. 'I'm sorry,' I said. 'I didn't mean to offend you.'

As I spoke, the tension drained a little from her face.

'You're English?'

'That obvious, huh?'

She didn't answer.

'We should be inside, it's freezing.' She looked down, shaking her head. 'You'll die out here,' I said. '*I'll* die out here.'

'No, please.'

'You left your coat in there. Besides I want my jacket back.' I smiled to show my words weren't serious.

She nodded ever so slightly. I put my arm gently across her back to guide her and was shocked at how light she felt. She looked up and I saw her clearly for the first time. A slender face with high cheekbones which left shadows on her pale skin, and wide brown eyes which refused to blink when they met my gaze. She wore little make-up and her hair, tied loosely, fell around her neck in silky waves. No pretensions. I felt awkward suddenly, out here holding this woman I didn't know, gazing at her stupidly and her looking back probably wondering why this strange man had followed her into the cold night. But I didn't want to let go.

When we got to the entrance, she slipped free. Glancing both ways down the road and seeing nothing, she sighed with what appeared to be relief.

'I am alright now,' she said.

'Who were you expecting?'

'It doesn't matter,' she said sharply.

'I don't mean to pry. You seem nervous that's all.'

She didn't respond to my prompting, maintaining a polite silence all the way back. And why should she? I thought. I was a stranger, and in Moscow you don't make small talk with stangers.

When we returned to the box, the show had reached the interval.

Talbot stood up at our entrance, 'Aha! The explorer returns.' There was a leer in his voice that made me wince.

'You didn't miss much,' muttered Frank.

'Introductions, boy, introductions?' Talbot's fat face beamed as he swaggered over. Then to me in English, 'Wearing your clothes already?'

Awkwardly, the woman gathered her belongings. 'I must go,' she whispered to me.

'So soon?'

'I have my things, now I go.'

A waiter swished in, carrying a silver tray of *hors d'oeuvres* and vodka in iced glasses. Her eyes followed the food and the waiter glanced at her with contempt.

'Delectables!' Talbot bellowed, stretching past us to pluck a *bliny* from the tray. He stuffed it in his mouth 'This is why I come really,' he said between swallows. 'I mean the music *is* a joy but the tucker's the best in town. And all for a dollar tip!' A dollop of sour cream dribbled down his chin. A tongue darted out and scooped it up.

'Now are you going to tell me her name, or do I have to be forward?'

While he bantered she edged to the door, her furs hanging over one arm.

'Please, stay for the rest of the show,' I said.

'I should not be here.'

'Why?'

'My friend did not come.'

'Then join us instead. We're staying at the Metropol, you could have dinner with us later.'

She hesitated, but she had already made her decision. 'This is not for the public. Everyone is Party here. A friend got me good seats, you know how I mean? I could lose my job if they caught me here.'

I nodded, thinking, I don't care what the reason is, just stay a little longer. A silence followed. It hovered between us, compelling me to break it, but I couldn't find the right words.

'What do you do then?' I asked eventually.

'You ask a lot of questions.'

Her eyes again, steady, unblinking. One minute nervous, the next so sure.

'I – '

'He didn't come,' she interrupted me, though it was hardly an interruption since I was opening my mouth just to keep the conversation going. 'So . . . ' she said, moving for the exit. Talbot was too busy cramming caviar by the shovelful into his mouth to notice, but I saw Frank watching the proceedings with an amused expression. They could go hang.

'You were very kind,' she said at the door.

'I was very rude.'

'No, I don't think so.'

She opened it, was halfway through when I said, 'Wait. I don't even know your name.'

'Ileana Petrovna.'

'Brian Grover.'

I offered my hand. She took it gently. My palm tingled at the touch of her fingers.

'Enjoy your stay,' she said and disappeared down the stairs.

FIELDS OF LIGHT

I returned to find Talbot ranting about the show.

'Incredible. What a mind, Brown, to conceive of that sound. Don't you think? How could he hear it in his head and then put it down on paper?'

'Beautiful,' Frank said drily.

'You can't just say beautiful. It's . . . it's more, an *experience*.'

'Saved you a cream roll,' Frank said to me.

'It's a *bliny*,' Talbot insisted. '*Bliny, bliny, bliny*.'

'I'd prefer a vodka.'

'Looks like you need it,' Frank said.

'You could say that.'

'Well?' Talbot slapped his stomach. 'What was she like?'

He beamed at me all chummy smiles and innuendo. I wanted to hit him.

'We talked, that's all. And for your information *I* followed *her*.'

Talbot knocked back another short and swayed slightly from the effort. 'So where's your jacket then?'

Stupidly, I looked down at my shirt and bow tie. 'Christ.' I'd forgotten all about it.

'She take it as a keepsake or was she just trying to rob you?' he sneered

My wallet and, more importantly, my papers were in it. But even as I thought the worst, I was sure it couldn't be true. She wouldn't have done it deliberately, After all, I put the jacket on her. She didn't ask. Besides, the whole thing didn't seem to fit. The way she'd been shivering out by the pond, her discomfort in our box without her friend. It couldn't have been planned.

'Hope she was worth it.' Talbot winked at Frank, who thankfully wasn't sharing the joke. 'I think we'd better contact the police,' he added, suddenly serious.

'No.'

'She's robbed you, old boy. Can't you see that?'

'It's a misunderstanding I tell you.'

He sighed. 'Whatever you want. All the same, you can't go far without your respectable foreigner pass.'

'She'll return it. I'll stay in my room tomorrow.'

'No you damn well won't. You've got important deliveries to do.'

'Dock my wages then! Better still, do them your bloody self. You need the exercise!' I stormed off leaving Frank cooing, 'Easy, easy,' to an irate boss cussing at my back.

I stayed in all day, as planned. Frank did my rounds in exchange for an IOU. I read a cheap thriller, cover to cover, twisting the pages, hardly aware of the words. I propped up my watch on the side table, checking it every quarter of an hour, waiting for a knock on the door. One o'clock came and I ordered trays of caviar and beef stew, though I wasn't hungry. I picked at it, then watched it go cold. Three o'clock came and went and I decided I really should get dressed. I killed half an hour sorting out shirts, which tie would go with what, noticed with a sigh the half empty hanger for my evening suit. It grew dark outside. I switched on the lights. The street lamps came on. I switched off the lights and sat out on the balcony, gazing across the city. It was a still evening with no snow falling. They would be thankful for it down there, working on the first Metro line. Along Prospekt Marksa, groups of heavily clothed workmen gathered around the drill site, toiling to keep warm. They went up and down the hole like ants. Dumptrucks laden with debris edged along the street. I followed their progress, admiring the resilience, the determination to keep the city moving. Across Red Square, St Basil's Cathedral rose against the dark sky, its domes capped white like icebergs. I wondered where she lived in this sprawling place. And I wondered what she'd do if she knew I'd been thinking about her all day.

I joined Frank for dinner, thanked him for putting himself out. He didn't need to ask if she'd turned up. The answer was obvious. I responded to his chatter with one word grunts and straightfaced his jokes. 'So you gonna tell the authorities, or what?' he asked finally.

'Maybe she couldn't make it.'

'Maybe she doesn't want to.'

'I could wait another day.'

'Wake up man. This is Russia. The woman robs you and you don't report her? You give her a chance to make amends, she doesn't bother. You put yourself at risk by delaying the obvious, you rile your boss and what's more, you're pissing me off too.'

'I'm sorry, really. I'll take the weight next week, I promise. It's just . . . I like her.'

Frank let his spoon drop into his bowl. It landed with a hollow ring. 'You *like* her. God sometimes . . . Listen Brian, we've enough problems as it is without you pining for a woman you've known for ten minutes.'

'I'm not pining. I'm concerned.'

'Well save a bit for you. And me. Talbot's stringing us along, and that's him being friendly. We get on the wrong side of him, and we're out. And what happens if the police do a check? Considered that?'

'They won't.'

'And if they do?'

'Trust me.'

'Name one reason why I should.'

'She'll come, alright?'

He pulled his napkin from his neck and scrunched it into a ball.

'OK, round two to Grover. I'll be messenger boy for you tomorrow but that's it. No more. Agreed?'

'Agreed.' I smiled weakly. I was in no position to haggle.

He'd done enough for me already, and his reasoning was indisputable, but logic played no part in my thoughts. I didn't care how many times I'd been wrong before (the list stretched from here to London and back again), I'd be right this time.

'I mean it,' he said.

'I know you do.'

Lunchtime the next day, Talbot paid me a visit. He made it clear he was disappointed in me but was prepared to give me another go. I wasn't aware that my first one had ended, but I took the hint and apologised. Strangely his mood changed after that. He admitted he'd said a few things out of turn himself, must be the drink, you know the score, no hard feelings. He expressed a sincere hope that she would return with my visas by tomorrow morning. I got the gist. When he left, I ran through our conversation again and it struck me for the first time just how much he needed us. He was in the middle of negotiating a huge deal with some nameless face in the agricultural department and he couldn't cope with the paperwork by himself. There was no way he'd sack us, as Frank had thought. In fact, we could turn our usefulness to advantage, pressure him to make the contacts he'd promised.

She came late afternoon.

'I asked her to leave, but she insisted she must see you personally,' the manager informed me as I rushed down the stairs. Russian snobbery was alive and flourishing even in this new age of Stalin Enlightenment.

'I'll decide who I want to see, not you. Next time get her a drink.'

They had planted her on a draughty seat beside the entrance. She looked as though she'd been sent to the corner of a classroom. When she saw me she rose unsteadily, half-smiling, half unsure, I think, at what my reaction would be. I noticed immediately that she was wearing the same dress as the other night.

The jacket was under her arm. 'I meant to come sooner,' she began, 'yesterday morning, but I couldn't be late for work. Last night, I was here but they wouldn't let me in. It was an accident. I only realised when I got home and it was too late to go back. Your papers are in here. You didn't report it, did you? It was a mistake, I didn't mean . . .'

'It's alright, it's alright. Slow down. I knew you'd return it. The police don't know. It's my own fault for not noticing in the first place.'

She handed my jacket over. 'I thought you would be angry so I pressed it.'

'It seems I owe you a drink then.'

'In here?'

'Why not?'

She glanced at the manager. 'He won't like it.'

'It's got nothing to do with him.'

We went to the bar, Ileana looking over her shoulder to see if he would say anything. 'I've only seen the Metropol from the outside. It's beautiful.'

We took seats by the bay windows overlooking the street. I tried to catch the attention of the ancient waiter but he was busy polishing at the bar.

'He's had the same glass in his hand since we arrived,' I said.

She smiled. 'I don't think he knows we're here.'

'I don't think he knows he's here.'

Eventually he came over. I ordered a brandy, but when I asked her what she wanted she became edgy. 'Perhaps I shouldn't. Perhaps I should go.'

'Stop worrying. You're my guest. After all the trouble you've been to, coming over here, the least I can do is buy you a drink.'

She glanced out the window while the old man hovered, confused at the delay. A couple of workmen in overalls walked past, hugging themselves against the wind. 'I'm normally out there looking in,' she said.

'Not tonight. Please, choose anything on the list.'

'They're very expensive.'

'Goes on my room bill. Please.'

She chose the cheapest vodka, with soda. The waiter raised his eyebrows and gradually made his way back to the bar.

'He thinks I shouldn't be here.'

'You're not breaking any laws are you?'

She hesitated before answering. 'That depends on who's watching.'

We talked of small things, – 'What brings you to Moscow? Will you be staying long?' – and the afternoon turned into evening. The bar filled up with regulars and visiting business men, men in suits and hats and chain watches swinging from their pockets. We became less conspicuous hidden in the crowd and slowly Ileana relaxed, though she said little about herself. I thought she'd leave after the first drink, but when I offered another she accepted with grace. And when I asked her to have dinner with me, to my surprise and joy she said, 'That would be nice.'

Soon we were joined by Talbot and Frank. This time the introductions were done properly. Talbot took me aside and said, 'Seems I owe you an apology.'

Ileana rested the silver spoon delicately on the side of her plate. She touched it as though it were something almost alien, to be treated with respect and perhaps a little trepidation.

'I have never eaten so well,' she said. 'It is very good of you.'

FIELDS OF LIGHT

There was a guffaw at the other end of the table. Talbot had been joined by two business acquaintances and was telling another one of his anecdotes, Frank had slipped quietly away, bored by our boss's posturing and not wanting to intrude upon us. We'd been left alone to create our own little bubble, sipping champagne, working our way through course after course of fine food. Inhibitions fell away and we talked. I told her everything I knew about myself. It was like a great release, relating stories of my childhood, sunny days at Charterhouse and Cambridge and my wanderings around the world. She listened eagerly as though each story were a nugget to remember and treasure; her world was so different to mine. I told her about the first time my father took us out in his car and how it refused to start as soon as my mother got in. And her eyes opened wide when I described a house in Abergavenny I had lived in when I was a boy.

'Eight bedrooms!' she cried. 'And you really had maids to do your washing and make your food!'

'It seemed the normal thing to me. I was only a child. I knew nothing else.'

'Don't apologise. Tell me more. What was it like living there?'

'It was quite lonely actually. My parents rarely spoke to me and other children my age lived miles away. So I made my own entertainment, I used to go exploring, pretend I was a trecker in the Amazon. There were three massive yew trees at the bottom of the vale just near a little hotel. I built a tree house there from planks of wood and watched the people going in and out. Sometimes I'd stay there all day making up stories in my head, pretending the visitors to the hotel were spies from Germany and we had to keep an eye on them in case they were involved in some dastardly deed.' I chuckled to myself remembering.

'You were a happy child. You had everything you wanted. When I have children, they will grow up with smiles on their faces too.'

'That wasn't how you could describe me. I had *things*, but I didn't have hugs from my mother or play fights with my father. That sort of thing was just "silly". They were typical English eccentrics, just like you'll find in your schoolbooks.'

Ileana waved a finger at me. 'No, no. In our books you are all fat and wear bowler hats.' She cocked her head to one side like a parrot, contemplating her next words. 'You should be wearing yours.'

'Oh, I've got it safely tucked away. It only comes out in emergencies.'

'Like when?'

'Well, if I'm posing for a photograph for a Russian schoolbook about strange Englishmen, perhaps. Or going to see my stockbroker.' I didn't know the word in Russian so I said it in English.

'What's that?'

'A vile capitalist institution.'

'It can't be so bad. Do they force you?'

I laughed. 'I think we may have a language problem here.'

A waitress wobbled up to us bearing a massive tray of coffees with biscuits and cream-filled chocolates and flavoured vodkas to wash it all down. She looked as though she were about to topple over under the weight. But she was doing the rounds at each table, a sure way to supplement her meagre earnings. All it took were a few westerners to feel sorry for her as she grimly tried to smile through the strain. She probably had a wad of hard currency up her sleeve.

Ileana's eyes followed the sweets as they were laid down. It was plain that she couldn't believe her luck. So many luxuries, such undreamed of affluence in the centre of Moscow. The Metropol was an oasis of hard currency wealth. The more I talked to her, the more I understood her initial fear at entering the building. She knew she did not belong.

She took a wafer mint and nibbled at it like a squirrel. It struck me that she was restraining herself. She was still hungry. Not just peckish, but *hungry*. It had been staring me in the face all night, but I only now realised. She was too thin. The dress had hidden it at first, making her look small.

I pushed the plate towards her. 'Take as many as you want, nobody's counting.' And she did, the tempo of her munching increasing with each biscuit until she stopped abruptly with the realisation that she was very full indeed. She looked embarrassed, as if she had done something wrong.

'Enjoy things while you can.' I filled our glasses with more champagne. 'All this time I've talked about myself, but I know nothing about you,' I said.

She picked up a knife and twisted it in the air. I caught her reflection, distorted on the metal. She stared at it. 'There is nothing much to know, compared to your life.' There was no bitterness in her voice, no self-pity. It was just a statement of fact, of acceptance. The old Russian complaint, 'What is to be done?' which has so often been met with a shrug and another glass of vodka. 'About what?' comes the inevitable reply.

'I have never left my country,' she said. 'I would like to see other places. When I was a girl I loved maps. My mother used to say I would go on great journeys and marry a foreigner. She warned me against Germans, "They are full of beer", and the French "too unreliable" she said. "But an Englishman perhaps" .' Her voice squeaked as she imitated her mother. 'But now,' she whispered, 'we can't go anywhere without permission.' She took a large gulp from her glass. 'It is no matter. Anyway you don't want to hear about me, it is nothing interesting.'

'Actually I could listen all night.'

She blushed. 'You flatter me.'

I pressed her and nothing interesting turned out to be a great deal. She had lived through the chaos of the revolution, seen the looting, the riots and the massacres at first hand. She told me about her family, which just as strange as mine. Once she started, it came out in a stream.

'We had a baby brother who died young of heart disease. The rest of us were girls. It turned Mother very strict. One time, she brought us all together and told us she would happily trade her four daughters for the life of her son. It made a deep impression on me, made me want to prove myself. When the troubles hit St Petersburg, we were forced out of our house. Petr, my father, was a postmaster. A simple man but he made for us a little home that we loved. The mob came in and requisitioned it for the people, which meant wrecked it. Eventually, we left with many others as the famine hit. All the food was going to the army to fight the civil war. I wanted to do something to help. Not the cause. The suffering. That's how I became a nurse. I trained on the front line. It was terrible. They saw things in terms of right and wrong. There was no middle. They never took Whites into our hospital. Whites were considered traitors and left in the mud to die. But I saw them just as people screaming in pain. I didn't care what they thought. But I was forbidden to go to them.

'When it was all over I came to Moscow. And now I live in the suburbs in a tiny flat and I go to work in the hospital. And in the summer the sky is blue and I go swimming with friends in the baths. In the winter, people stay indoors unless they have to go out, eating their jars of pickle and barely surviving. Occasionally, I meet a foreigner like you and they tell me of the things they have done, the places they have seen, but then they go again. Occasionally, there is a knock on a neighbour's door in the middle of the night and they are gone too. I've never had that knock, thank God . . . I make it sound gloomy don't I? It isn't. Really, I'm quite happy. The hospital is a good place to work, I have some friends, I have enough money to live.'

She stopped, out of breath.

'Then why are you so hungry?' I asked her.

Ileana looked down at her fingers, started picking at them. 'I traded a week's food coupons for the dress and now there isn't much in the cupboard.' There was an embarrassed smile on her face. 'It was stupid, wasn't it?'

'You have to treat yourself sometimes, otherwise you'd go mad. But when was the last time you ate properly?'

'I have soup, and my friends share, but most days they have hardly enough for themselves. They understand though, they don't begrudge me.'

Our tables were cleared except for yet another bottle of sweet Georgian wine that Talbot had ordered. I filled Ileana's glass up and we drank good health and happiness to each other.

Then the lights dimmed slightly and from the corner of the room music started playing. It was a gipsy band, all stringed instruments and drums. Soon, couples were going to the clearing between tables and dancing. One of the band members left the stage and came round selling poppies. I bought one.

'Can I?'

She looked at me questioningly. 'Can you what?'

I threaded the poppy into her hair. 'Do that.'

'You just have.'

'It goes with your dress. You look beautiful.'

A song started up again. 'For that, I will let you dance with me.'

She led me by the hand to the floor. My feet bounced on pockets of air.

'I'm not very good. Especially after all this wine,' I said.

'Don't worry, nobody's watching.'

She moved smoothly and I, awkwardly, tried to follow. I kept tripping over my feet and I cursed myself inwardly for never having taken the time to learn. A hundred lessons for this moment with her would have been worth it. She didn't seem to mind though. Occasionally, she would giggle as my limbs struck out at weird angles in a vain attempt to keep time with the music. Then the slow numbers came and cautiously I held her around the waist. She pulled my right arm out straight, threading her fingers between mine, and whispered in my ear, 'Pretend it's a waltz. Everybody can waltz.'

'Everybody except me.'

We swirled around the room, sometimes bumping into other couples, collapsing into each other's arms when the song stopped. From the sidelines Talbot clapped and cried 'Bravo!'

'What do you wish for more than anything else?' I asked in a lull between songs.

She looked at me directly, answering immediately. 'I'd like to meet a man who wasn't just passing through.'

I squeezed her hand. 'Maybe you will,' I said. 'Maybe you will.'

It was getting late. The customers dwindled until all the tables had been cleared and we were the last group left. The waiters lingered prominently in the background, and when Talbot asked for one final brandy all round, 'just to celebrate a spectacular night, mind you,' he received the curt reply that they were temporarily out of stock.

Even he got the message. So we left, glowing from the wine, good food and even better company.

I led Ileana down the marble steps to where a horse-drawn cab waited to take her home. I'd asked Talbot earlier to arrange it for her. He was only too willing to help, still feeling a bit embarrassed by his behaviour at the Bolshoi. I wanted her to remember this night. I wanted her to remember me.

The driver was scowling and muttering to himself as we came out. I offered to accompany her but she declined.

'People might get the wrong impression.'

The wind clawed into my face, but alcohol warmed my heart and I felt bold. 'And what impression might that be?' I asked.

The driver shook his reins, made a display of clapping his hands together. 'You want to turn me to stone? Get in woman, or I'll find another fare.'

'Another at this time?' I called back. 'Not a chance. Here's the money in full, plus that for yourself.' I gave him a note. 'Can we talk for a few minutes? Uninterrupted?'

He grinned through his beard. 'You can talk all you want on a fine night like this.'

I returned to Ileana. 'Well?'

She bowed her head. 'I don't know what you mean'.

'I haven't laughed so much for years. It was lovely when we danced. When *you* danced and I stumbled.'

'You're not so bad. You just need practice.'

'Will you teach me?'

Hair blew over her face. She pulled it away with a flick of her hand and laughed. 'I'm a nurse,' she said as though it explained everything.

'I'd like to see you again,' I said. 'Teach me to dance.'

'When?'

'Tomorrow.'

'I can't. I work double shifts, right through.'

'In the morning. Six o'clock. We can dance along the river.'

She shook her head. 'You're mad, Mr Grover. If your blood weren't so hot you would surely freeze.'

'But will you, Ileana?'

She was silent for a moment then she said. 'If I have to take you to hospital afterwards as my first patient of the day, don't blame me.'

'Taganka Square,' I called out as she got into the carriage. She leaned out the window and beckoned me forward. 'Don't forget the Russian farewell.' She took my head in her hands and kissed me on both cheeks. Our hats clashed and fell to the ground. I stooped and picked them up, brushing the snow off with my gloves. 'Thank you,' she said as I handed hers back. 'And you can call me Lena. My friends do.'

I watched the carriage as it disappeared. That night I dreamt I was weightless, floating over the world. When I woke up the next morning the feeling was still there.

III

I was ready by five. The doorman was slumped on a chair, hidden away in a corner and snoring loudly. I slipped out quietly into streets yet to wake up. With a thick scarf wrapped around my face, fur hat covering my ears, and *sapagi* snug on my feet I made my way to Taganka Square. Every other lamp was off, another efficiency drive to safeguard Stalin's five year plan. The streets were eerily silent. No-one passed me on the way.

I waited. She did not come.

Hunger left me. A hole lodged inside that couldn't be filled by food. I did my work in a daze. I woke up, went to Talbot's office, picked up his brown-papered packages and delivered them. I crossed Moscow a hundred times by tram and trolley bus but no image of it stuck in my mind. I stopped going out, preferring instead the confines of my hotel room where I could think about her in peace. Why hadn't she turned up? What had I done to upset her? I played events over and over in my head, dissecting each nuance of meaning in our conversation but found nothing. We had met, we had dined, we had danced. That was all.

But it wasn't all. It wasn't enough. I couldn't shake off the magic of that evening. When I contacted every hospital in the area, each gave the same reply. 'We cannot give out such information.' I checked with the box office of the Bolshoi to see if she'd left an address for ticket collection. They knew of no such person and besides, if they had, they wouldn't tell *me*.

I kept quiet about it, of course, but the change in me was all too apparent. Within a week both Talbot and Frank asked whether anything was wrong. I fobbed them off, explaining that I was tired. And in a way it was true. I was tired of trying to work out what had happened. I was tired of the unfamiliar yearning that had lodged in my gut. Frank had casually inquired if I'd seen Ileana again. I told him it hadn't worked out. I told him it's no skin off my back. I'm not sure he believed me, but he let the matter pass.

On a late afternoon at the back end of March, I sat down in a café on the corner of Taganka Square. I'd often go there now after my deliveries to wind down and watch the world go by. Spring was coming. Snow had melted like memories, leaving holes scattered in a grey slush.

The city that had astounded me only a month before now passed by in a blur. Workers trudged along pavements just as they had in Charing Cross. Clumsy trucks spilled down side streets, leaving the air solid with diesel fumes. I saw for the first time that they were knocking the heart out of the city, all traces of pre-revolution elegance flattened to make way for the new beginning. But to me the rebirth was still-born.

What was I doing here? Frank had been right. This was a dreadful place to live. Nobody smiled, nobody chatted, the coffee was sour. You had to bribe if you wanted anything done. The cold had lifted but the damp was still here. It permeated everything – the bed linen, the walls, the soul.

Frank was meeting me at three so I had half an hour to kill. I took a recent copy of *The Times* out of my briefcase. So they were setting up a coalition, in the national interest. What good would that do? A bunch of clubby politicians politely arguing over which of their failed policies should be given another go. And, yet again, the crossword was impossible.

I ordered another sour coffee from a waitress who served me with the relish of someone cleaning out a toilet. Outside it started to rain and within seconds the streets had cleared.

When she hurried past the front window it didn't register at first. My eyes and mind were out of focus. But into my hazy daydream her face appeared, a side profile distorted through the wet glass. I came back to the world with a start and looked again. It was definitely her, eyes screwed tight against the rain. Two shopping bags laden with food pulled her arms almost to the ground. I threw a few roubles on the counter and rushed out of the café.

'You owe me a dance,' I called. At the sound of my

voice she slowed for a second then sped up. She did not look round. 'I nearly froze you know.'

'Go away.' Her voice was small against the pounding of the rain.

'I waited and waited.'

'Go away!'

I caught up with her. A stream had formed on her head, following a clump of hair down her neck. She scratched it away, but it returned in seconds.

'I waited for you all morning. *Ten* policemen asked me what I was doing.'

'Then you are stupid. You should have stayed in your nice hotel.'

We came to the end of the square and she turned sharply down a narrow alley I hadn't seen before.

'Why won't you talk to me?'

She walked on, the heavy bags dragging through the pools on the pavement. I followed down one street, then another, a zig-zag into the old part of the city where rows of houses and dusty-windowed shops squeezed the roads thin.

'You'll hurt yourself, going so fast,' I said, 'let me take one.'

'No!' She yanked the bags away from me. Then she said quietly, exasperated and tired, 'Please, leave me alone. I can't see you.'

'If you let me take you for a drink you could see me better.'

Finally, she stopped. 'Thank you for last week and I'm sorry for not meeting you. It was a wonderful evening. You were very thoughtful.' She fixed me with an impenetrable stare. 'But that was last week, today is different. Today is today.'

'What about tomorrow? Can I see you then.'

'Tomorrow is today too, you understand?'

I didn't. 'And next week?'

'The same.'

'And that's it?'

She nodded.

'Why?'

'Because . . .' She was about to say more but changed her mind. Her face became closed, no expression. 'I'm going now, don't follow me.'

'You can't leave me here.' The streets were empty, old brick walls crumbling over the pavement, turnings that led to nowhere. 'I don't know where I am.'

'You're a grown man. You'll find your way home.'

'I don't have my papers. What if I'm picked up?' Her eyes flickered, recognition lodging there. She understood the danger, and however much she wanted rid of me she felt perhaps a little sympathy. For a moment I thought I had won her confidence again, but then with a little snort she walked off.

Again, I ran up beside her. This time she did not wait for me to speak. 'And what if we are both picked up, yes? You are alright, you're English, you're passing through. They will ask you questions, then let you go. What about me?'

I said nothing for a while, wondering what to do next but unable to give up and let her disappear again. She ignored me but stopped protesting. A small triumph, I reasoned. Soon, the dingy alleyways widened into roads and then into a main thoroughfare. I recognised an office block at the far end, one I'd seen from my hotel room. We were about half a mile from the Bulvar ring, I reckoned. It had stopped raining.

'Go left here, it will take you all the way back.'

A tram rattled past, slicing through the puddles.

'I don't want to.'

'*I* want you to.'

'For the last two weeks all I've done is think about you. Tell me why you didn't come. Surely, I deserve that much. At least I'll know then. Tell me, and I'll go. Promise.'

'You don't understand. People talk.'

'Is that it? You're scared of gossip?'

She looked around warily. 'It's not safe. You and me. It was different in the Metropol.'

'It can be different anywhere you want it to be.'

'Not here. If you run, you can catch the tram.'

'I'm not going anywhere.'

'I explained! You *promised*.'

'I lied. We like each other Lena. You can't worry about what might happen. Life's too short.'

'It will be if I keep seeing you. Leave me or I'll call the police.'

'Call them, let them cart me away.'

She picked up her shopping and began to stomp off.

'If you won't talk to me I'll sit down on the line and wait for the next tram.'

She ignored my threat.

'Look, I'm doing it,' I called.

I lay across the lines, waving my arms. On the corner of the street, under the canopy of a vegetable shop selling only carrots for the day, a group of people gathered to watch the proceedings. They weren't laughing.

Her face appeared above me, upside down and stern. 'Get up!'

'Not 'til you promise me you'll teach me to dance.'

'People are staring.'

'That's because they're bored. Do you promise?'

She clenched her fists, shook them by her sides. She looked funny upside down and I couldn't help laughing.

'Why are you doing this?'

'Because I like you.'

She looked at the crowd nervously.

'Someone's coming over. Pretend you've hurt your leg.'

'What?'

'Just do it!'

I clutched my knee and contorted my face in mock pain. She knelt down beside me. 'Put your arm around my shoulder.'

'With pleasure.'

'Hobble when you get up.'

'Huh?'

'I'm not joking.' She cursed under her breath and lifted me with surprising strength. 'We'll get the tram.'

'I'm happy walking.' Upright again, I saw the man she was talking about. He was striding purposefully in our direction and looked intent on giving us a hard time. 'Perhaps you're right.'

Lena grabbed her shopping with her free hand. 'Come on.'

A tram arrived on the opposite side of the street. We passed the man on the way. Before he could say anything, Lena snapped 'Space please Comrade. I'm a nurse. This man is extremely ill.' He wilted at the authority in her voice and we squeezed through the doors as they were closing. Lena pulled me to the back seats, faces turning as we stumbled down the aisle. She plonked me in a corner. 'Say nothing,' she whispered.

That was fine by me. For ten minutes, the tram rattled towards the suburbs and every time it rounded a corner, I felt Lena's body press against mine. That was all the medicine I needed.

I was good and nobody spoke to us. We were just another silent Russian couple.

We got off at a square of four red-brick apartment blocks surrounding a treeless patch of mud. *Ploschad 1905*, declared a bent metal sign on rusty railings. I limped beside her and she said in a level voice, 'You can drop the pretence now. And you can take a bag.'

'You're angry.'

Her brown eyes blinked slowly. 'If I was angry, Brian, I wouldn't be inviting you in for tea.'

Her flat was small and dark but she had made the best of it, covering the walls with multi-coloured cloths which she said her uncle had brought back from the south when she was a child. A square oak table with two bare chairs sat by the window. On it was a photograph of a young man in full army uniform, smiling broadly. I picked it up. She entered with a tea tray.

'My father,' she said. 'Before the World War.'

I nodded. 'Looks like he was as enthusiastic as mine.'

'He was always full of hope.'

We chatted all afternoon. The tea was sweet and strong. I apologised for embarrassing her in the street. 'It was the only way to convince you.' She apologised for leaving me alone that morning in Taganka Square. 'It was cruel, after such a lovely evening. But I came home and the flat was dark and I had work to face next day and I thought, it isn't possible. I have my life and you have yours. I thought, keep it as something to remember. He will only go away again. But it was very rude. I should have contacted you.'

'Well, that's one each.'

She smiled. 'It's not a good start.'

I felt my heart thump. She'd said start. Perhaps that meant it was official. 'Looks like I'll be here for quite some time, actually,' I said. 'My friend promised me work but it hasn't materialised. I'm stuck in Moscow. We could always meet up again.'

'I would like that,' she replied. 'Very much.'

That night the mild south-west front crumbled and a cruel wind from the Siberian plains seized its chance. Spring, caught in a false start, decided it was too early to make the running and crept back under the ice. By morning, Moscow was enveloped in snow again. For a week, Lena and I spent every free moment together. And with each meeting, we became closer. We skated on the solid Moskva, we ran rings round the poplars that skirted the parks; in the evenings we snuck into state cinemas and hid away on the back seats while the newsreels droned and, before the sun rose, we walked through the old city to the light of the streetlamps as everyone else slept. We held hands like children, swinging our arms between us, I took her to the café on Tanganka Square where I'd seen her rush past in the rain. She said the coffee was factory sweepings, the worst in Moscow, didn't I know anything yet? Sometimes I thought she saw me only as a friend, quickly changing the subject if I tried to get too close, sometimes I thought there was another Lena underneath that wanted to come out yet was too scared but, all the time during that week, I didn't want to leave, I didn't want this to end. And when, on the first Thursday of April, Lena said she had to work the whole weekend through and would not be able to see me until Monday morning, I felt restless. Three days. I'd planned nights out at the theatre, lavish evening meals, perhaps a picnic in the country. She kissed me lightly on the cheeks, told me I was a hopeless romantic but Monday would be worth waiting for. Before dawn we'd go down to the banks of the Moskva and she would teach me to dance.

But on Friday, suddenly everything changed.

'Didn't even need to meet him yourselves. He was *very* impressed by your Curriculum Vitaes. Know what else?

I made a deal worth twenty thousand yesterday.'

We were in his office. Talbot sat at his desk, rotund and proud.

Frank let out a long whistle. 'I've got to hand it to you, I suppose.' He smiled at him for the first time.

Talbot handed us each an envelope. 'It's all there. Last week's wages, train tickets, permits, everything you could possibly want from the man who always delivers. Contract runs until the end of the year. Should keep you happy.'

The Grozny plains. The Caucasus. A thousand miles away.

'You leave Monday afternoon,' he continued. 'I know it's short notice.'

'Shorter the better,' Frank said. 'Talbot – buddy, friend, pal – I take it all back.'

'What's it like down there?' I asked, stunned.

'Never been,' Talbot said. 'But I'm told they've got the best wines, the best women and the best weather in the whole of the Union.'

'Sun? I'm going to see the sun again?' Frank was ecstatic.

'Is he always like this when he gets his way? Brian . . . Brian?'

I was already out of the door.

We walked along the embankment. The Moskva was frozen at our side. Lena slipped her hand inside my glove and curled her fingers between mine.

'It is still on the surface,' she said. 'But underneath it keeps moving.'

I pulled her arm close to mine so we could feel each other's warmth. The trees were dark bones, fleshed with birds on shaky branches. They chirped and clucked, burrowed heads in ruffled feathers. Every now and then they would shoot up, specks of black dotted on a white sky, the trees erupting with the beat of a hundred wings, each bird blindly following the first as if it were safer that way.

Other than that the only sound was the crunch of our boots breaking the skin of virgin snow. There was no-one else around. It was too early and too cold.

Soon the embankment fell away and we were on a narrow path overgrown with bushes. Lena brushed her hand along the tops and laughed as blocks of snow thumped to the ground. She pushed on ahead, then suddenly stopped, spun round and landed a great lump on my back. I chased after her slipping and sliding, making snowballs as I ran. Lena skidded to a halt and waited for me by a wooden bench, giggling at my unsuccessful attempts to stay upright. I raised my hand, fully laden with ammunition.

'No, I'm unarmed,' she screamed. 'It's not fair to get me.' I dropped the snowballs. 'Now we're warm we can sit for a few seconds,' she said.

I wiped the bench clear.

'I come here in summer and pick *Klyukva*. Lots of people do it. It's a lovely sight, all the women lined along the bank with their bags.'

'Yes, it must be,' I said weakly. I had to tell her but I didn't know how.

Later, as the sun rose above the treeline, we came to a loop in the river and suddenly Moscow ended and the countryside began. Before, behind the veil of trees on either side, there had been building sites where cranes lay still on banks of mud. Here, the land stretched flat and unbroken for miles to the east.

'Does it ever make you feel small when you see this?' I asked her.

'Sometimes. But sometimes it feels good because I know it is there, and I know I could cross it if I had to. Do you see those two trees? They're over a hundred years old. The locals used to say that if you walked in a straight line between them and kept going, you wouldn't meet another town until you reached the Sea of Okhotsk.'

'Is it true?'

'No, not now anyway. Most of them never went more than a few miles out of Moscow. They'd never seen the sea. They probably thought it was just a big lake.'

I loved the way she talked. Slowly, so I could understand but not so I felt like an idiot. Sometimes she would talk and I would lose track of the words and just watch her lips, the way they pursed together and slid apart.

How long had I known her? Two weeks altogether, and those broken by a month of guessing. Two weeks in a lifetime. It wasn't much. I wondered what her lips would say when I told her I was leaving. Perhaps nothing at all. Perhaps they would remain still, a flat line telling me, more than any words, what she felt.

They were moving now. Two words. But I hadn't heard them. She lifted a finger to my mouth and flicked snow from the end of my nose. She looked over her shoulder both ways.

'Kiss me,' she repeated.

I took her head in my hands, brushed my lips on hers. They were cold, but her breath was warm. I squeezed her against me. We stayed like that, snuggling inside each other's coats to hide from the wind and ice.

'I was going to teach you to dance, remember?' she said.

It seemed an age ago.

'But my partner never turned up.'

'Perhaps he assumed too much.'

'Perhaps he hoped too much.'

Moscow, February – April 1931

So we danced, and the ground crunched under our feet, and I told myself *remember this moment, whatever happens next remember this*. And while we danced, I kissed her again, eyes and mind closed to everything else but the feel of it, until there was nothing but the sense of touch and we stopped the dance, lost to this particular point in time.

'If we don't move we'll stick to the ground,' she said eventually and kicked my feet. 'Look, you'll have to stay here until it thaws.' But I wouldn't let go.

'Lena, I'm leaving this afternoon.'

There, it was out. But it didn't feel better. Her body tensed and she stepped away. Her face, flushed pink from the cold, looked puzzled.

'Where?'

'Grozny.'

Her expression hardened. She shook her head, hid her face in her hands.

'You knew, but you didn't tell me,' she murmured.

'That's not how it happened.' I tried to pull her hands away but she would not be touched.

'You said you were staying in Moscow!'

'I didn't know, I thought I'd be here longer. It was as much a shock to me. Lena, come with me. It's warm in the Caucasus. We could work in the day and have all evening to ourselves.'

I saw it all. I even half believed it.

'You're like everybody else. You know it's impossible. You just want to say goodbye nicely.' Suddenly tears were streaming down her face.

I put my arms around her but she broke free and ran back the way we came.

I called after her. 'I mean it Lena! Lena! I mean it!'

I tried to run after her but kept slipping over. She did not turn round. Soon she disappeared behind the trees and all that was left were footprints in the snow.

Part Two

STORM

GROZNY
May – December 1931

I

In Moscow, the new Russia had been selective in what it revealed. The old city, sprawled in rings around the Kremlin, had suffered only the very beginnings of Stalin's onslaught. I had revelled in its ancient beauty, marvelled at the levelling of the snow. In the winter, everything was beautiful, but everything was hidden. Here, on the oil fields of the Grozny plains, everything was visible and, so, inescapable.

There was a sea out there, a sea of dark spikes thrusting out of arid ground. Oil derricks broke the skyline for miles in every direction like a massive bed of nails. And underneath them, an ocean, thick and black and aeons old. Forests the size of the Amazon, decayed then compacted by time, by the weight of sands and rock blown from vast deserts. Layer after layer, each foot marking the years, deep-down crushed. The earth and the people who worked it were simply a means to an end. Used and then discarded.

In the two months since we'd arrived, quotas were raised mercilessly, experts were at best shunted to backwater units, at worst denounced as intelligensia and removed. Column after column of army trucks and jeeps of blank-eyed soldiers swept across the Caucasus and descended on villages, rounding up farmers and their families and carting them off to the Collectives. There, they would till the soil until it turned to desert, rearing crops only to feed the bellies of the 'real workers' in the cities, while they starved on paltry rations. We didn't know all this. Not then. The truth came out years later, but we saw the effects, we saw the inescapable signs of disruption, we overheard the talk. Occasionally, we chanced upon a bone-thin peasant from an outlying district stumbling through Grozny's town centre where we were all round-faced and well fed. We saw the results of incompetence when machinery collapsed from neglect, when trucks broke down because the wrong grade petrol had clogged up the tank because there was nobody who knew what to do. We knew these things were going on but we didn't piece them together.

Sometimes you can be too close to see.

Each day that passed, though, my eyes were prised open wider. I understood now Lena's fear and felt her resignation. Not just understood, but visualised it, at times had witnessed it. She had experienced in Moscow what I, as a foreigner, had been shielded from. I understood, now, why she was so nervous about me coming to her flat. She had lived through the upheaval since the revolution and found herself a niche in which she could survive. Not a bad life, perhaps, with her fulfilling job in a leading hospital, a wonderful city to enjoy, even a trace of anonymity if you were discreet. Not ideal, but better than most. For a few weeks I had disrupted it, offered something else, and just as she was beginning to believe me I had left. Another stranger with golden promises. Another stranger just passing through. I'd had no choice but it made no difference in the end. Where was her choice? I could leave and she had to stay, peeling off the hope I had wrapped around her. Her country was mutating, its people in a constant state of flux, and its final shape a distant utopia glorified incessantly through the papers, the radio, the posters that screamed on every street corner. Throughout it she would survive, the less contact with foreigners the better. For her, any life was better than none at all.

It was two months since I'd said goodbye. My letters went unanswered and I understood. But in understanding I found no escape.

I gazed out through the refectory window at the vast plains. Outside, the air sweated oil and the dust-battered buildings coughed out men. The shift-change. A convoy of trucks chugged up the main track spewing a cloud of dirt in its wake. Every now and then, one veered off to a tributory lane tipping out workers at their designated well. The trucks were open-backed, filled with clean faces that stood out as bright specks in a wash of grey. Below me, the small line of people waiting to get into the refectory for a well-earned meal had mushroomed into a crowd, hungry but, as ever, patient. Black-faced, regulation tunics crusted with grease, they stood chatting, passing round cigarettes, laughing, grimacing. Some were down on their haunches, arms spread behind their backs; others, standing alone, stared the thousand-yard stare. They were thinking of showers, of bed and the next twelve-hour shift.

Above them was a veil of cloud, under their feet a bottomless black hole. In between, the thin strata that housed us all. I wondered how they coped with simply going backwards and forwards every day, year in year out. Perhaps, when there is no choice, what you have is what you have.

In the distance, the trucks disappeared in a spray of

dirt, grey on grey, as though they had been wiped out by a painter's brush. Moments later, the cloud ripped, a seam forced open by the sun. Metal glinted, grey turned silver and the wells looked like diamonds set in concrete rings.

Frank eyed his black bread and eggs with dismay before plunging his knife into the yoke, watching it spread in a pool across the plate. He mixed a dollop of caviar into the yellow mess and sighed. His skin sagged loose on his face and his hands were shaking so much he had to keep putting them in his pockets for fear that he would knock something over. The product of another brain-shrinking vodka bout down at Lily's, no doubt. He closed his eyes, took in a deep breath then let it out with a shudder and a shake of his head.

'It's no good,' he said, snapping his eyes open, 'I'm still here, I still feel lousy. And what am I given to see me smiling through the day? Alcoholic bread and a bowl of goddamned salty fish roe – with extra added salt to bring out the flavour!'

'It's Buluga,' I said wearily. Leaving him to discover sobriety at the bottom of a dozen cups of thick black coffee, I turned back to the window and my thoughts.

Her hair flows wildly as she weaves through the crowd. Finding a space, she spins in the air, her arms stretched up like a spire, then lands on one foot in a delicate swerve that makes me dizzy. The move turns into a straight line, picking up speed towards me, muscles tensing then relaxing with each push. As she nears the bank she leans, the blades digging into the ice with a satisfying crunch. She stops, panting, and calls to me. 'Come out it's fun.' Her cheeks are flushed and her eyes are smarting from the cold and I think, God you don't realise how beautiful you are.

'You can't stay on the edge like that. You look silly.'

'I look silly if I move. I keep slipping.'

'Look,' she says. A boy no more than five zooms past. 'It's easy.'

'The confidence of youth.'

She skates over to me, effortlessly. 'Mr Grover, you are not so old. Here.' I like the way she calls me Mr Grover when she is making a point. She smiles and pulls me out to the centre. At first I stumble and she has to keep holding my arm up to stop me from falling. 'Watch. Push out with your right, lean to your left, push out with your left, lean to the right.' I follow her steps and soon I am mesmerised by the rhythm in the movement. 'That's it, that's it! she cries. 'Stop looking at your feet.' And then I realise she is ten feet behind me. I keep going, concentrating on the rhythm. The air rushes at my face and my ears burn.

We skate along the Moskva all afternoon until the sun slinks away from the short day. A few minutes ago the ice was teeming. Now it's empty except for Lena and I. The crowds are wise, it is becoming impossible. As soon as we stop moving we freeze.

On the bank, Lena wriggles her furs on and skates off with accustomed haste. She smiles at me all the time she is doing it. I don't know what she is thinking, but I think I am in love with her.

A spoon bounced against my forehead. 'Hello? Hello-o?' Frank waved his hands in front of my face.

'Sorry?'

'Thought we'd lost you there for a moment. You really must make more effort with the natives. Andrei asked you a question, didn't you Andrei?'

The man nodded, extending a hand.

'Daydreaming. 'Scuse me. Didn't see you sit down.'

'It is alright,' he said in good English, looking at me earnestly with deep blue eyes that darted in little stabs with every movement I made. Andrei had introduced himself to us on the very first day, showed us our 'special' rooms in the complex, explained how, and at which specific hours, the rusty shower could be persuaded to expel tepid water, and generally made us feel at home. He was our contact. Barely out of his teens, fluent in English, French and German and inconsolably eager to please, for the last two months he had crammed Russian grammar and vocabulary into our heads to the point at which even Frank could spit out a full sentence without faltering. In return we let him wheedle as much information out of our heads as possible. It was an unofficially official set-up; that is, it wasn't written down in triplicate in the local Party rule book governing liaison with foreigners. But the big boys turned a blind eye as long as there weren't too many smiles exchanged between nationalities.

He smiled at me now (he hadn't yet reached his quota) and said: 'Will you join us for the projection tonight?'

'Probably,' I replied. 'But we may be too tired.' Frank looked at me. We knew what it would be. Undisguised propaganda extolling the virtues of collectivisation, and the unparalleled achievements of the first two years of the first five year plan. The previous show consisted of a formidably large man in a greying lab coat who stood facing the camera and delivered an hour-long speech on the importance of personal hygiene to the success of the revolution – replete with diagrams.

'It would be very nice if you could.' Andrei said leaving to find more recruits.

When he'd gone Frank pushed his plate away. 'Don't know about you but I'm going down Lily's tonight, get some proper food. Coming?'

'No, think I'll stay in.'

Behind us, plates clattered in the kitchen, water gushed into deep basins. They were getting ready for the next influx of hungry mouths.

'You think too much.'

'*Please*.' I sighed and let my shoulders drop.

'She's having a party. We're all going down,' he coaxed. 'Do a bit of mingling, meet some new people . . .' And then, getting no reaction, 'We're only on afternoons tomorrow, which gives us a chance to recover.'

'Thanks, but . . .' There was no point explaining. What could talking do? He meant no harm and I owed him a lot but I didn't want to go through it all again, not now. She was in Moscow and I was here. And there was nothing we could do about it.

He had a pen in his hand now, wiggling it between his fingers. Wherever he went he had that pen. It was gnarled at the end through years of biting. When he was in conversation, he would put it in his mouth, bite it, rattle it on his teeth. In Sarawak, he'd tap the girders with a special code to signal to the men that beer hour was nigh. It was the first time I'd seen it in a long while. Knowing it emerged only in times of crisis, a prop to channel the ensuing conflict, I watched wearily as it travelled inevitably into his mouth. He started to chew.

'How long you been in Russia?' he asked, after a few moments.

'Five months.'

'How long have you been blind to any other woman except Lena.'

'Four months.' I blushed. 'Well, not quite.'

'M'lud, I rest my case. The man clearly suffers from diminished responsibility.' He rapped the pen on the table. 'Send him to a bordello!'

'What's wrong with Lena?' I snapped.

'She not here. She's lovely, she's beautiful, but she's just not here.'

'You think I haven't noticed that?'

'Look, I'm having fun,' he said. 'Lily's a great girl, but it's nothing serious. We both know that in a few months I might have to shoot off. She can hardly come with me. So we just enjoy things as we can. But you, there always had to be more. You had a fling and now it's ended. She's a Ruskie for Christ's sake! She knows the score. She belongs up north and you, eventually, do not. It's as simple as that.'

I groaned. It was always 'as simple as that'.

A bell rang behind us and there was an immediate eruption of scraping chairs. Time to work. I made to get up, but Frank pulled me back down. I wanted to leave, lose myself in the job.

'No, stay a second.' He looked serious. 'We aren't a part of this.' He gestured with a sweep of his hand, everything I could see. 'It's *work*. And after work, we play, and there are rules that we must play by. You know what the golden one is?' He leaned forward, tapping the pen against my nose. 'Don't get in too deep.'

'It's not that easy.'

'Oh, it is,' he said in a low voice, 'and you should make it easier. You've already got problems, little lady by the name of Madeleine remember?'

'Look I'll sort it out, alright!'

'You won't do anything 'till you sort your*self* out. You mope around, hours on end with your eyes glazed over. Your work's suffering. Maybe your judgement too. What about the charts last month eh? Days wasted because you didn't read them right. You make another mistake like that and you're out. They won't even bother to contact the Embassy boys. Just "Bye, bye Brian, hope you like salt."'

82

He leaned back in his chair, drained the last dregs of coffee from his cup and licked his lips. 'I know what the trouble is. You feel guilty. Because you never told her about Madeleine, because you had to leave just when things were beginning to click, because, ah I don't know, because you're English!'

I didn't answer.

'Am I right or –'

A sound in the distance interrupted him, dull like the thump of a log dropped on grass. The sort of sound that is quiet when you hear it, but you know instinctively is deafening at source.

We turned to the window, and it seemed that everyone turned with us for by the time we rose there was a mass of bodies squeezed in tight and jockeying for position. At other windows faces were pressed against the glass, breakfast forgotten, ladles dropped.

A mile away, Number Three had blown. A column of fire, oil and gas touched the sky. A thousand feet up, at its apex, a sponge of black cloud spread out like a tumour.

Wherever they were, people stopped. Trucks screeched to a halt, men atop their rigs downed tools, wiped their brows and stared. The crowd below us waiting for their meals turned, thinned out into a long horizontal line. Some great hand had placed a finger on the cog. We froze, rabbits staring into the light.

A piece of debris flew off the top platform, smoking from the heat. It rotated in mid-flight, grew arms and legs which scrabbled frantically for something solid in unresisting air.

Nearly fifteen years later, when I heard of the drop on Nagasaki, I remembered that moment, everyone facing the same way, still and quiet, watching. I could understand the people who (from a distance) witnessed the city evaporate. They said they had to stare. It was beautiful and terrible at the same time. It was impossible to close your eyes, pretend it wasn't happening. It was a magnet that drew crowds. In Nagasaki, the light that vanished eighty thousand lives in a second looked like a ladder from heaven. Some were blinded by it because they watched too close or too long, but I'm sure the image remained with them, scorched on the back of their retinas.

The awful silence was sliced through by a wail. 'Misha! My little Misha!' A small woman with mousy hair tucked back under a headscarf forced her way through the group. She was round like a barrel, with stout legs that looked as though they could carry twice her weight. Down one side of her face there was a port wine stain. I recognised her as one of the kitchen-hands who spent her whole day chopping vegetables behind the serving counter.

She went to the window and pushed her face against the glass. 'My son, they killed my last son. It was Dmitri, I know!' Her hands went up to her cheeks and she started pulling at the skin under her eyes. All the while she moaned his name, 'Misha, Misha.'

Andrei went to her. Gently, he held her with his arms, pulled her away from the window, murmuring, 'Come, you don't know, you don't.' For a few seconds she stopped her crying and all we could hear was our own breath. Then she whirled on him.

'You watched him die,' she screamed. 'All of you. Just like you watched those vermin take over our country.'

'That's loose talk Oksana Ivanova!' someone called from the group.

'Loose talk? I had two sons and a farm and a man.' Her voice cracked. 'My other son was sent to fight for *this*. He didn't want to go. He was for the Whites I tell you. The Whites!'

I tapped Frank's arm and whispered in his ear. 'We'd

better get over there, see what we can do.' He nodded solemnly and we left the screams behind.

By the time we were outside, things had started moving again. The alarm had been sounded, setting off some built-in trigger mechanism that activated a sustained crescendo of blind panic. People jerked into action everywhere, shouting orders, waving arms or just running to and fro with expressions on their faces that signalled only complete confusion. They might just as well have closed their eyes, clasped their hands and prayed for the problem to go away.

We stood on the main dirt track that cut a swathe through the field, watching the chaos. 'They don't know what the hell they're doing!' Frank yelled above the noise. It was true, I could see it in their faces. They were all scared. Yet it was a fear born not of the prospect of physical danger, but of the possibility of blame.

We ran. A truck passed us on the way. The driver recognised us, screeched to a halt and shouted to get in the back.

'What happened?' Frank asked above the roar of an engine that clearly had not been serviced for years.

'Gas pocket. They went down too quickly. Pipe came out like toothpaste.'

Gravel pinged under the back wheels. Something knocked against my feet as we took a curve. In the gloom I leant down to steady it. My hand touched something wet and sticky. I peered closer. Poles of wood with canvas in between. Makeshift stretchers. Four of them piled one on the other. The sticky stuff that I had felt was blood. The driver was on his way to the well for the second time.

'How many hurt?' I asked.

'Too many,' he replied.

FIELDS OF LIGHT

There was no sky. A column of pure white heat rose where the tower had once been, one thousand feet from top to bottom. Where the flame ended, a thick blanket of toxic smoke formed. And underneath, the air was thin, the fire burning the oxygen out of the atmosphere. When I opened my mouth to breathe, I sucked in sound. For a whole square mile around the well, nature had created for itself a miniature hell on earth. Sixty-one tons of high tensile steel had crumpled under the strain. Foot long bolts, two inches thick, had shot into the air like primitive artillery. Girders that had taken ten men to fix in position had kinked and snapped as though they were no stronger than bits of a child's model. The main structure of the derrick was twisted and curled over to one side, like a mangled monster crawling from the heat. Around the base, sections of pipe which had been forced out of the drill hole by an ancient pressure of gas lay scattered on the steaming ground. I heard Frank let out a small whimper as, helpless, we watched metal boil. In a decade of working the fields, I had never seen anything come close to this.

Near the site office they were arguing frantically. I heard one voice above the others. 'You do as I say, or we *all* die.' There were shouts of protest and the voice rose again. 'And you know what I mean by that, don't you. You get your orders and you follow them!' This seemed to calm them down. As we approached, Edvuard Nikitich, Chief Driller for the south section and one of the few experienced oil men as yet untouched by the Party machine, pushed his way out of the throng.

Frank shook his head and whistled. 'Jesus! Look at them biting. Bit of a radical cure for a hangover.'

Nikitich stormed over to us, his face flooded with anger, 'Come to gloat, huh?'

'We've come to *help*,' I said.

'You touch nothing. You're not authorised.'

'Who cares about authorisation? Look at it!'

'Get back to your soft beds and read a book. You shouldn't be here.'

'We've got the experience. We've handled this sort of thing before,' I lied.

'Really?' he spat. 'And what do you suggest? Mr Brown here can plant his great arse over the pipe while you paw over the wrong charts?'

At this Frank stepped in. 'You think that rabble know what they're doing? I seen every damn well from Texas to Borneo but I've never seen a sonofabitch this big. You need all the help you can get.'

Nikitich raised his arms in frustration. 'Yes,' he said, simply. He must have seen the logic of recruiting our hands and heads. He glanced back at the crowd. 'They're just boys. They should be in school.' His eyebrows, a bush that travelled right across his forehead, lowered as he squinted at us. 'What can you do?'

'Whatever you want.' I looked up at the fire licking the sky that was no longer visible. 'What's the plan?'

'The plan is we confer with Comrade Sirienko and follow his advice. Follow me,' he barked and set off through the mud to the office. Sirienko? The Party man, the bureaucrat of bureaucrats? He ate production figures for breakfast.

'Surely *you* will advise *him*,' I prompted.

'You want to help, I do as he says and you do as I say. That's how it works.'

'But – '

'Leave it, Brian,' Frank warned.

As we walked, smoke from the fire suddenly enveloped us. It stuck to our skin, and with each breath took hold in our lungs. Frank bent over, hacking at the ground. 'I'm too old for this,' he cried between splutters.

'Here,' I handed him a handkerchief. 'A gentleman never goes anywhere without one.'

Lights from the office appeared through the gloom. The door was shut firmly. Nikitich knocked, no reply, knocked again. Millions of gallons of oil were spewing into the stratosphere, one man was dead, several gravely injured and here he was following protocol.

'Go in!' I shouted.

Nikitich gave me a withering look.

'Does he know what's happening?'

'It's all in hand. Comrade Sirienko will see us in his own time.'

'I don't believe it! I just – '

'*Shut up* will you,' Frank hissed. 'There's nothing we can do. We go in, we give 'em some advice and they follow it or they don't. That's all.'

'*There are people burning out there*. You saw Dmitri.'

'I know, I know.'

And then we heard a faint 'Come!' and we entered the Party lair. Sirienko was at his desk. Behind him, nailed on the wall, was a portrait of Stalin gazing benignly over the proceedings. A small bust of Lenin looked straight back at him. Long lists of quota figures fluttered as the door slammed behind us. There was silence as the man rearranged his desk. Edvuard shuffled his feet uncomfortably, uncertain whether to speak before being addressed.

'Well?' Sirienko said finally. He looked up and the lines under his eyes said it all. Fear. Who to blame? He leant back in his chair trying to look self-assured. 'You've come to tell me what to do. Isn't that right Drillerman? We need help from the experts, good capitalists, yes?'

'With respect,' began Edvuard, 'we come to seek your advice. The men are ready but we must act quickly. What do you suggest?'

'Concrete.'

Frank grimaced openly at me. This was simply unbelievable.

'After all, we have a lot of it,' he continued. 'Snuff out the flame. Just like *that*.' He slammed his hand on the table.

'How old is the well?' Frank asked.

'This is the new field. You've forgotten that?'

He ignored the jibe. 'How deep?'

'Deep enough to get oil and the occasional pocket of gas.'

That was enough. 'Look out there!' I demanded of him. 'What can you see?'

Sirienko smiled condescendingly. 'On a good day I can see the mountains. Today is not so good.'

Now I exploded. 'This isn't a bloody game!' Frank pulled me back, saying rapidly, 'Please excuse my friend, he's upset, he saw Comrade Kirov fall, he was a colleague.'

'Perhaps he should go home?' Sirienko said, a glint of malice under his concern.

'He is very knowledgeable, I think he should stay.'

'Very well.' Sirienko turned languidly to Nikitich. 'What –'

'Please listen,' I interrupted. 'you must take out the fire first. Concrete's no good. Before we get close enough to hit it, the heat will incinerate us. If there's another gas pocket there could be a second explosion. With steam we can put it out quickly, then work on halting the flow and capping the pipe.'

Sirienko went silent. I think he realised it was the only way but did not want to admit it. He was scared, but he was too damn conceited to realise the fact. He turned to the Chief Driller. 'And what do you think with all your knowledge?'

This was the litmus test. Frank and I turned to the driller. His face was set, his eyes blank.

'I think we should try concrete first,' he said without hesitation.

FIELDS OF LIGHT

We worked into the evening, and then into the night. There were at least fifty of us in tandem, the shirts pulled off our backs because of the heat. We bolted makeshift ramps around the well, using winches and pulleys to carry great sheets of steel. All the while, the oil streamed out of the ground, igniting some fifty feet up. From a distance it looked like a massive blow torch, and the men that worked around it, moths fluttering to the light.

Dump trucks came, laden with the quick-setting concrete they used for the bases of the towers. They reversed up, getting as close as they dared. The concrete poured down the ramps, inching towards the source.

By about nine o'clock it looked like we were making real progress, so Frank and I took a breather for a drink. We were standing by the water urn filling up our glasses when the sixth truckful arrived. Suddenly, Frank grabbed me by the arm. 'Look.' The urn was trembling on the table. The ground juddered underneath my feet and I felt myself falling. Then the world turned over and a vacuum of night sucked me in.

The ground was wet and sticky in my hands. There was a pressure under my arms. I was being dragged along the ground. I opened my eyes. My head was fuzzy. It felt like there was a bump on the back of my head as large as a cricket ball.

'Get up!' Frank screamed at me.

I pushed myself onto my elbows, forced life into my legs and scrambled to my feet. Around us, men were running everywhere, blind with fear, aimless, bumping into each other like slapstick clowns.

Then the air became fire and the fire became furnace.

Petrified, we watched the dark backs of the men, shadows against an inferno wall. Then we ran.

Grozny, May – December 1931

The ground trembled and behind me came the roar again, I felt the power of it at my back, trying to dig into my neck, to drag me down. But I kept on, feet fighting pools of mud, kept on until the air was cool against my face. Only then did I turn and confront the devastation.

The men staggered out of the heat, coughing, spluttering, some screaming as scalding oil stripped their skin, others clutching arms smashed by lumps of flying concrete. A thin sheet of flame shot after them wide and low across the ground as if desperate to claim more lives. It almost reached the heels of the last man before folding back in on itself with a pop.

Nikitich stumbled towards me, and then sank to his knees. The man could hardly speak, and I don't think he knew it was me, but I thought I heard him say, 'I had no choice.' I wanted to shout at him, wallowing in his self-pity while other men burned, but then I saw the bubbling black patch on the crown of his head and I could not touch him, could only turn away and empty my insides onto the scorched grass between my feet.

The stretchers lay hideous in an orderly row by the site office. Men were screaming to be taken away. Like chunks of meat on a slab, pleading to be carted off. I ran past them, not knowing where to look, blind with rage, and sick with the smell of scorched flesh.

I stormed into Sirienko's office, not caring anymore. 'Are you satisfied now? Come outside and take a look at your lovely regulations. Come on!'

He was slumped over the desk, hands ruffling his hair. He lifted his head and said very quietly, 'The apparatus is ready. Do what is necessary.'

Six boilers, connected together like carriages, forced steam through the long elbow-shaped pipe. A gang of roughnecks directed by Frank aimed the high pressure jet fifty feet up towards the base of the fire, then worked up and around. As we got closer, the heat became ferocious. I felt the skin on my arms beginning to blister. But we kept going, knowing that with another explosion we'd all be dead. High-pressure steam smothered the flame with almighty cracks as drops of solid oil showered around us. Then, with a sigh, the furnace collapsed into nothing.

Two minutes. That's all it had taken. Everyone cheered, some even thought it was over but although the immediate danger was gone, oil was still spewing crazily from the severed pipe duct and it would keep going for years unless it was cut clean so it could be capped. No-one knew how to do the job, except for Frank and I. Nikitich was injured, Sirienko had abandoned responsibility. All eyes looked our way.

'Fancy a long oily bath outdoors?' Frank asked me.

'Gentlemen never make a public show of themselves. But one can hardly expect a drunken Texan to understand such subtleties.'

'I'm sober, boy, believe me.'

'I hope so,' I said. 'I sincerely hope so.'

We armed ourselves with a two-man hacksaw and a pair of goggles each. Three roughnecks followed behind, struggling with hose pipes as thick as constrictors, while all around the well, two-foot wide arc lights had been set up. They cast magnificent ghost shadows against the night sky, dancing in massive, jerky sweeps, aping our movements, multiplying them ten times over.

The roar of the oil became almost unbearable. Frank mouthed something to me but I couldn't catch it. He took a rag stuffed in his jeans belt, ripped it and scrunched the pieces in his ears. I followed suit. It drowned out the worst but the dull rumbling that was left enveloped me like a cocoon so that after a few minutes, it felt like there had never been any other sound. It merged into the back ground, became part of my thinking until I hardly noticed it at all.

There was only one way to finish the job – cut the pipe by hand. I clambered onto the concrete table that housed the drill pipe and helped Frank up after me. Close up, the scene was surreal. Girders twisted out from the centre, looking as if they had crawled along the floor to escape some dreadful torture. Some had endured such intense heat that they had welded together upon cooling. They rose up like deformed sculptures with angular limbs. Above us, what was left of the derrick shuddered constantly from the onslaught of gushing oil. Fifty feet above, a sheet of metal from the platform swung to and fro. Everything was black – the air, the concrete, the pipes. A hole that sucked in all light. At the centre, the drill pipe snaked out of the hole, mangled by the explosion. We stood either side, hacksaw poised between us. Frank motioned to the men with the hoses and we were hit by blasts of water from all sides. Any spark from the blade, metal grinding against metal, would end us.

For two hours, on and off, we heaved into our work, each thrust taking bare millimetres off the pipe. Soon we got into a regular rhythm, leaning back, pushing forward, leaning back, pushing forward. Rivulets of oil, thinned by sweat, trickled down my forehead and stung my eyes. Water slammed my back and sprayed in a hazy cloud off the hacksaw blade. Fingers curled around the handle felt like brittle stone that could be cracked off at the merest touch. Legs aching, arms lead, tendons in the neck ready to snap. Muscles bulged in our cheeks. We kept on and on, wiping the muck from our goggles with every other push until the movement took on its own life and the only thing that mattered was getting to the end.

When the final resisting piece of metal came free, we collapsed backwards on the concrete table, nothing left to offer. I looked up at the clean column of oil, letting the mess spray all over me. For minutes I could not move. Then I got to my knees, saw Frank still lying on the other side, completely motionless. I crawled over, shook a stiff leg. 'Time to go,' I shouted though I knew it would be impossible for him to hear me. No response. I got right up to him, slapped his face. He was out cold. Not knowing what had happened to him, I shoved my arms under his, heaving his great weight away from the centre, mumbling all the time, 'You can't stay here, old man,' and 'You're on a diet, as from tomorrow' – as much for myself as him. I'd gone about a foot when I felt something catch. I looked over and saw that his foot was stuck under one of the girders, and a nail jabbed into his ankle. 'Jesus,' I said to no-one. He must have blacked out from the pain. I crawled back, got my fingers between metal and concrete and, summoning reserves I didn't know I had, heaved it off him. The nail gouged at his flesh as it exited the wound. I winced. The shock brought him round with a scream so loud it was audible against the roar.

Bit by bit, we made it to the edge of the table, Frank groaning all the while and gripping my shoulder with each step. We staggered down. I could see nothing, the arc lamps shining directly in my face. I lifted an arm to shield my eyes, pulled Frank along with the other. In the distance the whooping and cheering started. Taking heart, Frank broke free and stumbled ahead waving his arms in the air like a maniac. I reached the mud and abruptly the cheering stopped to be replaced by urgent cries but I couldn't hear the words for the roar behind me. Frank turned on his good leg. I remember his turning, the pain in his eyes, the look on his face of utter relief that it was over and then how it changed in half a second, less, to one of shock. I took a step towards him, ready to run, thinking it might be a seizure. His mouth opened and I saw his teeth, then

I felt it. A small rush at my back and with it a hissing like an arrow cutting the air. Then a bone-crunching thud. Frank's face loosened slightly.

'Stay there! Stay absolutely still!' he shouted. I stood rigid. I heard the crowd gasping. He hopped up to me, used my shoulder as support and took a look behind.

'What is it? Damn you, tell me!'

He panted in front of me, 'You think my injury's bad? Just a nick compared to what you just missed. An inch! You're the luckiest mother alive.' He chuckled. 'You can turn round now.'

I did and there before me was a foot-wide iron girder, planted vertically in the ground. A grave marker for someone who should have died only moments before. I stared at it a long time, not saying anything.

Soon they were all crowding round us, smiling, asking if we were alright. I felt claustrophobic, I needed to get away from them, from the wells. I just wanted to talk to Lena. I just wanted to see her, feel her warm against me. I would write to her one final time, plead with her to let me see her in Moscow again. I'll do anything, I thought. Say anything to me but just say yes to that.

The next morning when the pipe had been capped by an outside team, I went back to see if the girder was still there. It had been pulled out and towed away. But the hole remained, six foot deep. I picked up a piece of rubble from the explosion and dropped it down. It made a tinny clunk on the bottom.

Someone tapped me on the shoulder. It was Andrei.

'It's a fine, fine day,' I said to him.

He smiled. 'You and your friend are in the papers. *Pravda, Isvestia* – all of them.'

'I saw. What a night.'

'We are very grateful.'

'I'll make a good comrade yet.'

We talked a while, then I asked him how Oksana was and he went silent. 'She's gone,' was all he would say and suddenly he had turned and was trotting off down the road. I waved at his receding back.

Later, I asked the same question of a group of men working round one of the boilers. They shrugged their shoulders, looking away. 'Doesn't anybody know?' I said.

Eventually one of them said. 'She went mad. She was disturbing the others in the kitchens. So she was sent to The Sanctuary.

'What's that?'

Steam hissed across his face, disappearing in wisps.

'It's an asylum,' he said finally. 'She'll be well cared for there.'

II

I would stand before a crowded court twice while I was in Russia, though the circumstances of each occasion could not have been more different. In the late summer of '31, the Weimar Republic was crumbling, the US was wavering again but Frank Brown and Brian Grover had achieved the recognition that Talbot had suspected they would – engineers *extraordinaire* in the limelight. For a precious few weeks after the fire, we were elevated to the status of local heroes. Hacks from the surrounding areas swarmed on us, demanding to know every detail of our lives. The suspicion that was usually offered by the residents of Grozny to foreigners – a suspicion that was never overt, just sidelong glances or off-hand comments that could always be interpreted at least two ways – gave way to a curious and unsettling respect.

The old courthouse in Grozny nestled incongruously between the municipal swimming baths and a construction site for a new heavy-burden bridge over the river. A left-over from Tzarist days, it was intricately designed inside and out, lavishly detailed as though someone, using the smallest chisel they could find, had started on the bottom brick and found they could not stop. The gold leaf was peeling from years of neglect but this only added to the effect. The building overlooked a central market square lined with poplars that curled permanently to one side due to the storms from the south which shook the town every year. Proud and majestic, the courthouse was also a meeting place for locals; old men stood rubbing rough tobacco and stuffing it in pipes; large women rested their weary legs, dumped bags of food and gossiped on the bottom steps of the entrance; gangs of boys, hoofed their tattered footballs repeatedly against the side wall. The interior doubled up as the local Party meeting hall, where protests against American imperialism were staged by sweat-sore men from the factories going through the motions. Lectures embracing topics as divergent as the power of the proletariat and how to spot the first signs of potato blight; commemorations of Lenin's death; ecstatic celebrations of Stalin's birthday; meetings with unanimous passings of ensuing resolutions, these were the boasts of municipal life.

Now, a month after the fire, and a week after Lena had sent me a two-word letter saying, 'Don't write', Grozny was celebrating. The galleries were packed solid with faces peering in our direction. There was a bustle of expectancy. This was something special.

I scanned the rows for faces I knew. Just about everybody in town was here. Edvuard was there, looking ridiculous with a bandage wrapped round his head. Close by sat Andrei, alive with anticipation and chatting to a couple I did not know. A few rows behind was Bob Lewis, another rigger from California newly arrived and yet to make his presence felt in social circles. Looking slightly uncomfortable, he was surrounded by a group of Americans who had been drafted in to help with the refineries. They had their legs up against the back of the chairs in front, leaning back with hands at their necks. They appeared to find this whole set up slightly amusing, as if they were no part of it. And in a way who could blame them? We were all aliens. But we had work, we had positions of responsibility and that was more than could be said for many of our trade in the West. You had to adapt. And if you did it brought new rewards. Frank and I, along with a few others, were becoming accepted. It helped if you knew the language, or at least made an effort. These new recruits would always be set apart. They did not embrace what the local population had to offer. They came to a country and created a little America inside it and wondered why they were ignored. I'd seen it happen with the British in Sarawak. Frank, of course, had always been a law unto his own.

On the benches sat the heads of the local party; three officials looking bored and tired. They were round like balloons, stomachs pressing hard against their uniforms and, if you looked carefully, you could see the white of their vests between the buttons. All three of them sported bushy mustaches, the Party fashion of the time. Perhaps they all wanted to be little Stalins. They fitted the part, they lacked the essential element that set him apart. An aura of terror. They seemed merely comical, benign middle-party local managers with aspirations that would never be met.

Above them was a poster pinned to the wall. It was a beautifully printed, highly stylised picture of lean men toiling against the elements – evidently for the national good, risking life and limb so that Russian families could sleep warm in their beds with bellies full and hopes alive. They had square jaws and determined eyes that looked to a blissful future on the horizon. The first held a scythe swung back full tilt, the second a hammer striking an anvil, and the third, with arched back, shovelled coal into a blistering furnace. In the distance, factories stood proudly black against a blood-red skyline. Heavy type across the top shouted in joy:

FORWARD! WITH THE CHILDREN OF THE REVOLUTION

Frank grinned when he followed my gaze. 'The dream . . .' he nodded his head at the poster '. . . and the reality.' He glanced at the Three Wise Men. One of them stood up and shuffled a fistful of papers in his hand, then smiled in our direction and opened his mouth to speak. And just as abruptly snapped it shut.

Suddenly, there was a hush in the hall. Heads turned down the aisles as the great double doors of the old court creaked open. A young child started to winge. 'It's *boring*', I heard him say before he was slapped roundly across the legs.

The man who strode in was immaculate. His dark hair perfect and parted from the right, eyebrows that looked like they had been combed, chin shaved so close you could almost see your own reflection on it. His tunic was hemmed in by a wide leather belt buffed to a shine and his boots glistened in the shaft of light that came through the doors. Perched on the end of his nose was a pair of gold-rimmed spectacles, over which his eyes stared. As he walked, his feet clicked on the floor. The sound saturated the air. All eyes followed him.

The officials, who were now rapidly making a new space for the guest at the centre of the bench and clearing the desk, had evidently not been expecting him.

'Who's *he*?' Frank whispered.

'NKVD, GRU, *Cheka*, whatever they call it. Come to rally the troops, flush out the doubters.'

'How do you know?'

'Just watch . . .'

The officials lined up to greet him, each shaking his hand as though they were touching royalty, their knees bending as he passed before them. He smiled at them in quick stabs, the muscles twitching slightly in his face as though more would have been a wasted effort. With a calm grace he swept past them and turned to the crowd leaving a slipstream of charged air in his wake. Then he exuded the charge before him, casting it over his audience so that they sat rigid with attention.

'Today is a great day,' he began. 'That is why I am here. To celebrate with you an achievement that proves to the world the proletariat's march of progress is unstoppable. Why, you may wonder, should we have cause to applaud the rectifying of what should never have happened in the first place?' He paused, scanning the people along the front row and lingering just a little too long on Sirienko.

'Indeed those blood-sucking leeches, those self-congratulatory fat-cats of the imperialist West, always quick to laugh at us, will ask the same question. Well, I shall answer them simply . . . They are right.'

A murmur rippled through the audience. Heresy from a top man? Maybe a test? Whoever agrees first, is noticed first.

'It is true that such accidents under the Czar would have been been unthinkable.' I saw the officials at the bench going very red indeed. They looked most uncomfortable, their fawning smiles transformed to thin-lipped straight lines in a matter of seconds. But this man who held the people in his awe, this man whom I had never seen before and did not know the name of, knew exactly what he was doing.

'It would have been unthinkable,' he went on, 'because before the revolution we *had* no oil fields. Only a small trickle, a little boy taking a leak.' The tension left the hall. The Wise Men chuckled, and the audience caught on that they should too. Soon it had turned to raucous laughter, some rocking in their seats with tears streaming down their faces. The man raised a hand and the noise evaporated.

'There are those, however, who will look back on the old days with bourgeois affection. "The good old days." It was Marx who said people always thought the world was better when they were children . . .'

I whispered in Frank's ear, 'It was Socrates actually.' He looked at me puzzled, as if to say, 'Who the hell's he?' and I thought perhaps the old man had been right.

'. . . Nostalgia is a dangerous affliction. It blurs the sharp edge of reality.' He hooked both thumbs under his belt, striding across the stage in a loaded display of contemplation. 'Twenty years ago, where were we comrades? A nation on the verge of greatness? A people content at work and play? No? I'll tell you where we were. In the dark ages! Nihcolas and his *kulak* cronies licked the cream in Leningrad, while honest workers, you! and you! and you!' he stabbed his finger out in time to the words, 'with not a crumb in your heaving stomachs, licked the mud. And if you protested, the capitalist boot pressed against the back of your neck, pushed your face further in. Did our country thrive? Did we lead the way in industry? Did we walk with our heads held high, our faces smiling as we went to work? The answer is no, comrades. No, no, no . . .'

'What? Is he talking to us?' Frank sniggered.

'. . . So let the West mock. I say, let them! Behind their superior smiles lies the tight grimace of fear. For they know they are beaten. Their system is crumbling. The tide is turning our way. In London, affluent London, workers queue up in their thousands for a bowl of soup no thicker than water. In Munich they riot for bread because the money they are paid might as well be stuffed in cushions for all it is worth, and across the United States of America whole families travel in search of work that isn't there. In the end, they are forced to scrabble in the earth like pigs nosing out scraps. And, even then, they find none. And the banks and the grasping bourgeoisie gloat as the hope in their eyes flickers and dies. Snuffed out.'

Some of these self-same workers now began to shuffled their feet. It was a rousing speech, but even this great orator had not learned the vital lesson that you can only rouse for so long. As he paused to conclude, one poor peasant thinking the end had already arrived, actually stood up to lead the rapturous applause. Nobody followed him and the arm of a severely embarrassed wife pulled him back down in his seat. He'd broken a golden rule: never voluntarily stand out from the crowd.

The orator, however, ignored this minor incursion.

'We comrades, together, are fighting for a better future and we, together, are secure in the knowledge that our cause is just. Each and every one of you is at the heart of the fight. We must modernise our machinery and our factories, build up our industrial strength until we are the envy of the world. We must work all hours necessary, make the breaking of quotas a matter of personal pride, until we have achieved that aim.

'But we can not do that without oil. Oil is the lifeblood of the nation. When a well blows, it is like a pistol shot in the heart of the Motherland; when it is put out, it is like a healing hand.'

Finally, he turned to us and I shuddered suddenly. His eyes were dead. It came to me in sick realization. He no more wanted to thank us than he would if the Czar himself had been standing here. We represented the enemy, we had done them a good deed and, employed correctly, we were good propaganda tools but we were still not one of them. Rewarding us was necessary, it fitted into the scheme of things but when I shook his hand it was limp and cold. And even as he was saying, 'These men are converts to our cause. They know we are right, that is why they joined us,' I felt we were being singled out in another way. The sub-text to us was, don't overstep the mark.

I stared out at the crowded galleries and the heaving chambers in confusion.

More than anything, I wanted Lena to be here, to witness this moment so that she could believe I had become a part of this life, but even as I wished for it I knew it was a lie. We would never be accepted. Living with a foreigner might be tolerated for a while, but to expect to join the pack? That was a pipe dream. And Lena had known this. She had spelled it out to me so clearly when I'd followed her through the Old City but I had bludgeoned on, blind to the problems I might be causing her. And in the end, like a persistent salesman, I'd got my prize. She trusted me, she saw hope through me and then she saw the back of me.

Satisfied?

'They are examples to us all,' his voice blared on. 'Bravely, heroically, they risked their lives to ensure the aims of the First Five Year Plan are met. Yet they expected no reward. We are here today to hold out our arms in welcome and thanks. Brian Grover, Frank Brown, it is the wish of the Communist Party of the Soviet Union and the working people of Grozny that you are awarded the highest honour for your selfless act . . . Heroes of the Soviet Union.' The court erupted with applause as he pinned a simple red star onto our lapels.

His eyes clicked as he did it, a mental photograph to

store away perhaps for some future occasion. I grinned obsequiously. He pressed an envelope and a black box into my hand.

'In the box there's something for a real celebration, Mr Grover,' he said, in unfaltering English. 'Good lemon vodka, you won't find it anywhere else.'

'Thank you so much, Comrade – ?'

'Beria, Laurenti Beria.'

The name meant nothing to me then, nothing at all.

Frank and I stood either side of Comrade Beria clutching our money and displaying our medals, looking like little schoolchildren who had just won a form prize. Press photographers came forward, bulbs flashed our faces white. Beria took the opportunity to lay his long arms across our shoulders and squeezed us into his sides.

'Admire them,' he bellowed. 'Emulate them. *Beat* them!'

A few minutes later, the crowd began to disperse and with stifled goodbyes (now that no-one was listening there was no need to pretend) the Party officials disappeared into their layrinthic offices. Frank slapped me on the back. 'Our finest hour, boy and there's my Lil now. Just look at those curves.' He rubbed his hands. 'Aaalll mine! See you later, little boy.'

Then his voice changed. 'Hey, you want to come with us?'

I shook my head. He walked up to Lily, put an arm around her waist and started his sweet talk. I couldn't hear the words but I could imagine the general standard of the conversation. I watched their backs as they were swallowed up by the slow procession of people moving through the double doors. Little by little they disappeared back to their real lives, sucked into a bottleneck of daylight like sand in an egg timer.

I felt hollow. Frank had been right that morning before

the fire, when he said I was in too deep. Without Lena, nothing was solid. I'd received accolades that would make any man proud but without Lena as witness, like Bishop Barcley's tree, they might as well have never existed.

I decided there and then to walk out of that small-town court room, pack my bags and go. Frank could bask in the glory, lap up the affections of Lily and keep his broad grin to himself. I wished him well. I would return to Moscow, say thanks to Talbot but it didn't work out and knock on the door of Lena's little apartment and, if she agreed to see me, say goodbye to the one really decent thing in my life.

The hall was empty now, the crowd were just voices outside trailing into nothing.

I closed my eyes, contemplating my lowly voyage with glorious self-pity. When I opened them, she was standing there.

We met in the centre aisle. Her hair, dark and shining, peeked out from under a felt hat and curled around her cheeks. I looked at her, saying nothing, blinking repeatedly, each time believing she would disappear.

We embraced. Her fingers dug into my back and I knew she was real. She buried her face in my chest and clung to me with animal strength. I prised her away, cupped her face in my hands, rubbing my thumbs over her cheeks, staring directly into her eyes. Words tumbled together in my head, a manic whir of thoughts that would not turn into sentences. Finally, I forced my mouth to move and croaked, 'How?' but she put a finger to my lips, hooked it round the bottom one and pulled me towards her.

'Not now,' she whispered, and kissed me deeply. 'There's something we have to do.'

FIELDS OF LIGHT

III

The window was open, curtains fluttered in the breeze. Black shapes on a black background. A simple dresser, a basin, the end of the bed. But as my eyes became accustomed to the dark, blur coalesced to detail. Wallpaper loose on the walls, a stain on the ceiling shaped like Africa, her suitcase lying open on the floor, clothes scattered in crumpled heaps. My tiny compartment in the complex, home for the last three months and finally, as it was meant to be, occupied by the woman I had needed so badly since I came here. She had forbidden me to speak all the way back, and once the door was closed behind us, she'd pulled me into the bedroom and silently undressed herself and then me.

Outside, cloud split into thin strands and the moon came out. It cast a silver glow over her like a second skin. Shadow nestled between her breasts. I traced a finger along her shoulders, down her side. She was all soft lines. A bead of perspiration nestled in the hollow of her back. I licked it off, savouring the salt on my tongue, then moved up, kissed her neck, her lips. I nestled my nose in her hair. It smelt of autumn. Slowly, tentatively I entered her and she closed around me. The muscles in her thighs tightened and relaxed in rhythm then her arms were around my neck and her ankles pushed the small of my back down so that we hardly moved. And it seemed that we had melted into each other and our skin had glued together, squashing the air between us until the contours of our bodies formed a solid. We rolled onto our sides and pulled even closer, hardly drawing breath. I buried my head in her neck, and we stayed like that for a long time pressing and shifting back in tiny movements. Lena closed her eyes and I felt her shaking inside, squeezing me, pulling me into her until a wave of heat rippled up my legs, spread to the tips of my fingers and I gasped out.

For a long time afterwards, there was nothing except the sound of her breathing dying down to a regular rate and the touch of her chest rising and falling against me.

'Now we can talk.' She lay on her side. Her hands were dug under the pillow, her legs twisted up in the sheets.

'I don't know if I can,' I said between breaths.

'You don't have any questions?'

I nodded. 'How come you're here?'

She tossed her head with mock petulance. 'If you don't want me, you should have said so in your letters. But after that, you'd better.'

'Believe me I do.'

'Good. I'm here thanks to your friend Talbot.'

'Talbot?'

'And, I suppose, to your persistence. Your first letter went straight in the bin. I was angry. You hurt me Brian, badly.'

'But – '

'Ssh, I know what you're going to say. Wait. By the time your second letter arrived, I'd cooled down a little so I kept it. I didn't know whether to open it or not. I wasn't sure I wanted to know you any more but all the same I couldn't bring myself to throw it away. It hung around the mantlepiece gathering dust, staring at me every time I went into the room. A few weeks ago I received your last letter. That decided it. I was being stupid. You either face it or forget. I chose the first and opened them both. I believed you. I read your words and I found myself wanting you beside me. I remembered what you said before you lay down on the tram lines. Life can be different anywhere you want it to be and I thought, what do I have, what do I really have?

'Next day, I went to Talbot's office. You told me he

knew everybody. I put the information to good use. He was surprised to see me, he hardly remembered me in fact. He was even more surprised when I asked him to get me transfer papers. At first he wasn't very helpful, he thought we'd only met for two nights. I explained to him how we'd wanted to keep it discreet. I showed him one of your letters as proof. I hope you don't mind.'

'It's not a pleasant thought, I admit, but I'm not really in a position to argue.'

'He told me that you'd had no choice in leaving. You had to take the job, once it was offered, if you wanted to stay in the country. The head of *Soyuz-Nyeft* is a very powerful man, he said, and wouldn't take kindly to a rejection, especially from a foreigner. That settled it for me. I knew I was doing the right thing.

'Your friend said he would see what he could do, no promises. Two days later my transfer papers arrived.'

'And now,' she leaned across me, resting her chin on my chest, 'I'm here.'

'I love you,' I said. The words came out strangely, like a frog croak. I hadn't said them in such a long time.

Lena laughed. 'Prove it. Tell me what you love.'

'I love the way my nose fits into your belly button.' I pushed my face into her stomach. She rolled over onto her back.

'That's not enough,' she said.

'I love the way you smile, because your body smiles with you, everything curls up in a grin.'

'More.'

I placed my hand around her ribcage, 'And the way you pretend you're not ticklish. You go rigid, your face tightens and you try to fight it but if I count to ten . . .' I wriggled my finger. 'One . . . two . . . three . . .'

'That's not love,' she screamed, 'it's torture. You're no gentleman.'

'Whoever said I was a gentleman?'

Her eyes opened wide and her mouth dropped. 'Puh! *You* did.'

'You're mistaken,' I said loftily. '*That* must have been some other virile young male.'

She went quiet then and looked away.

'Lena?'

It was only for a second, an eye-blink, and she was smiling again. 'If you were a gentleman, you would profess your love to me in a long speech.'

I shuffled onto my knees. The mattress sagged under my weight. Lena's naked body bounced as I moved.

I clasped my hands together, looked up to the heavens and said whatever came into my head. In English.

'Once upon a time there were three bears who were particularly fond of asparagus soup. Unfortunately, there had been a run on that very vegetable which made them extremely angry indeed . . .'

Lena shook her head. 'What? What are you saying? In Russian? English is no good.'

'It's a beautiful language.'

'In Russian.'

'It's difficult enough in my own language.'

'It shouldn't be.'

'Help me then.'

'I know the thing.' She rolled over onto her front, stretched an arm into her suitcase, her feet stuck up in the air as she did so, and brought back a bottle of vodka and two glasses.

'A toast.'

'Snap.' I showed her my presentation case of lemon vodka. 'Courtesy of Comrade Beria.'

Her eyes lit up. 'Beria!'

'How come you know him? He's local.'

'I've seen him in the papers, he's a rising star.'

'Anyway, a double toast.'

109

'You must do it the traditional way. "*Litotska*", we say. Fill it half-way.' The liquid glugged from the bottle, deep and resonant. Her fingers were slim around the glass. 'Before you drink you must cross the glass, like this.'

'Why do you do that?'

'When you open your mouth to drink, the devil can leap in. The cross drives him away.'

'You don't believe that, surely?'

'You think you know me?' she reprimanded. 'How can you love someone you don't know?'

'I love finding out,' I said.

We clinked glasses. 'There are no devils,' she said. 'Not real ones. But it is custom, I like it. It reminds me of my grandfather and St Petersburg before the revolution. He would sit me on his knee, the bottle in one hand, a glass in the other, tell me stories all night then sing the drinking songs. The women there used to call vodka "orphan's tears" because the men would work all week and spend their wages each night in the taverns. They never came home. He told me that while he breathed his fumes over me.' She chuckled, remembering. 'But the tradition is good. It is old. Untainted.'

She handed me a glass, put her own between her knees. She dipped her finger in the vodka, swirled it around then leant over and rubbed it on my nose, then ran it down over my lips and into my mouth. I sucked the sharp taste off.

'So', she said, 'a toast. To all things old and all things pure.' We crossed our glasses and threw it back in one shot.

'To Talbot,' I returned. 'Old but not so pure. Mmm.' The air bit at the back of my throat as I breathed in.

Ileana tutted.

'*What?*'

'You've forgotten something, Mister Grover.'

'What?' I repeated.

'Your speech. In *my* language.'

'That's not fair.'

'I won't believe you unless you do it.'

'OK, you win.' I took a deep breath. 'When I first saw you, I thought you were pretty. When I saw you again, about two seconds later, I realised you were beautiful. And when you opened your mouth and spoke, a tingle ran down my spine. It's true!

'I spent an idyllic evening with you and a not so idyllic morning without you in the most wonderful city in the world. I spent two weeks dreaming of you, wondering where you'd gone, and one week wishing I'd met you ten years ago. Then I spent three days wondering how I was going to tell you I had to go and I've just spent three terrible months hoping you would write to me.'

'I did, I said don't write.'

'That wasn't what I had in mind. Why *did* you do that?'

'Weakness. I suppose I wanted you to know I'd received your letters . . . But your speech.'

'Alright, you ask me what do I love? I love the tiny hairs under your chin that only show up in this light and I love the space between your toes, and the space between your ears, the dimples in your cheeks, the ridge of your back, the furrows on your forehead when you frown – I can't do this in one go, the list is too long. You make me laugh, you make me lose my inhibitions, you ask me questions that make me think. But if I had to pick one thing, one thing that proves it – when we're together, the world seems better. Everything bad, unfair or cruel disappears and there is only here and now and that is so perfect, everything else is forgotten.'

Lena closed her eyes, flopped back in the mattress. I waited. It seemed as though she were weighing it all up, taking it in. Then she got up on one elbow, and like a child who cannot stop asking 'Why?' she said:

111

'More.'

So I leapt on her.

When I woke up the curtains had stopped fluttering. The air was still and dense. Through the window the sky glowed purple, paling by the minute. Lena's clock clicked away beside my head. I stretched over, squinting at it in the dim light. Five AM, but I felt wide awake. Faint leftovers of a dream clung behind my eyes as dots danced around the room.

I sank back into the pillow.

'There was a thunderstorm before.'

I started. Lena was staring at the ceiling, her arms straight by her sides.

'I thought – '

'I didn't mean to make you jump. Sorry . . . It woke me up and I couldn't get back to sleep. I was just thinking. Things racing round my mind.' She paused. 'Sometimes you can't stop them.'

'What sort of things.'

'Oh, nothing important.' She rolled over to face me.

'Really.'

But there was something behind her expression, something hidden, folded over a hundred times into a tiny square.

'You can tell me,' I said.

She smiled. A beautiful one that said, you would not understand. 'There is nothing to tell.'

'You don't trust me?'

'It's not that. It doesn't affect us.'

'Aaah, so there is something.'

'Brian, please . . .'

'You admitted it!' I tried to sound jocular, cajoling. As though it were just a game. But there was more to it than

112

that. I wanted everything from her. My love was selfish. It required everything. And the last three months had left a thirst that demanded to be quenched.

'There are secrets that should be left alone,' she said quietly. 'And you try to get it out of me!' Her face tightened, angry and confused. 'Is that why you came to this country? You like the way people's private lives are pulled from them?'

I looked down at my fingers, dug bits from under my nails.

'No, that's not what I meant.'

And then she was hugging me, rocking back and forward. 'I'm sorry,' she kept saying it again and again. 'I know you're not like that. I know you're not. I'm sorry. But we all have secrets. You do too. Everyone does. Sometimes talking about them just makes it worse.'

In the silence that followed I felt ashamed. She was right. I had a secret too. And it was a lot bigger than hers. I was sure of that.

We lay there, silent and thinking, until there were sounds outside – vehicles rumbling down the road, people chatting before they went on shift. Finally, she said to me: 'Some day I will tell you, if you promise one thing now.'

I gripped her hand, slipped fingers through hers.

'I'm sorry Lena. It was wrong of me. You don't have to make a deal with *me*. I don't deserve it.'

'No, listen! I want you to promise.'

'Anything.' I would have done anything at all.

'Will you take me away from here? Not now. One day. To England. Will you promise to do that?'

I grinned. 'Cross my heart,' I said in English.

'What does that mean?'

'It's an English tradition. It means yes. I promise.'

FIELDS OF LIGHT

IV

Madeleine is in her study again, writing. A shaft of light streams through the french windows. A million specks of dust dance over her head. I try to grab them but they slip past in mocking swirls every time.

I am standing in the doorway, watching her silhouette. She is a statue in the sun. The sun doesn't touch her. It can't compete against her own cold light. When she walks through the town on market day, it's as if she has no shadow. She inspects the stalls, rubbing cloth between her fingers, tutting. She never buys. The locals steer clear of her now. So do the other families. She is alone. She likes it that way. We haven't spoken for a week.

There is a pulse behind my ears. I have not noticed it before.

And now she moves, lifts her fountain pen slightly and taps it against the mahogany desk. The echo bounces around the room like machine gun fire, tat-a-tat-a-tat. She holds the pen higher and this time slams it into the wood. The nib screeches against the grain and I cover my ears. Suddenly there are thousands of scratches on the desk, criss-crossing over each other. She writes furiously, the same line over and over again, deep into the polished surface. I can't see what it says, but I know the words. 'Get me out of here, get me out of here'. I stick my fingers right into my ears to block out the sound, but it will not go away. It merges with the pulse in my head. I try to shout down the noise but find I can no longer speak. I try to run away but my body is rigid; the weight of thick air pushes me down, stifles all movement. I grunt, thrust my neck to the left, to the right then the pressure snaps with a rushing release.

I opened my eyes. Blankets, coarse wool against skin, sweat matting hair on my forehead. A banging coming from the kitchen. A throbbing between my eyes.

'Breakfast! Breakfast!' Lena tumbled into the room, wielding a frying pan which she hammered with a spoon. I felt sorry for the spoon but even sorrier for my head. I pulled myself up, the sheets ruffling comfortingly around my legs.

'What did I do to deserve this?'

She mistook the meaning of my question and smiled. 'I thought an early breakfast might soften you up. When you sleep you are like a plank of wood.' She held her arms stiff by her side. 'Like this. There was no other way to wake you.'

She was still in her nightshirt. I watched her legs as she flitted around the room. Smooth cream skin, skin I dreamed about. She pulled the curtains, up on tiptoes, the muscles in her calves hardening as she stretched. Last night I had kissed those legs from the heels to the top of her thighs.

She cleared a side table of last night's debris, two wine glasses with dried red sediment stuck to the base, a fat cigar stubbed after a few puffs, a pocket mystery unread since I'd arrived; and I thought how familiar we have become. The guards on both sides had slipped, leaving an easy warmth between us that demanded no explanation.

After the first few days Lena left my room at the complex and went to stay with Lily. It was better that way, fewer questions. I'd arranged it through Frank, asking him to ask Lily if she wouldn't mind. I needn't have worried; Lily had been surprisingly amenable to the idea and they took to each other immediately. Lena set up camp there in a spare room and made it her own. I remained at the complex in a cubicle which most definitely wasn't my own. The distance between us was about eight miles, but the journey always felt short. Lena settled into her new job, working all hours tending to patients who had fallen from towers, got their hands caught in lathes with no safety guards or their skin scalded from boilers which leaked from lack of maintenance. Sometimes she would become frustrated by the hopeless regularity of the injuries, but she knew she could not speak out. To suggest better precautions, to make the most even-handed of observations might be taken the wrong way. I fared little better. The wells demanded most of my time; our exalted status after the fire soon fading to an attitude of 'If you're so good, work some more.'

We lived for Saturdays, the only full day we could spend together. We fell into a routine, maybe snatching a few hours in the evenings, trying to keep out of the way (and prying eyes) of others. But on Friday nights we'd all get together, Frank, Lily, Lena and I and we would salute the fine things in life in a tavern close to Lily's house. Saturday mornings, like this one, were reserved for the market. It was a ritual we never tired of. Whatever the weather, we'd go into Grozny and lose ourselves in the crowd. It was a way of becoming a regular, both part of the scene and lost in it at the same time.

In the spring, before Lena arrived, Grozny was mild and grey with a plodding numbness that could have made it any small mid-continent town around the world. When the heat came, its character changed. The river cleared after the winter spates had dredged the thick mud from the bottom and fresh water from the Caucasus mountains replaced it. The transition from brown to blue was miraculous. The town became charged. Couples would promenade along the banks staring into the cool expanse. Gangs of children with scuffed knees and grubby faces skidded flat stones, forever trying to reach the other side. Old men with old memories sat by the bank gnawing at great hunks of bread with toothless gums. On cloudless days it was simply too hot to be unhappy. People fished and swam and took boats up to the dam; they became vibrant, they lived again.

The other change was the Chechen, a tribe that had travelled the Plains for thousands of years. In the summer they came down from the mountains to sell their wares and swamped the town in colour and chatter. They were a law unto themselves and one which the authorities could not cope with. Numerous attempts were made to bring them to heel but their will was too strong. The system was intrinsically alien to them. For them, there was no such thing as property in the traditional sense. Land was there to be used and nurtured then left again as the community moved on. Material possessions were minimal and anything that was made was solely for selling or bartering purposes. The idea of 'property is theft' meant nothing to people who had no property. But because they, for the most part, kept to themselves they were tolerated. At one time the police, like eager missionaries, made regular sorties into the hills to convert them. They soon stopped when their comrades never returned. The persecution went in cycles. There would be long periods of calm in which they were left alone, then some new career bureaucrat would hit upon the novel idea of making a name for himself and start the crackdown once again.

So each summer, as though the world had not moved on, the Chechen came down from the mountains and set up market in the central square of Grozny. They sold wonderful food, distinctive because it was fresh, and on the sides of each stall they would drape beautiful woven cloths of yellow and red with sparkling gold threads. The locals flocked. Money was saved through the winter for the occasion. Such was the popularity of the event that no attempt was made to break it up. After all, the police had their wants too and this was probably one of the few chances they ever got of buying something decent to wear and something delicious to eat.

For Lena, the market days at Grozny represented everything that she had been denied in Moscow – the freedom to wander, to pick and choose at random, not to have to queue for hours. It was a different world, an idyllic haven. Within weeks of Lena's arrival we began to live as though we had been here together for the whole of our lives. The summer passed in this way with hardly a blink. And suddenly it seemed, it was November, one month until my contract ran out.

Lena brought in a tray of coffee and a plate of fried food. I watched her as she placed it carefully in the space she'd cleared and thought *five months*. I wanted another five, and then another. I was sure it could be arranged. I was working hard enough, and they certainly seemed to need me at the wells, but I felt uneasy. Perhaps it was just the after-effects of that dream again. I'd been having it a lot recently, always waking in a sweat and a wave of relief. Perhaps I was just anxious about a warning from Bob Lewis after the medal presentation. 'Watch your back, they get jealous you know.'

Lena sat on the bed by my feet, folding her legs underneath herself. 'Big day today. Party at Lily's.'

'Again?'

'You said you would help out.'

'*Again*?' I clutched my forehead. 'What else did I say last night?'

'Oh nothing much.'

'I know what that means.'

'Only that you shouted out that Sirienko was a bumbling idiot fit for nothing better than a janitor's assistant. The place was packed, Brian.'

'Didn't everyone agree? I seem to remember them nodding their heads.'

'It was your head that was nodding.'

'Ah.' I fell back on the bed and covered my face with a pillow. 'I might as well end it now,' I said. 'Is it possible to deliberately suffocate yourself?'

Lena pulled the pillow away. 'I wouldn't let you, even if it were.'

'That man was there again, wasn't he?'

She nodded solemnly, then added quickly. 'It's nothing, He's just another face.'

I'd first noticed him a few months ago in the works' canteen. Thirty-something, blond hair cropped short, smooth pale skin, unusual for an area with such fierce summers, and a thin angular frame. He sat in a corner by himself reading a copy of *Pravda* and sipped a coffee for over an hour. I remember thinking, maybe he likes it cold. He was dressed in the regulation works tunics, but they were spotlessy clean and didn't seem to sit well on him. I gave him a friendly nod when I left for my shift. He didn't acknowledge me, instead buried himself into his paper. I thought nothing of it. Just another new boy, nothing remarkable in that, even if he did look a little odd. But then I didn't see him for another week which *was* strange. New recruits were normally introduced to the rest of us, taken into the fold. Although we were many, we just about knew everyone else by name, thanks to Andrei. When I asked him, he looked bemused. 'Nobody new here that *I* am aware of.' I let it pass. It was no concern of mine. Later that month things started to go missing around the wells I was working on. Small things: charts, files, tools. Occasionally my team was disrupted for an hour or so because of it. Puzzling, but again I thought it was a case of petty thieving. It was to be expected in a place like this. A few weeks after that an engine broke down halfway through the drilling of a new bore-hole. It set us back days. Then heavy equipment

119

started to go missing, boilers ruptured, bolts in the rigs were loosened – all manner of small calamities disrupted the operation of the field. And many of them centred around my area. At the meeting about the loss of production I explained that I'd asked around, but nobody knew how these things had happened. All eyes stared my way, and I felt suspicion rising. In the end, however, Sirienko just said, 'Work harder to make up the time.'

As we left the meeting, Edvuard Nikitich took my arm. 'No longer the golden boy huh?' There was a smile on his face that was no smile at all. 'It happens,' I replied. I wasn't too bothered to be honest. It was a Friday, the tavern beckoned and so did Lena. 'See you Monday,' I said. 'Perhaps,' he said.

Then two weeks ago, I saw the man from the canteen again. I was walking across the market square, in a world of my own, when I noticed him sitting on a park bench under the poplars. We were perhaps fifty feet apart. This time he was wearing a suit and he was staring directly at me. When I met his gaze he took out a book and non-chalantly relaxed back against the seat, as if enjoying the evening sunshine. A perfectly natural thing to do. I changed my direction, started walking towards him. He put his book away, got up rather hurriedly and disappeared behind the line of trees. Not so natural.

So when Lena confirmed he'd been there again at the tavern, I thought about it all again. Little episodes that seemed insignificant at the time, were beginning to form a pattern. 'He's not just another face. We're being watched.'

She lifted her hands. 'So?'

'So my contract is up soon.'

She gave me a hug. 'Let them watch. They'll renew your contract. They need you.'

'Perhaps.'
That's what Nikitich had said.

Refreshed after a mammoth breakfast and a long overdue shave, I stuffed my pockets full of roubles and a few dollars in case they were the flavour of the day. Lena drew up a list of what we needed which consisted mainly of Chechen spirit (a dynamite concoction) and vast quantities of fresh fruit.

Outdoors it was warm and clear. The block where I was living was reserved for foreigners and most took the privilege of a lie-in on Saturday mornings. So when we slipped out it was quiet with just the occasional chug-chug of distant wells and infrequent smatterings of half-caught conversations carried on the air.

We walked into Grozny in silence, down the long dust track that wound gently around the slope of our hill. By ten o'clock the sun was slamming the ground. Waves of heat rose up, buckling the horizon in all directions. This was not the Russia I had been told about. It was tropical, exotic, with an oppressive heat that forced one to be lazy and take one's time. Every now and then, Lena stopped by the roadside to pick wild flowers. Within an hour she had a massive bunch.

'You'll have no room left to carry the food,' I said.

'*You're* the one who's helping Lily. You carry the food. I'm happy holding flowers.'

I lowered my head and pretended to sulk. About a mile down the road a truck trundled towards us, a small speck on the skyline. Lena turned to me.

'If you must pickle your brain with vodka, then you must pay the price.'

This wasn't exactly fair. It was rare for me to get *very* drunk – I avoided it because the alcohol gave me a loose tongue – but Frank could be a very persuasive drinking companion. I've never had a high tolerance, so my idea of excess was Frank's idea of a swift one. I vaguely remembered an avalanche of plans for food and lists of guests and, luxury of luxuries, the setting up of a gramophone that Lily had mysteriously acquired. After that things degenerated into an unfavourable blur. So I was roped in, much to Lena's amusement, and she was determined to play it for all it was worth.

The truck was much closer now, its engine spluttering and coughing as it negotiated the incline. It reached the brow of the hill, but instead of speeding up it slowed right down, almost to a stop. At first I had assumed it was from the fields but as we approached it became clear it was police issue. There were three men in the front. The driver leaned on the steering wheel staring at us and smiling.

At any time, in any country, however free it proclaims to be, facing authority is an unnerving business. The power of the uniformed man over the commoner is psychological more than anything else. But in the Soviet Union the effect was more pragmatic. People disappeared.

As we walked towards the truck, I remembered our conversation the night I first met Lena: the constant fear of a knock on the door. Two of the men hopped out sending little puffs of dust into the air as they landed on the road. I approached them with a confident smile. I didn't know what else to do. It was obvious they wanted to make life difficult for us. Otherwise they would have just passed on. Then again, perhaps they recognised me from the award ceremony, perhaps there was still mileage in the temporary fame I had bathed in?

The driver was laughing now. A quiet chuckle to himself, as though he knew what his comrades were up to, had seen it all before, and was going to sit back and enjoy the show. They looked like normal people who, in another more normal time, would have held down dull jobs. But their uniforms had tainted them; the small kernel of self-importance that lies within us all had, in them, grown out of hand. They had power and they liked to use it.

They stood blocking our path until we were within an arm's length. Lena looked down at the ground.

I held out my hand. 'Good morning,' I said. They stared grimly at it until I was forced to drop the pretence.

'Name?' the first one said.

'Brian Grover.'

'You're not Russian. Nationality?'

'British.'

'Papers.'

I had learnt from the very beginning to carry my documentation with me everywhere. Nervously, I produced my passport and visa papers. The officer plucked them from my hand and painstakingly pawed through every page.

'What are you doing here?' he asked.

'I work on the derricks.'

He nodded and whispered something to his partner. When he turned back to me his face had transformed from a placid, slightly amused expression to an impassive stare.

'Someone is sabotaging the wells.'

That was a dramatic way of putting it, but I wasn't going to argue so I said, 'I know.'

'It is funny, don't you think, that all this happened after you came here?'

'What do you mean by that?' I felt blood rushing to my cheeks.

He waved a hand in dismissal. 'It is only an observation.' He glanced at Lena, looked her up and down. 'How long do you intend to stay here?' The words were directed at me.

'Indefinitely.'

'Then you may need to extend your visa.'

'I intend to do that.'

'Of course, it might be revoked.'

'I hope not. I'm happy here.'

He gave Lena a sidelong glance. 'I can see that.'

There was a pause, as if he was contemplating something more. Then he held out my papers. I reached for them and he let them slip from his hand. The passport landed face down. I stooped to retrieve it. He placed his boot on the cover and pressed it further into the dust. I looked up at his impassive face and he said, 'You must look after your documents. They are valuable.' I nodded, and reached again for my documents. This time he let me take them.

'Well,' he said. 'That's all for now . . . hero.'

The driver started up the truck, a smirk underneath his scowl. The two officers turned on their heels and walked away.

As they passed us the truck stopped again. The driver leaned out of the window and called, 'If you're such a hero, why do you bed with the whore of Grozny?' And he started laughing. 'The hero and the whore. We know everything you do. Everything. I've seen it with my own eyes – '

I watched them as they disappeared into the distance. Lena buried her head in my side. I felt her tears soaking into my shirt.

'They were just bored.' I told her, but my voice lacked conviction.

Lena looked up at me then. I wanted to lick the tears away. 'They *hate* us. Because I am with a foreigner they don't trust me, they call me a whore. Because you were successful they are jealous. Don't you see? And once they get onto you, you're in trouble.

'Ignore it. You said it yourself this morning, let 'em watch. We've done nothing wrong.'

'They don't need a reason.' She opened her hands and

124

deliberately let the flowers fall to the ground. 'You don't understand,' she said. 'You don't know how difficult this is.'

I didn't. I wasn't sure what she was referring to – something general or something specific?

'We'll need these for tonight.' I scooped the flowers from the dirt. 'Come on, you spent ages picking them.' Slowly, she knelt beside me and helped.

She had planned to put the flowers in a vase by the gramophone at Lily's where everyone could admire their beauty. Now, she said, it was pointless. She felt defiled by their comments. Her honour had been questioned. It didn't matter who by. It didn't matter that it was their job to make people feel uneasy. Normally, she would shrug things off but this had bitten in deep. The months we had spent together had been as near to problem-free as we could hope. We had immersed ourselves in each other. We took languid evening strolls in the park, had candle-lit meals with sweet Georgian wine at Lily's flat; we went, as lovers do, to work in the morning with grins across our faces. But now our little bubble was punctured. We'd ignored the signs: the mutterings from passers-by in the street, the cool stares if we went into a shop together. Nothing, we thought, could touch us. But it could. I should have known that the moment you think you are safe is the point at which you are most vulnerable. And unless you react, it is also the point when you lose your footing, the current grabs at your ankle, tries to pull you under.

Instead, the problem could wait for the moment, I thought it would be alright. Life had always swung to my favour in the past and it would do so again. We could still enjoy tonight. We had friends to meet, dancing, sumptuous food. But somehow, this time, there was a darkness at the edge of things.

FIELDS OF LIGHT

We lost ourselves in the crowd. The market was a blaze of colour that covered the central square. Canopied stalls ran in lines that spilled into crooked back streets. Everywhere tradesmen and women clucked out the price and exceptional value of their goods. Each stall competed against the next with a good-natured but intense rivalry. Pots, pans and bric-a-brac, knick-knacks and shawls, hats and ripe fruits and unheard of herbal concoctions were thrust under our noses. The place was a riot of capitalism.

Every now and then, amidst the jumble of bodies, we could spot a uniform. Just a reminder that this orgy of non-conformity was a temporary safety valve. It was all under control, and we were too. The Chechen were another world, they did not count. We could touch and we could see, but we could not become.

I gripped Lena's hand as shoppers surged past us towards a trader declaring an auction of floppy hats and ornamental cushions. His head was smooth as a conker and his eyes creased into a web of wrinkles as he held high his merchandise and yelled into the *mêlée* of eager customers.

Lena whispered into my ear, 'Look at him. He knows he is free. He has escaped and yet he is still here.' These were her first words for an hour.

'Let's get our "moonshine" and go see if Lily's out of bed yet,' I said.

'What's "munsheen"?'

'The drink. It's English for illegal home-made spirit.'

She tried the word out again, rolling around her lips. 'Munsheen. I like that.'

'Is it good?'

'Very strong. I might use it in hospital to douse the wounds.'

For the moment everything was forgotten. As we ambled back to her house arm in arm and laden with shopping, I prayed that the moment would stretch to eternity.

Lily's place was a small cottage on the south side of Grozny. From the outside the house was nothing remarkable. Square-faced with shuttered windows and walls blackened by a sticky layer of grime carried on the air from the factories, it stuck out of the ground like a blistered thumb. But it had a quality that marked it out from the rest – away from the main roads and surrounded by rolling fields it offered privacy. Here, we could talk about what we wanted as loud as we wanted. We could listen to music that anywhere else we would not dare to admit liking. We could break the shackles of everyday life and let ourselves loose. It was an oasis of normality and it housed parties that were the talk of the oil fields.

Only a select few were invited, of course, those trusted to be discreet. Riggers and refiners and mechanics who knew a good knees-up when they saw one and weren't likely to blab in case it was stopped. They were mainly Americans, some French, a lone Canadian named Cahl Tyrone, a couple of Brits who had followed much the same course as me and were happy just to be working, and lastly (and, for the lusty Yanks, by no means least) Lily's numerous girlfriends who flocked there for the attention, the affection and the lavishly bestowed gifts that were heaped on them by the decadent representatives of the bourgeois West.

Lily herself did it for the fun. She didn't fit into the slot that Time and Place had allocated her. To me, she seemed an image of the Twenties. She was long and slim with short blonde hair that curled into little tubes behind her ears. She plucked her eyebrows thin in high arches and she wore bright red lipstick that glistened when she spoke. At her parties, she became a social magnet flitting from room to room to ensure full glasses and lively conversation, and wherever she stopped people accumulated. She glowed in the adulation without ever expecting it or showing it off. She was just a natural extrovert who found fun in life and expected, no *demanded* that everybody else should too. It was natural that she and Frank would become partners because they both saw their lives as there for the living and little else. Together they made a pretty convincing argument for it.

Lena was her foil, and I loved her for it. She rarely wore make-up and was quite unconcerned about elaborate dresses or catching looks from admiring passers-by. It was this that had drawn me to her in the first place. Many might have thought that Lily's exuberance would have smothered Lena, but Lena felt that she had found a friend she could trust completely and one who would never let a single moment be dull. If Lily was the flame then Lena was the ember. Most are attracted to the flame, but long after the flame has burnt itself out the ember is still glowing.

When we arrived, Lily was in the living room still in a dressing gown and beginning her nightly hour-long session with her make-up bag and hand mirror. Frank came out to greet us, half-covered in shaving foam and muttering something about Russian razors. We sat down for coffee and made plans for what needed to be done by the evening. Through the window the blue mountains of the Caucasus beckoned, sharp and brilliant in the midday sun. I caught Frank glancing wistfully at them as the women went through the lists.

'You got roped in too?' I asked in English.

He chuckled, chewed on his ever-present pen and, looking apppraisingly at Lily, said: 'Believe me, young Grover, it's a price definitely worth paying.'

'Aha!' I had him, I finally had him. In my most condescending manner possible I said, 'Correct me if I'm wrong but what was that you said to me not so long ago? "Don't get in too deep" wasn't it?'

His lips tightened, his jaw muscles flexed but no words came back. Eventually he acceded, 'Yup, you've got me there. I think that makes the score one hundred to me and one to you.'

I had been to three of Lily's 'gatherings' as she liked to call them. ('We're gathering tonight' she would say in a hushed whisper to those lucky enough to be selected.) Each had been a memorable occasion. People sang songs, performed tricks, played cards or generally just lazed on sofas sipping drinks. With the lights down low and snacks passed round on beautiful hand-painted platters you might have thought you were at some high society party in London except that at Lily's, everything was a little rougher at the edges. There was no need for silly rules of etiquette or polite small talk or dressing up in ridiculously stuffy evening wear. People came as they were and left in the small hours. It amazed me that they had never been broken up by the authorities. When asked this by new and nervous guests Lily airily declared that 'nobody told and nobody heard.' True or not, the atmosphere was such that for a while you just did not care.

This time, however, the party took a different turn. Lena and I seemed just to be going through the motions. I planned to take Frank to one side and tell him all about our rendezvous with the police and the man we thought was spying on us. But in the end I didn't get a chance.

By eight o'clock the room was full of guests forming in small groups, discussing the good old days and the strength of the punch that Lily had concocted. Lena was in the kitchen spooning out caviar from great metal tubs and Frank was popping open bottles of wine.

It started with a faint commotion at the door. We could almost sense it before we heard it. The hum of conversation changed tone, rose up a pitch and suddenly became a wave as the realisation that there was going to be trouble set in. Then a voice shouted above the din, 'Frank!'

He was there immediately, pushing through the confused throng of party-goers. I followed in his wake, trying to see who was at the door. Then I heard a voice that I recognised. 'Let me in! I'm telling you it's for your own good.' It was Andrei.

'*Idyi*! You're not invited. Frank!'

'He's OK Lily. He's a friend,' I called, but at first she didn't hear me in all the confusion.

'I've got to speak to Brian.' Andrei tried to push past but was blocked by a wall of arms and bodies.

There was a further scuffle and I saw Bob Lewis's head appear above the others at the door. I caught up with Frank who was saying again and again. 'What's wrong Lily, what's wrong Lily?' so rapidly that she couldn't get a word in edgeways.

Finally, she broke in. 'He pushed me against the wall, he grabbed me. I thought – '

'You did what?' Frank made a lunge for Andrei but Bob stepped between them, grabbing Frank around the chest. He looked him straight in the eye and said, 'Just shut your mouth and listen. There's no time. The police are coming, OK?' Bob let him down, angry at the confusion. 'That's what Andrei was trying to tell you Lily.'

'I don't understand.' She flapped her hands in the air. 'I don't understand!'

'It's not what you think.' This time it was Andrei addressing Lily. 'I wasn't – '

'For Christ's sake everybody shut up.' Bob screamed this in English but I think the message was understood. 'You've all got to get out. Now. The police are going to make out this is some sort of brothel. Andrei heard it all. Nikitich set the whole thing up.'

'Edvuard?' I said.

'I overheard them,' Andrei said. 'Sirienko and Nikitich.

They were in the site office and I heard them mention a raid. They were laughing about it. They tipped off the police about tonight.'

'Why?' I asked.

'They don't like you . . .' he started, lost for the right words. 'They don't like you doing this. Especially you.' He seemed embarrassed. 'You and Ileana, it sets a bad example.'

There was panic in the house. People rushing for their coats and leaving by the back door, drinks spilt on the carpet. In a sickening haze I made my way into the living room. Lena was there. 'What's happening, Brian?' There was fear in her eyes.

'Get your stuff together. We have to leave. I'll explain later.'

She hesitated, not wanting to understand.

'Please, just do it!' She disappeared into the chaos of scared people.

Andrei's warnings came too late. Simultaneously, as the window in the living room shattered inwards, screams started up outside and a clipped voice through a loudhailer commanded, 'Remain where you are. Do not attempt to leave the house.' I heard thumps coming from outside and looked out. On the path, a few of the guests first to leave had been herded into a tight circle. Around them strode a group of officers. They swung their batons into the shivering bodies repeatedly. A woman fell to the ground, blood running down her neck. An officer went over to her. For a second I thought he was going to help her up. He kicked her as she lay there. Amid the confusion. Frank came by my side murmuring 'Jesus, Jesus.'

Suddenly, they were in the house, a swarm of them, ten, maybe fifteen uniforms, pushing people to the ground, pulling pictures from the walls, smashing plates, hurling chairs through windows. Nobody moved as the police went about their business. We all stood rigid, fearing who might be singled out next. Frank was by the entrance to the hallway, rubbing a bruise on his cheek.

The destruction stopped abruptly as a senior officer entered. He paced around the room staring at each one of us in turn, saying nothing, just looking us slowly up and down. He lingered by me. I felt his sour breath against my face. 'Party's over,' he whispered. Then he turned and pointed at Andrei, snapping his fingers. Two officers grabbed him, pulling his arms roughly behind his back. He was thrust to the centre of the room. The senior officer looked at us all again, his face relaxed, as if this were the most normal thing in the world, and punched him in the stomach. Andrei doubled up. His head was jerked back by the hair. The officer lifted his baton and swung it at his face. I heard a crack and looked down. There was blood on the carpet.

'You only get one warning,' the officer said to us all. Then they left, dragging Andrei unconscious into a waiting van.

A silence descended over the house. It was punctuated only by the sound of Lily's new gramophone. The needle had stuck. The same words played over and over again, rising and falling then abruptly cutting off. It got too much for Frank who leapt across the room and flipped the record off the turntable. It made a deathly screech.

For five minutes nothing happened. People were too shocked. But when we were sure the police had gone and were not going to return, we started to move. Bob got a broom and started to sweep. Others took the cue and set about restoring the place to some sort of order, happy to have something to concentrate on. Lily and Lena emerged from the bedroom. I took Lena in my arms, squeezed her tightly. At least we're alright, I kept saying to myself, at least we're alright. Someone asked, 'What about the people outside?' But the party-goers who'd been beaten there were gone.

Slowly everyone filtered away, saying little. By midnight only the four of us remained.

The silence sank into the walls. This was the end of a special part in our lives. What had been before could not be restored again. We knew that. It did not need to be articulated.

'What will happen to Andrei?' Frank asked no-one in particular.

'We won't see him again,' Lena said.

Lily picked a picture up off the floor. The frame was broken, the glass was cracked. She put it back in position above the fireplace. It hung slightly askew.

People disappear from your life like raindrops in a puddle. The picture is distorted for a while in the ripples but soon it returns intact, unaffected. I never found out what happened to Andrei, or why he was singled out, or even why they were content with only smashing the place up as a warning to us all. We weren't going to stay around while someone explained. I handed in my resignation which Sirienko accepted without comment. Frank said he'd work out his contract, then see what happened. We tried to convince him that it was a bad idea but he wouldn't budge. We wished him luck. I think he realised that the raid was really for mine and Lena's benefit. They'd been setting us up for a long time. We were lucky to get away with an 'official' warning.

Lena couldn't leave without papers, so a train was out of the question. We left two days later in an unmarked truck. No-one asked any questions. Lena hid in the back under sacking all the way.

Our beautiful summer had come and gone all too soon. If Grozny had been our oasis, now the desert was blowing in and even the blindest of loves could not ignore the portents.

Moscow and its grim winter beckoned. But at least, I thought, we could lose ourselves in its midst.

MOSCOW
August 1933

'It would certainly raise your chances.'

We were in a smoky restaurant off the Bulvar Ring, one of Talbot's favourite dives. 'Besides,' Talbot continued, 'I could invite you round for dinner parties, then you'd be respectable.' He drained the final drops of wine from the final bottle into our glasses: 'This deserves a toast. To a modern-day Rasputin. May your reputation crumble before you.'

As we left the restaurant, Talbot put a drunken arm around my shoulder, 'One thing I've learnt recently and you should keep it in mind. The problem with the world is that love is monogamous but lust is universal. Don't do the same as me. I mucked it up.' He'd spent the whole afternoon telling me how his wife had left him after he'd had an affair in London with his new secretary. I'd spent the whole afternoon resisting the urge to tell him about Madeleine. He was a miracle worker, but even he couldn't have sorted my life out. 'If you love your Lena,' he said, 'and I know you do, make sure of it.'

Talbot hailed a cab. 'Home,' Talbot said.

FIELDS OF LIGHT

I wondered where that was, where it would be in ten years time, and if Ileana Petrovna would be a part of it. For one drizzling afternoon, Talbot and I had pondered the might-have-beens and what-ifs that sweep through everybody's lives and now I was going to seal them up in a bundle and post them like a dead letter. I would marry Lena, if she would have me. I knew that I wanted to spend the rest of my life with her.

For a year and half since leaving Grozny I had wrestled with our situation. I'd spent days thinking it through, but never quite coming to a conclusion. How could I marry her? I was still, technically, married to Madeleine. If I left Lena in Moscow while I spent months in London trying to finalise a divorce anything could happen to her but if I stayed and we got married, it might make life easier. Every day, the newspapers ranted about betrayal as more innocents were put on trial for crimes against the revolution. Any excuse was used. As the lover of a foreigner, Lena would be considered especially suspect. We'd seen that already in Grozny, and even in Moscow we couldn't remain anonymous forever. But if she was the wife of a British subject, she would be legally protected. They wouldn't touch her as long as I was with her. As Talbot said, we would be more respectable. Would it secure a passage out of this country together? A possibility, I'd thought, but I had no guarantee. And if it could, what then? We'd return to London, a bigamist and his illegal wife. If anyone found out, she might be sent back. In reality, the situation was impossible. And it had been made worse by my own refusal to face the truth. I had never been able to tell Lena about Madeleine. Many times, I'd been on the verge of it but couldn't bring myself to make that final push. I couldn't risk losing her. And now, things were so good between us that I didn't want anything to ruin it. It had been better to pretend that the problem did not exist. I had pushed it into a quiet little corner of my mind until it disappeared. At times, I believed that the Brian Grover who had married Madeleine Jacobs in the States six years ago was a different man altogether from me now. I knew that the two of me were inextricably linked and that they were both presented with an inescapable dilemma. I *shouldn't* marry Lena until I'd left the country to divorce Madeleine. Lena *couldn't* be safe unless she was married to me.

Talbot's parting comment and the difference between 'shouldn't' and 'couldn't' had finally decided me. He said marriage would raise our chances of leaving together one day. I'd only thought it might. He'd confirmed it. But even married, how could I leave her alone here, while the purges continued, while every second look was over our shoulders? At least we could stay here safely together, in relative peace, until it was safe for me to go to London and sort out the other half of my life that I tried so desperately to forget.

If I was a modern-day Rasputin then Talbot was King Midas. Recent personal difficulties aside, everything he touched turned to gold. The hard work he had put in over the past couple of decades was reaping dividends in the middle of the depression. In Moscow he was seen as a miracle man. If they needed some piece of vital machinery which could not be made in Russia they would turn to him and he'd sort out the supply. In England, companies fought for his contracts. In a time when protectionism had swept the world and stifled trade between nations the word export was almost a dirty word. Nevertheless business was needed desperately. The Soviet Union was virgin territory and with Talbot's help British firms could ravage it.

FIELDS OF LIGHT

When Lena and I had first arrived back in Moscow, Talbot had been very helpful. After our explanations about the raid, he exuded copious amounts of grease getting Lena a work-transfer permit back to her old hospital, while warning us that this would be the last time before serious questions might be asked. In return, (there was always a return) I agreed to work for him again. This time I was to be a salesman. It had taken a long time to learn the ropes but in the end it was worth it. A few weeks earlier I'd secured one of the largest commissions Talbot had ever had the pleasure to benefit from. It was simple really. I had simply applied his ultimate rule: spot the gap and fill it.

One of the things I had learned about Russia was that the systems by which they ran their industries were hopelessly inefficient and dangerously short-sighted. On the oil fields we were constantly running out of the most basic tools, even though they had a workshop on-site. If they could not organise demand and supply on a local level, then nationally there must be massive room for improvement. I considered my target. What changes had taken place in the last few years that had not been met by similar industrial changes? Stalin's first five year plan offered an unending list of upheavals to look into. The most glaring was his modernization of agriculture.

For centuries, Russians had lived off the land, the peasants using hand-held tools to till the soil, and scythes to cut the wheat. There had been no need for improvement. Before emancipation, the serfs had worked for their lords at near starvation levels and there was no incentive to do more than the necessary minimum. Afterwards, most concentrated on being self-sufficient, with perhaps a little extra to sell down at the local market, or a barter here and there. Why modernize and grow more than was necessary? Collectivization changed all this. Farms were to be run like heavy industry. Stalin wanted to drag the peasants screaming into the twentieth century. Accordingly, millions of tractors were built in the first couple of years of the plan and sent off to the collectives where nobody knew how to use them. Or, more importantly, maintain them. Within two years most had broken down: the engines clogged up, metal fatigued, gears crunched. Unfortunately for them, no-one could fix them. Fortunately for me, I knew of a factory in Britain crying out for trade in engine parts. I applied Talbot's Law and linked the two together. This led me to an order of 10,000,000 crank shafts from the Soviet Agricultural Ministry to replace worn out parts in their tractor engines. When he heard, Talbot blessed me like some modern-day saint. I didn't complain, for genuine compliments from the man were rare indeed.

Ileana Petrovna and I had moved into a flat together in the suburbs shortly after returning to Moscow. It was nothing much, two square rooms with a bed, a brown-stained sink and a broom cupboard. Paint flaked off the ceiling, the windows would not shut properly and the corridors on the block smelt of bleach on a good day and rotting vegetables on a bad. For all that, it was a home, a place where we could be together without interruption from the outside world. With the money I had from an insurance policy which had recently matured in London, I might have wheedled us into a posher complex but we felt it would have been riddled with inner-Party members snooping around until they dug up what was required. Besides, Lena wanted to be with the real Moscovites, with people who lived from day to day, not knowing what the next week might bring. To escape, to move away, was the step we both wanted to take, but that was not yet possible. So we went about out lives like any other couple – living a mundane, but blissful life.

Grozny had been dreamy at weekends, Moscow was

dreamy every day. With my new-found wealth I worked only when I felt like it while Lena now only had to suffer the occasional night shifts. We lived a leisurely life, spending whole afternoons at the swimming baths, lying with our feet dipped in the water, telling each other stories while the sun baked our backs. When it got too hot we'd slip back in the water. Later, we might take a stroll through one of the parks, then jump on a tram rattling into the centre and shop at GUM, the large store catering for the less communists and foreigners. There, I would treat Lena to real coffee which, unlike the dusty grey powder that passed for a drink in the normal food stores, was freshly ground from beans. Every time I opened a pack she would snatch it away and stick her nose inside, inhaling deeply. 'The smell,' she once said, 'that makes me believe in heaven.'

Then, in the evenings, we might catch an opera or a new play at the Bolshoi, and wash the night down with a fine meal. We became accustomed to living in a pocket of fantasy whilst all around us the country was in turmoil. I make no apologies about the fact that we turned our backs. Someone with a conscience would have got involved, would have campaigned for the downtrodden, fought against the corruption that lay at Russia's heart. The person with a conscience would have been bundled into prison to rot for the rest of his days at his very first protest. If there had been a choice, we would have left the country completely, set up home in England or Europe or Africa – any place that might let us be. But there was none: Lena could not leave, and I would not leave without her. So, though we talked about a different life, we took refuge in leading a grand existence in the eye of poverty and persecution. We wanted for nothing. We made new friends through Talbot's connections, both foreigners and natives, believers and double-thinkers. Lena took me to dinners at the houses of her colleagues; young women and men who worked at the hospital and talked of bright futures for all. For many of them I was a novelty. They wanted to know what I thought of Russia, indeed why I was living there when I was so obviously a capitalist. I said that I admired the Russian character, I loved the people, their open friendliness and I wanted to be a part of it. There was no point in explaining the other side of my argument, they would have been offended or I would have been reported. You had to learn, especially in the city, to be tight-lipped. If you said anything that could have a double meaning, let alone clear-cut criticism, it would come back to you. Lena was probably already marked so we had to be extra careful. No-one was safe but no-one seemed particularly bothered unless it directly affected them.

That day, as I rode with Talbot in the back of a cab, I thought about all this and believed that we would be safe. He dropped me off beside an old woman selling flowers, I bought the largest bunch I could hold.

It wasn't the most romantic of settings. When I arrived home, Lena was standing at the cooker frying onions. Even before I opened the door I could hear the familiar scrape of the spatula against the pan.

She was wearing an apron tied tightly around her waist and making such a clatter that she didn't hear me come in. So I watched for a while. It summed up everything I adored about her. Even in drab clothes she was elegant. Her silky dark hair, left to grow this past summer, hung down in long waves over her shoulders. When she leaned forward, it fell away over her front and I wanted to bite her neck. Instead I crept up on her, silently laid the flowers on the sideboard, and slipped my arms around her tiny waist.

She didn't flinch, but inclined her head until our lips met.

'Turn right round,' I said. She twisted in the circle of my arms. I reached over for the flowers, placed them in between us.

'They're beautiful!' She went all doe-eyed. 'Are they for me?'

I put a finger to my lips. 'Not a squeak.'

She wiggled her body as though a shiver went down her spine. 'Ooh, I love it when you get masterful.'

'I'm serious!'

She rubbed herself up against me, her eyebrows raised in surprise. 'I know you are. It's not *that* difficult to tell.'

Clearly she had no intention of taking me seriously so I lifted her off the ground and carried her out of the kitchen. Picking someone up with ease is always a nice way of asserting your authority.

'What are you doing?' she laughed.

'I'm taking you to the sofa where you will remain silent until you hear what I have to ask you. Do you promise?'

'I promise.'

I set her down, thrust the flowers into her open hands and knelt down before her like a true gentleman.

'Ileana Golyius Petrovna,' I began.

'Petrovna Golyius,' she corrected.

'You've broken your word already. How can I say what I'm going to say if you break your word so easily? . . . Ileana Petrovna Golyius,' I tried again, 'will you marry me?'

The flowers fell to the floor and I took her hand, kissed it lightly with my lips. Her nails dug into my palms. When I looked up her face was wet and the muscles in her cheeks had gone taut making hollows that caught pools of shadow. Her eyes were closed, the lids squeezed tight and fluttering as though she were dreaming.

You are the most beautiful thing I have ever touched,

I thought then. Say yes. Say yes and it will be alright. It will be solid and no-one will be able to take it away from us.

For a long time I was aware of nothing except waiting for her lips to move. They were all I could see. Two pink lips, smooth and full and edible, two lips that would form the simple syllable *Da*. They had to. I willed them. But they didn't.

'Brian, you ask such stupid questions!'

I flinched at the words, at the exasperation in her voice. Then she said, 'Of course I'll marry you.'

I hugged her, I squeezed her, I span her round the room. Suddenly there was no gravity, my legs felt light, I thought I might even be able to dance. This woman who made me laugh, who made me think and feel, this woman who was as warm inside as her skin was out, who was raw and real and more complete than I could ever be was going to marry me. My head went woozy as though I'd downed a dose of laudenum. I felt invincible.

'You're crying,' I said as we hugged each other. 'You should be happy.'

'I am,' she said. She sniffed and wiped her eyes. 'It must be the onions . . .' Her expression crumbled into panic. 'The onions!' She leapt up and ran into the kitchen. As soon as she opened the door, black smoke billowed into the living room.

Dinner that night was a little on the charred side.

There was a long line of us, men and women, dressed up in our finest waiting for the big moment. Only, in the Soviet Union of 1933 there was no big moment. Marriage in Moscow was definitely creeping out of fashion. It was too bourgeois, too irrelevant. There were factories to be built, fields to be ploughed; who cared about a ring on a finger?

The registry office was as bleak as a railway station toilet. At the end of the queue was a pane of glass behind which sat a dour attendant with about as much goodwill as a pike eyeing up a baby frog. In fact, she looked like a pike. Her nose pointed out hard and beaky and under her mouth hung a sack where she stored all the resentment and bitterness of her years.

Smoke hung in the air and bridegrooms flicked ash absentmindedly on their trousers while the brides with immaculate hairdos briskly brushed them down. Looking at the faces of the people around us it seemed to me that they didn't consider this to be so special an event. It was more something to be done. They were the transitional society, young and old who were bowing to the new way of doing things with meek acceptance yet could not rub off the echoes of a previous age. Tradition does not die, it is manipulated to suit the needs of the present.

The queue dwindled achingly slowly. Every half an hour there would be a shuffle of feet on polished tiles then a resumption of hushed, tired talk as the wait continued. In between each processed couple there was a long wait while Pikeface pulled down the shutter at the cubicle, ostensibly to do paper work but more than likely just to annoy us, hope we would get bored, think again, and disappear. Each time the shutter went up again, Pikeface sighed. Written large across her face was a neon sign saying: 'JUST GO AWAY'. But we didn't budge an inch. One couple had come prepared, knew they were in for the duration. With smiles they took out a lunch box crammed with finger snacks and fed each other. It set off a domino effect with many others following suit. Those that had no food were offered by those that had and soon we were all munching.

Typically, in Russia they had the reception before they had the wedding.

Lena looked stunning. Her hair was pinned up in a bunch on top of her head. Little ringlets, curled meticulously in the morning, hung down each side of her face. For once, she wore make-up, though only a little. Her eyes were orbs that could suck me in with a glance: they didn't need painting. But it was her dress that stuck in my memory. It was the same red, flower-print dress that she had worn on the day we met. And this time it didn't hide an undernourished body, it hinted at the beautiful, curvy woman underneath.

The 'ceremony' itself was very bleak. We were given forms to fill in that demanded revelation of every conceivable personal fact, signed them at the bottom and handed over five roubles. A simple transaction.

When it was done Pikeface let out another of her gutteral sighs and pronounced in monotone: 'You are now husband and wife.'

I whispered into Lena's ear, 'See how her nose twitches when she speaks?'

Lena laughed out loud but cut it short when Pikeface started to scowl. She stared us out waiting for us to go but there was one final thing to do. Wedding rings had been outlawed in the Soviet Union. They'd been pronounced bourgeois. I took Lena's hand, made a ring with my thumb and forefinger and slipped it over her fourth finger. Lena swung her arms around my neck and we kissed. 'I have something for you too.' From her pocket she produced a square silver case. She placed it in my palm.

'Open it.'

Inside was a miniature portrait of her in watercolour. 'I had it done by a street artist in the market at Grozny. I was going to give it to you on your birthday but I forgot. The case is hundreds of years old. It's an heirloom.'

'It's beautiful.'

'You must keep it on you all the time. It's instead of a ring. Do you promise?'

'I promise.'

There were coughs behind us, others were waiting. Pikeface looked me directly in the eye and said, '*Nyet*'.

As we strolled across Red Square that day, her feet tapped the cobbles in time with mine. I remember the sun stroking our backs as it sank behind the Kremlin wall and how we danced at the edges of sharp shadows cast by Spasskaya Tower, the tower of the saviour. Small groups stopped to watch. Some smiled, some clicked their tongues in disapproval but I think at one point we even got a clap. She taught me finally how to dance properly, there and then, humming Tchaikovsky's December Waltz to keep me in time. We pressed against each other and I trod on her toes, clumsily, but this time it didn't matter. We danced for what seemed like hours and slowly I became sure of the movements, the simplest steps in the book but for me a mountain to scale. Soon we were spinning round, the Kremlin barricades looming over us dark but irrelevant. Little girls and boys and old women and men gawped at the curiosity, then moved on. I knew we were just a fleeting moment in their lives but that I would remember this day for the rest of my life.

We stopped, breathless, Moscow a mere blur in the background. I rested on Lena's shoulder and gasped in great lungfuls of air. Lenin's mausoleum stood before us and I remarked how it looked like a pile of matchboxes stacked up. She frowned at me and said, 'Don't be so disrespectful' and I laughed at the smirk behind her scowl. But I also knew she was being careful for just across the cobbled stones a queue snaked up to the place where the man had been laid to rest.

Lena grabbed my hand and yanked me through the crowds. 'I want to show you something,' she cried as we ran through the gateway to Sobornaya Ploschad. 'There,' she said, and pointed to the white bell tower of Ivan the Great. I let out a deep whistle of admiration, even though I had seen it before.

'Don't pretend,' she said to me. 'It's obvious you know it. That's not my surprise.'

We went right up to the base of the tower where the enormous Czar Bell lay. Hoisted in the tower, it had been left where it was made. She walked around it, tapping her nails against the metal. 'Listen!'

The chimes came in quick succession as she tapped, tight and metallic at first then folding over themselves and building up to a deep rumble like a far off thunderstorm. She ran around the bell, now banging it with her fist. I chased after her and as she speeded up, the rumble turned into a roar. When I caught her, she flopped back against the bell. The vibration thrummed through our bodies.

'It was cast two hundred years ago, almost to the day,' she told me. 'This sound is centuries old,' she whispered. It's for us, don't you see? It's our celebration.'

'But the bell was never tolled,' I said.

'I know. That's why I'm doing it now.'

I looked up to a see a uniform striding purposefully towards us. 'I think we'd better go,' I said. We sent him a friendly wave and ran off. He was too fat to chase us and too lazy to get someone else to.

Later we met up with Talbot at his flat. We knocked on the door and it swept open immediately. He'd been standing there waiting for us, had dressed for the occasion in evening dress and glistening, starched shirt with a bow tie that hurt the eyes. He bowed down like a servant.

'Greetings good lord and wife,' he said humbly. As we walked in he nudged the door a little further and a bucket flipped over on a string above him. Confetti showered over his head. He stood there rigid as it fell, his pristine black jacket becoming covered in flecks of every colour.

When the last piece had dropped lightly onto his shoulder, he calmly brushed himself down. 'That,' he said, 'was not meant to happen.'

I whispered to Lena, 'They say in England, "It's the thought that counts".'

Talbot turned on his heels, 'This way lady and gentleman.'

He must have spent the whole day cleaning the place up. Normally, it was a nightmare of old newspapers heaped on chairs and scattered correspondence 'filed' on the floor, but today his flat glistened. Along the hall ornamental lamps glowed dimly, their brass fittings glinting from a recent polish. We turned into the dining room and there above the fireplace hung a banner printed in blue. It said simply 'Good luck'.

Lena leapt into his arms, smothering him with a hug. 'It's a lovely surprise,' she said, smiling.

'The surprises,' Talbot declared grandly, 'haven't even started.'

For once, he wasn't exaggerating. He then carried in tray after tray of luxuries: chicken, steak, caviar, of course, champagne and a gargantuan cake encrusted with thick layers of chocolate. Talbot was our humble servant and it made us feel like royalty. For one night in our lives we were treated as king and queen and Talbot was the best best man I could have wished for. After he'd finished his last mouthful he began to talk, giving us advice on making the most of married life as if we were a naïve young boy and girl with no idea of what should happen next.

Finally, when the air was woozy with alcohol and the candles had burnt down to the wick, Talbot heaved himself up from the table and informed us with a slur, 'Almost forgot.' We groaned, our insides tight and hard from over-indulgence.

'I can't eat anymore, I can't drink anymore and I don't think I can even speak any more,' I said.

'I should have given you this at the beginning of the evening but with everything else it slipped my mind,' he said.

He walked up to Lena, stood behind her then placed a garland of flowers around her head. 'To show you how beautiful you are Lena. The flowers are nothing by comparison.'

'You flatter me, thank you.' She looked at me. 'But we women like being flattered. *Some* men know that.'

'My dear, you should be flattered that I married you at all,' I replied in my most pompous voice. For an answer Elena threw a napkin at my face. I ducked and it missed me. I grabbed her and drew her into my arms.

Talbot, hovering in the background, said: 'She's quick off the draw, man. You'll have to watch your step.'

Midnight came and went, the last bottle was drained and finally we bade Talbot goodbye, thanking him a thousand times. A horsedrawn cab was waiting for us outside, just like the night we first met. He had thought everything out to the last detail.

I carried Ileana Grover, my Lena, giggling and tipsy over the threshold and into the bedroom. Then, falling onto the bed, with the lights down low, we made first night love very slowly, very tenderly and, for once, without a thought for the neighbours.

The next morning I tried to wake my wife but at six o'clock

her eyelids were still stuck down in sleep. She was curled in the blankets, a little cocoon of warmth that did not want to be distrubed until a more reasonable time in the day arrived. Unfortunately, her feet unprotected by covering were inviting me to tickle them. Naturally, I had to oblige. The result was a murmur which turned into a groan, which developed unnervingly into a roar and culminated in a violent leap out of bed.

Her eyes were open now, she was fully awake and she was angry.

'Explain,' she said.

'Alright, alright. We're catching a train at eight.'

'Where to?' she demanded.

'Ooh, I don't know, the name seems to have slipped my mind.'

'*Where to*?'

'Not telling.'

'*Tell me*.' And she dived onto me, her fingers relishing the torture.

After a while, she gave up. I wasn't going to tell her, no matter what she did. We packed in a frenzy, throwing things haphazardly into one bulging suitcase. As we stood looking around to see if there was anything we'd forgotten before we left, there was a click from the letter box out in the hall. Lena raced to it saying, 'It's probably a good luck card.'

She came back looking a little puzzled. 'It's in English. I thought you didn't tell anyone?'

My stomach dropping, I reached over for the letter. 'I didn't –' I said, then stopped. On the back, in a scrawled hand were the letters MG.

'Who's it from? Who's it from?' Lena asked, excited at the prospect of a letter from overseas.

I ripped it open. 'It's probably just an old mate from the oil fields in the States,' I lied.

'Who?'

'Mark. Mark Green.' *How can you do this Grover? You've been married a few hours and already you're lying through your teeth.*

'You haven't mentioned him before.'

It was getting deeper. A big lie can become a small lie over time. It's the small lies to cover the big ones that can get out of hand until you no longer know what is true. But I had to keep it up, to buy just a little more time. After the honeymoon, I told myself, I could clear the whole thing up. All that mattered was that Lena and I were together and we were safe. Why should a wrong decision, a terrible mistake from the past be allowed to tarnish me forever? I wouldn't let it happen. Not now. Not yet. We had a honeymoon to savour, just Lena and I with nothing to intrude. Later, later . . .

So I said, 'I'd forgotten about him. It's been so long. I'll write after we get back.'

'We'll send him a postcard together,' she said. 'He'll want to know about me.'

'Yes,' I said distractedly, trying not to worry about why she'd written, 'I should imagine he would.' I made an excuse, went quickly into the bathroom, shut the door and sat down to read.

So, I tracked you down at last. You're like a ferret Brian. You think you can slip in and out of anything. Well, I wanted to let you know that you can't. I'm not someone you can leave behind like a bad memory. I exist and I will be heard.

I have waited and waited but heard nothing. I got in touch with a private investigator. He's expensive but very effective. You wouldn't believe what he can do – he has contacts everywhere.

I know all about you, and the slut. I don't suppose she knows about me.

FIELDS OF LIGHT

Think on this. People aren't stupid. And nor am I. It just
needs a word in the right ear to confirm their suspicions . . .

I returned to the room, my toothbrush in my hand.
'Brian,' she said, 'how does he know our address?'
There was no answer to that. I couldn't exactly say to
her, well darling he's so keen to get in touch he's put an
investigator on our tails. 'I don't know. It's funny, I really
don't know,' I managed.
It worked. She just shrugged her shoulders and slipped
on her long fur coat. I would make amends, I swore to
myself, I would. I looked down at the piece of paper that
was now like acid in my hands. The final lines echoed in
my head.

I could make life very difficult for you Brian. And I will.
Come back to the States. Stay in Russia and you're finished.

Madeleine

I'd felt safe for precisely eighteen hours.

SOCHI
September 1933

The wind was a gentle caress at our backs. We were standing on the waterline in a deserted bay. It was midday and
the sand shone a brilliant white. Sea nibbled gently at our
feet. Along the beach were two sets of footprints. Soon
they would be washed away by the waves as if we'd never
been here.

'Imagine we are the last people on earth,' Lena said.
'What would it be like?'

'It would be lovely,' I replied.

'It would be lonely,' she said.

'But it would be lovely for a while.'

Our feet sinking into the wet sand, we walked along the
shore to where Ivan had his shed. Ivan had promised a
boat would be ready for us to take out.

'It would be good if you knew there were other people
but you only saw them when you wanted to,' Lena said
quietly.

I nodded, watching the water splashing over my toes.
Suddenly, Lena stopped, slumping down on the ground.
She put her hands around her knees. I sat down beside her.

'What's wrong?'

'I don't want to go back! Here, we can do what we want. The people like us and we like them. Why can't we stay?' In answer I hugged her. For 'We have to go back', was no answer at all.

It had been perfect. An escape for us both. For Lena, the first legitimate place to enjoy selfishly. For me, simply an escape from unwanted reminders of a distant life.

We'd arrived in Sochi weary from the journey but elated at the prospect of two weeks' holiday. Pulling into the station, we entered a dream world. The sun beat down on the brown-brick platform harder and hotter than any we had seen in Grozny. Laziness hung in the air like a dust settling slowly. Porters in dark, baggy uniforms might take your luggage, but in their own time. There was no point hurrying them, and there was no disrespect intended if they reacted to your requests slowly – it was simply the way things operated here. A faded blue sign hung from the canopy of a wood-slatted shack at the end of the platform. It looked like a holiday chalet that had been built in the wrong place and left untended for years. On the sign in a yellow hand-painted scrawl was the word *Informatsiya*. The front window had been closed with a rusty bolt.

We stood, surrounded by a pile of our clutter, looking, to anybody who had bothered to notice us, completely out of place. Lena surveyed the scene, stretched and looked up at the white-hot sky.

'I don't care where she is,' she said. 'I'm glad we're *here*.'

'She said she would meet us.'

'Who cares? We can leave our baggage in the waiting room and wander round for a while. It'll be safe.' It was true, we could have left it with a sign saying, 'Please steal me' for the whole day and returned to find it still there – most likely with additions to the pile, of food and wine from friendly passers-by. There was no malice here. Sochi, it seemed, was a little utopia in a world gone mad.

Somebody waved at us. A stout woman with a dark oval face. It was Mrs Sakharin, the lady who had arranged a flat for us. She waddled over, displaying a welcoming grin and outstretched arms.

'Greetings, greetings!' Her head bobbed as she talked, causing her hair, pulled back in a floppy bun, to lurch from side to side.

'Are we that obvious?' asked Lena, warming to the woman immediately.

'Anybody who has spent time in Moscow is obvious,' Mrs Sakharin whispered. 'Too much tension. They move like this . . .' She stuck her chest out, angled her arms like wings and strutted in a circle around us. Nobody seemed to think anything of it. The ticket inspector in his booth glanced up, shook his head and smiled but that was it.

She stopped abruptly, as if she had suddenly remembered she had an audience. 'I mean no disrespect of course – and you,' she pointed at me, 'are clearly not from Russia at all.'

'I'm English,' I held out my hand. 'Brian Grover.'

'We don't shake hands here,' she cried. 'We embrace or we fight. No in-betweens!' She hugged me with strong arms and nodded to Lena. 'I know you are just married dear, but I don't often get a chance to wrap myself around handsome strangers. And exotic foreigners are unheard of.'

Lena shrugged. She was too happy to care.

'I would hardly describe myself as exotic,' I ventured, but the moment had moved on.

'Now, let's get you to your flat,' Mrs Sakharin said, quickly disentangling herself. 'You will be hot and sticky, and newly-weds should never be hot and sticky – except at the appropriate time.'

FIELDS OF LIGHT

She snapped her fingers at a young porter lad, half-asleep in the shade. He came to with a start and rushed over.

'The trolley, idiot!' she barked at him and he ran back to get one. Both Lena and I flinched at her sudden change of mood.

'My son,' she explained with a dismissive wave of her hands. 'Heart as good as Christ Himself, but he's so *lazy*.'

'It must be the heat,' Lena responded helpfully.

'It is. Everybody is like that here.' She sighed. 'Better that I suppose, than the dreadful busy-bees up north.'

The trolleys were loaded and we trundled out of the station. Within a minute she was showing us to our home for two weeks. 'Close to the station and close to the sea,' she informed us. 'I deal in nothing but perfection.' She wasn't exaggerating. Inside, we stood by the french windows, which opened out onto a veranda, and were met with a beautiful, calming view. The sea stretched to the horizon, rippling, almost flat at low tide, the harbour curved in from left and right like two fingers beckoning the boats home.

'This isn't really a part of the Soviet Union,' Mrs Sakharin told us that first day. 'The grey men come here on vacation to restore their bodies and souls. They've wrecked everything else but they know this is a paradise they must not spoil.' She'd smiled at us then. She must have seen so many like us before. 'Remember what they've done. Remember what their real motto is: "Do as I say, not as I do." Well, now you can be like them, you can be king and queen here. Make the most of it while you have the chance.'

We had, but today was our last day and the two weeks we'd spent here were already only half a second's worth of compressed images. I took Lena's hand and pulled her to her feet.

'C'mon, Ivan will be waiting for us.'

An hour later we were in the sea up to our waists feeling bulbous in lifejackets and holding a yacht as it rocked against the waves. Ivan stood on the stone ramp that led from the boathouse to the water. He was an old man, seventy maybe, who looked like his craft had been carved into his soul. He was at home in his shed surrounded by lobster pots and fishing nets and shelves of waxes and polishes and old dusty clamps. It was so much a part of him, that it seemed to me it would fade with him when he died.

We had met him a week ago, as we took our morning walk along the beach. Patiently sanding down a minute patch of wood on the hull of a dinghy, over and over his hands went, until the surface was like glass, he was so engrossed in his job that we stood back, watching from a polite distance, so as not to disturb him.

His fingers were like gnarled twigs but they moved quickly, flicking off the dust then sliding over the same area again and again. It was deceptively hard work and his thin grey hair stuck to his forehead in damp curls. Eventually he stretched and surveyed his work, satisfied. He turned to us and said: 'It is not ready until it is as smooth as the skin of your first lover.'

His face collapsed into a sea of wrinkles from which appeared a huge grin. And he spoke completely unself-consciously in the way that only old people feel they can. 'You two are lovers,' he told us. 'You hold hands like tomorrow may not come.' We got to talking then and he wanted to know everything about us.

After that, we met him most days and on one fine afternoon we brought down a picnic. Later, when the wind got up, blowing our tablecloth and food over into the sand, we salvaged a bottle of vodka and retreated into his shed. The next few hours passed as we drank, told stories and listened to the wind rattling outside. I asked him if we could go out on the water sometime and he said, 'Maybe – if your vodka is always as good as this.'

Today finally, Ivan had given in to our pleas and generous alcoholic bribes. 'You can take *Alba*,' he said, 'she's my finest and oldest.'

'What does *Alba* mean?' I asked.

He grinned. 'Short for *Albatros*.'

'You can't call it that!' I cried out and Lena laughed.

'I can and I did,' he replied. 'Fifty years ago. The first and safest boat I ever made. It's all superstition, I have no time for that. Sea, wood and air that's the reality, that's what makes a boat stay up, not a name. My friends thought I was mad too . . . Take it or leave it.'

We took it.

But now, as we moved out of the harbour, it seemed that Ivan was having second thoughts. He was waving his arms and shouting to us. He wasn't convinced I knew how to sail and, admittedly, it had been years since I had taken a boat out by myself.

Ivan's accent was thick, each vowel sounding like a frog's mating call. He was pointing at us then at the sea frantically, yelling instructions that made no sense at all under the noise of the waves.

'What's he saying?' I asked Lena.

'He said the wind's changed. I couldn't catch the rest, but I think he wants his boat back.'

'Feign ignorance. I bought half the vodka in Moscow to do this.'

So we pretended to take his gyrations as some sort of farewell and with broad smiles waved back at him.

Soon, Ivan was just an ant in the distance, still scurrying up and down the ramp as if sheer persistance alone could bring us back. We moved out of the sheltered bay and the sails bellied out with the cold wind that tumbled down from the Caucasus mountains and swept over the sea in chunky gusts. The open sea was unexpectedly choppy, smacking against the hull like children clapping. I showed Lena how to adjust the gib rope so that the sail curved true without flapping. She soon got the hang of it and, true to her nature, was fearless of the water.

'Lean back over the side when you feel the yacht tipping forward,' I called to her. She did and almost fell in. I grabbed her and she gave me a petulant look.

'I did what you said!'

'Sorry, I forgot to tell you to put your feet in the loops.'

We were about half a mile out and still travelling in a straight line.

'When we turn, I'll give you a shout. Duck and go over to the other side OK?'

She nodded. The breeze was picking up, becoming more even. I turned the nose of the yacht into the eye of the wind and we tacked. Lena moved like a natural.

The sun was at our backs now, warming us up in between the bouts of spray that burst across the bows with every big wave. The nose cut the water, our legs were taut as we hung over the edge and I felt a strange elation. It was the ease with which it had all come back. How long was it? Ten years? Easily. After leaving Cambridge and between jobs I had travelled round Europe, staying by some lake in central France for a while – I forget its name – where I met up with a friendly group of rich young 'down and outs' doing the same sort of thing. A couple of them had been keen sailors. They took me out on the lake a few times and showed me the basics. Since then I had always vowed to take it up properly some day. But like so many other things the opportunity had never presented itself again – or I had never created it.

We tacked around the headland of our quiet bay. A a couple of miles to the other side was Sochi. Nestled close to the waterline, its clumps of white buildings were dissected by long, wooded avenues. From a mile out it looked tiny, like a planner's model town.

'Can we stop?' Lena asked.

'Sure. Why?'

'It would be nice to just sit and watch for a while.'

I let the sails flap, stuck the rudder full down and we drifted. Lena snuggled up beside me.

'It looks so different,' she said. 'From out here, everything looks quiet, no people, no trucks, the only sound is the water . . . I like it out here.'

I squeezed her hand. 'It gets cold after a while.'

'Not yet though. Where shall we go now?'

'Find a landmark. Pick one.'

'The church on the hill over there, with the tower.'

It was about three miles away on the next headland, standing exposed to the ravages of the seasons. It seemed a bleak place to worship. A long, steep walk unsheltered by trees. At the end of it, all you'd want to do is collapse in the pew and hope the priest had some words to warm you up.

Lena adjusted the sails as I pushed the tiller left and we headed for the church. On the horizon dark clouds were thickening in curls but I reckoned we had a while before we should turn back . . . .

On our first evening in Sochi we ate out on the veranda. The nights closed in quickly down here and we watched as a string of lights lit up on the piers. We spent the time chatting, holding hands, kissing – content just to absorb this rare, uncomplicated fragment of our lives. The temperature was dropping and the sky became clear. Lena leant back in her chair and watched the swirls of stars.

'My mother once told me that each star is a child that

might have been born. But that some children will never be born because the right people don't meet each other. They are the ones that chance never made . . . I would like a child, Brian.'

I was silent, surprised by her words.

'One day, when we can, when things are sorted . . . What is it Brian? What's wrong?'

I turned away. I didn't want her to see my face. I could not speak and I could not tell her why.

Now, I watched her adjusting her position to balance the yacht. Her knuckles were white with cold and her hair was salty and tangled by the breeze. She was laughing, lost in the rush of something new, something exciting. I thought of being back in England then, of taking Lena up to Windemere, perhaps, where we could rent out some country cottage and stay there as long as we wanted. We could go for long walks, sail in the evening, drink in a real pub – fool!

How had I let it come to this? It was so perfect here, so uncomplicated. The thought of a child was wonderful. There was nothing I could want more to give her. But for Madeleine I would have said yes immediately. Lena wanted to live in England. And to bring a child up there would complete our lives. But how could I go back now? As a bigamist, a cheat?

I yanked at the tiller and the yacht lurched in the waves.

Lena scrambled to the safety of the deck, suddenly unsure of the situation.

'Brian, perhaps we should turn back.'

'It's just the swell Lena. Nothing to worry about.'

We had lost our momentum and we were bobbing around like flotsam. I looked at the marker. The yacht was upwind of the church now. About two miles to go. It became a battle, a test of will. With the wind almost behind us we could go all the way there – the hardest way. I let the rope out a few degrees, until the sails flapped. I leant over to Lena. 'Now we're going to go *really* fast. But you have to lean right back.'

She looked apprehensive.

'Come on, you did it without thinking before.'

'I don't know.'

'It'll be alright. Don't you trust me?'

'I trust you, but I don't trust *that*.'

I followed her gaze. Black clouds broiled in the distance, – a distance that didn't seem so far away now. Between, the sea was a misty wash of grey. Which meant a squall. I knew that, but I didn't want it to beat me, so I refused to let it register. I gripped the rope and pulled it in hard.

'Ready?'

Lena gave me a quick half-smile.

'Lean out!'

I turned the boat so the wind was full at our backs and soon we were at full speed. I felt blood rushing through my limbs as I pumped the mainsail. The cold in my fingers was something physical, but irrelevant. The yacht cut the waves at forty-five degrees, yawing wildly sideways with each impact. I wasn't even in the yacht, I was hurtling down a tunnel and only the church, no longer brilliant white in the sun but smudged grey by the sweep of clouds, mattered. And in this cut-off world, Lena would come over to England, and my parents would love her, and Madeleine would agree to a divorce, and we would cruise past the obstacles in our way as though they had never been there –

'Brian, it's raining.' Lena's voice cut into my thoughts.

The swell was now ten feet. When we were at the low point, there was no land or sky, just a wall of water.

'We're wet through already, what does a bit of rain matter?'

162

Sochi, September 1933

'Brian, it's a *storm*. Turn us round. Please.'

'A few more minutes, then we can ride the swell back. It'll be fun.' The fact that I had to shout out the words did nothing ro reassure her. We carried on.

Then the real rain swept over us; a blanket of huge drops, driving near-horizontally, that stung when they hit my face.

Lena grabbed my ear, pulled my head round to face her.

'What the hell's got into you. *Turn around now*!' There was a hardness in her eyes, a speck of flint that I had not seen before and it snapped me out of my madness.

'Yes, you're right,' I said quietly but words were lost in an explosion of sound.

The gust hit the boat like a hammer. The air went solid so that for a second I could not breathe. I tried to turn into the wind, into the waves, to give us a few second's grace but, as I did, a wave crashed portside and both rope and tiller slipped from my hands. Unguided, the boat swung round. I caught a glimpse of Sochi but it was obliterated by the boom flapping past me.

'Lena! Heads!'

There was a crack as we did an involuntary jibe, and another crack as the boom hit Lena just above the ear. The force threw her overboard. She slumped face-down in the water, the lifejacket keeping her buoyant. I didn't have time to jump in after her. The next gust of wind blew the yacht straight over and it seemed as I hung in the air that she was plunging in nose first.

That's not –

Then I was under and the roar of the outside world was only a rumble, getting quieter. Something was dragging me down. I could feel the pull of the lifejacket under my arms but the sounds kept receding. Something was around my foot. I opened my eyes. I saw a blur of green, unformed

163

shadows, movement above then nothing. Then a lump grew in my chest. I want to breathe, I want to cough! Up there! No, it's your foot, idiot! Use your hands. I curled up, peering at the mess. Twist it out. Pull. that's it. Air. Lena? *Pull*.

My shoe ripped off, and I slipped free. I burst to the surface, gasping and retching.

'Lena! Lena!' I screamed as hard as I could but it was lost in the roar of the storm.

I saw her as I rose to the high point of the swell. The yacht upturned with the rudder sticking hopelessly in the air looked like a shark. Lena was on the other side. I struck out for her, losing sight each time surf crashed over the boat. Seconds were hours and I dreamed of us drinking hot coffee in our flat in front of a cosy log fire.

When I reached her she was limp. I grabbed her under the arms and pulled her back to the boat. There was a gash on the side of her head. Blood ran onto her face, only to be washed off a moment later. I pressed her up against the side, holding the rudder for leverage. Wrapping my legs around her waist I thumped her in the chest with my free hand. Water dribbled from her lips and she let out a gurgling moan. I did it again and this time she shook her head.

'Off – ' she said.

'Ileana, can you hear me?'

Her head flopped to the side. I slapped her cheek. 'C'mon! Wake up, please, wake up.'

'*Nyet.*'

'Lena. We have to pull the boat upright. Can you help me?'

Her eyes opened momentarily and I grabbed the opportunity.

'Think of a hot fire and a nice bed. If you help me now, we can get back. You can be warm and snug and you can sleep for as long as you want. Jut a few minutes, *please*.'

Life seeped into her, first her arms, then her legs began moving of their own accord.

'That's it. Hold the rudder. Hold it tight.'

She wrapped her arms around it as though it were a teddy bear. It would have to do for the moment. If we stayed in the water much longer we wouldn't be able to move at all. I clambered up onto the hull, slipping on the shiny surface. Damn Ivan and his damn polishing. A toggle was floating on the other side. I leant over, wanting to lunge for it but knew that I would only slip over head first if I did. It bobbed in the waves a few inches out of reach, mocking me. I willed it forward, splashed my hand in the sea trying to create some pathetic current that could compete with the ravages of the storm.

Attached to the toggle is the rope. Attached to the rope is the yacht. I get it, I pull it upright and we get in the boat and everything is alright.

I felt the boat dip suddenly, much deeper than before, looked up and prayed. In the second before the wave hit I locked Lena's hands in mine around the rudder.

It passed over in a roar, like a huge hand jerking and pulling every part of my body. I clung to Lena and the boat with all my strength. We tipped sideways and something slapped me around the shoulders.

It was the rope.

Lena was flailing in the water. She had no idea where she was. I grabbed the rope in both hands, stuck my feet against the hull and pulled. Slowly, the submerged mast came into sight, the sail ballooning behind it. I tugged Lena over beside me.

'Grab hold of the side – use your weight.'

She nodded slightly. Somewhere inside her confusion of pain and cold she heard me. Agonizingly, the mast tipped upright. I clambered in, rolling onto the tiny deck. Lena clung to the side, her hands like a corpse's.

'Cold . . .' she said.

What now? the gale was directly astern, the boom was swinging dangerously. I dragged Lena inch by inch over the side, careful to balance her weight. She flopped in beside me, a deadweight.

Rain like blades sliced at the back of my neck as I pulled the boomsail flat against the wind. The gib would have to flap, I didn't have three hands and the two I had were so numb they were near to useless.

The yacht surged forward as the sail snapped taut. Lena jerked on the deck with the force. I positioned her head between my feet to stop it from rocking.

'We're going to be OK,' I said to her in a daze. 'We're going to be OK and I'm sorry, I'm so sorry. I should have told you about her, I should never have lied. I thought you would leave. I should have told you about Madeleine . . .'

It streamed out like a crazy mantra, the same words over and over again, guilty fuel for the boat, the driving force to get us to dry land. Then Lena's eyes were wide open. She stared quizzically at my upside-down face. 'That's not rain,' she said. 'That's tears, you're *crying*!' And then she smiled as if the storm had moved away from her; she was basking in some sunny place in her imagination. 'Tell me about her when we get home,' she murmured and her eyes closed.

'Home' was a beach crowded with people waiting to see if we were still alive. As soon as we entered the shelter of the harbour, a group of fishermen went into the water, breakers crashing over their heavy waders. Ivan headed the pack, waving his fists in the air. The yacht ground to a halt as ten pairs of hands grasped stern and bow.

They all talked to me at the same time. I hung my head,

not wanting to meet their eyes, and avoided their questions by waving my hands helplessly. They lifted Elena delicately from the deck. I wanted to help them, felt I should, but there was only a hollow where my strength should have been. The sea had snatched it from me. Then a pair of strong arms heaved me from the boat. I closed my eyes, I was ready to go to sleep right where I was but the hands would have none of it. I was guided to shore, no longer feeling the icy grasp of the water, recognising only the sensation of my feet touching something solid and stable beneath me.

I collapsed on the beach and the man who had brought me ashore knelt down beside me. Then fingers prised my eyelids apart. I blinked. It was Ivan. He looked like a weather-beaten gnome crouching there on the beach with the storm hammering at his back. All hair and gnarled skin, but his eyes were alive and bright.

'You're a strong man,' I managed to get out.

Short smile. 'I'm seventy.'

My mouth felt thick and rubbery; there were things I needed to ask. 'Lena?'

'She will be fine,' he soothed. 'Just cold . . . and a hefty bump on the side of her head. She's with a doctor now.'

There was silence and then he said. 'You forgot to pull the rudder up when you came in.'

'I'm sorry. I've been a fool. Really I –'

'It happens.'

'What, fools or storms?'

He sighed. 'Sometimes . . . both at the same time.'

'I was angry.'

He raised his eyebrows and his forehead looked like the skin of an elephant. 'What about?' he asked.

I shook my head in response.

'You were angry at Lena,' he declared in a sure voice. 'What has she done?'

'No, no. It wasn't her. I was angry at myself.'

'Oh,' was all he said.

Back at the flat the doctor looked me over. She checked my pulse, temperature, blood pressure, each time writing the details carefully onto a clipboard. I noticed there were two leaves of carbon paper underneath her main sheet. Information was important even in this paradise.

She tapped my chest. It sounded empty.

'You can put your shirt back on now. Nothing wrong with you that a hot shower and a long sleep won't cure. Your wife will be up and about by tomorrow. Mild concussion, that's all.'

We both looked through the open door into the bedroom. Lena was lying on her back, blankets up to her nose and snoring like a foghorn.

'I've never known her make a noise like it,' I said, chuckling.

The doctor gave me a reproving look. 'Be thankful she's making a sound at all. You were both very lucky.'

'I know. Look, I'm really grateful for all you've done . . .' I offered her a handful of pound notes.

'That won't be necessary,' she said, her voice crisp and businesslike. 'I don't accept illegal currencies. One of the advantages of the Soviet system, you might say "a perk", is that healthcare is available and free. For everyone.'

'I meant no offence.'

'If you need any further aid, do not hesitate to contact me. I will see myself out.'

I sat down beside Lena. The movement woke her up. I leant down to kiss her on the cheek, but she moved her lips to mine. She ran her hands around my head. 'It's not fair. You have no bumps. My hero has no battle scars.'

'I'm not exactly a hero.'

'You saved my life.'

'Lena, I nearly killed you!'

'Why would you do something like that?'

'Sometimes, you're impossible. Is the invalid allowed to be leapt on?'

She shrugged. 'That depends.'

'On what.'

'You know.'

'I don't.'

She looked through the french windows, her eyes focussing on nothing in particular. 'Sometimes, you think you know someone and then something happens. They do a thing that surprises you, really shocks you. And you think: "Do I know him?" Then you watch how they react afterwards and you think, yes I know him inside out because you can predict what comes next and you can understand what they are feeling.'

'Lena –'

'Please, let me finish. And the reason you can understand what he is feeling is that you have felt it yourself. You have chewed at it until only gristle is left, pulled it apart heaven knows how many times trying to reassemble it a different way but it comes back the same each time. And you feel there is no escape because to do the one thing that would lead you through to the other side would surely destroy the image you have built up around you, an image which you even believe yourself. So time goes on, and it festers inside. It goes away for a while because you are very happy, but even that happiness is not complete because it is based on deceit. It is real at the time, but in memory it becomes false. It is tarnished with this thing that was never rubbed off.'

'Lena, you're tired, you got a nasty slap on the head courtesy of your hero . . .'

'*Don't patronise me!*' The flint was there in her eyes again. 'That is something I *wouldn't* expect from you.'

'I'm sorry.'

'Look,' her voice softened. 'I'm going to tell you a story and it's the only time I'm going to tell it, so please don't interrupt me. Let's find some coffee and go out on the verandah.'

'Are you sure you're up to it?'

'Quite sure,' she said, swinging her legs out of bed.

The aftermath of the storm had left the air fresh and clean. The cloud had broken up into little balls. Below us puddles were drying on pavements, the sun was sinking behind the Caucasus mountains and the Black Sea was mirror smooth. Mrs Sakharin had told us that given the right conditions, the mountains sometimes cast shadows across the sea. 'Like long fingers smoothing it out,' she had said. There were no shadows now, only a luminous glow that covered everything.

Lena stirred cream into her coffee, then rapped the spoon on the side of her cup.

'You know the first part of the story,' she said. 'About the little girl who grew up in St Petersburg before the revolution, who loved her mother and father, who trained to become a nurse because there was too much blood and too much hate. After that the story changes. This little girl grew up to be a woman who thought she could make a life for herself in a quiet little backwater, away from the turmoil. Somewhere warm and easy. Leningrad was too cold, too harsh and besides, how could she live in a place that couldn't even decide on a name for itself?

'Most people went to Moscow, if they could get a permit. It was the centre of the world, everything happened there. But not this young lady. It was too close to the carnage, too frantic. No, this lady applied for a position in a nice little hospital in the South, where people smiled at you as

170

you went to work, where the days passed slowly and you didn't have to wear ten pairs of socks at night. A place to the west of here . . . quite near actually. Her application was accepted, so she packed her bags, got on the train and went to Grozny. She was only twenty-two, much of the world was new to her –'

'But –" was all I got in.

'Please Brian, don't make it hard for me.' She stretched over the table and took my hands in hers. Her hair fell over her face. I wanted to move it away with my lips, to smother her, to squeeze against her so there would be no more talking, but that was not the answer. And I realised that Lena was stronger than I could ever be. She was forcing the moment while I ran from it.

'For six months, life carried on quietly. She felt happy there . . . for the first time in years she could see the results of her work. She was helping people, not patching them up so they could be sent out and butchered again. She decided she would like to stay there a long time.

'Then she met a young woman, about the same age as her, called Natalia Oblonsky. She was outgoing, very popular. Everybody knew her.

'You could say Natalia adopted this naive young woman. She took her everywhere, introduced her to a whole new set of friends. The young woman had buried herself in her work and her social life consisted of detailed conversations about debilitating diseases over a cup of coffee in the hospital canteen. Any diversion was welcomed.

'One evening, Natalia invited her round for dinner. She loved playing host. When the woman arrived, there was only Natalia and this older gentleman there. Natalia had said it would be a "gathering" and the woman certainly wasn't early so she knew something was up when Natalia said: "Now we're all here, we can eat." Natalia introduced her to the man, and the woman thought he might be a boyfriend or a brother. But he was too old, at least twice Natalia's age, and there seemed to be no affection between them. He introduced himself as a doctor. The woman was curious . . . she hadn't seen him around before which was strange. They got talking and she noticed Natalia became quieter, but when she looked at her Natalia was smiling, not in the least put out. Then it clicked, (sometimes this woman was very slow), her friend was matchmaking. She felt embarrassed about the situation but had to admit to being attracted to him. He was fatherly, sure of himself and for an older man quite handsome with deep brown eyes and thick dark hair. He knew what he wanted, he was a good talker and an even better listener.

'They . . . they started meeting up together, going for walks along the river. He took her to the theatre. He was . . . quite wealthy but he never flaunted it, never took it for granted. He told her all about himself. Before the revolution he had been a private doctor and was well respected locally so he escaped the changes forced on most in his profession. He had a sort of special status with the authorities because of his standing and they left him alone. And he had a private house which was most unusual. It was nice when they went back there alone, in their own place with no-one to tell them what to do. He was kind to her, he made her feel special . . .

'She fell in love and it seemed that he loved her. They got married within months of first meeting and naturally she moved in.

Lena paused for a while then. She was breathing raggedly, trying to calm herself. I said nothing.

'Then, about a year later, she woke up one morning and there was an empty space next to her in bed. The sheets were still warm and crumpled. Maybe, she thought, he was up early studying. She went downstairs . . . no sign of him. She went into the surgery – no luck. But his briefcase was gone. She went into the kitchen. The kettle was still steaming on the stove and there was a full cup of tea beside it untouched. Underneath it there was a note with a scrawled, "No time to explain". That was it. No love, no apology, no goodbye.

'That day she sat at home by the kitchen table going over the same questions – why? Why did she leave? What had she done wrong – again and again until it was evening and a rap on the door shook her out of her trance. Maybe it was him? Maybe he had come back to say it was all a mistake? She rushed to the door and swung it open. The police burst in. One of them grabbed her, shook her, shouted in her face: "Where's your murdering husband?" She could hardly speak. She shook her head. "He wouldn't murder . . ." The others were ransacking the house, ripping it apart. "He murders babies," he said. "You know where he is." She said, "No!" and the man slapped her, "Tell me and you will be alright." And she screamed: "I don't know. He ran away. He ran away. The bastard ran away and left me." And she crumpled in front of the men and she was ashamed of it. But they left her alone after that. One of them knelt down beside her and told her all he knew.

'It seemed her husband had been carrying out illegal abortions. That's where all his money was coming from. He must have found out that Intelligence was on to him.'

Lena stirred her cup of coffee, now cold. 'He didn't trust me Brian, he kept his secret and left me to face the consequences. I was garbage – nobody spoke to me. Except Natalia. You know her as Lily. I had to leave, start again in Moscow. I gave the house to Lily. I vowed that I would never deceive another person the way he did me . . . And I broke that vow when I met you. I never saw him again.' She rose and leant against the balcony, her back to me. A dog barked in the street below. It made sense. It explained how she'd heard of Beria, she'd covered that slip well. And it explained her rapid friendship with Lily. They must have had a lot to talk about in private. So many secrets. But who was I to judge?

She hadn't finished. 'This is very hard to say. A few weeks before I met you, I received a letter from him. I thought he was dead, or had left the country. He said he'd made a new life for himself. A new identity, a new woman, children, somewhere far away where no-one could touch him. He didn't say where, that would be too dangerous. He was coming to Moscow. He said he wanted to explain, to make it up. With the letter were two tickets to the Bolshoi. He was coming to ease his conscience. He was meeting me for himself, not to help me. I didn't want his money, though God knows he owed me. I just wanted him to know how much he'd hurt me. He didn't turn up. I just sat there with you staring at me, thinking *Where is he, where is he? He couldn't do this*. But he did.

'So now you know who the empty seat was for. I was scared he'd been caught. I thought you might be police waiting for him.

'When you said you were going to Grozny, I couldn't believe it. It was ten years ago, maybe all had been forgotten, but could I go back? And that first night with you, home again in Grozny – I nearly told you then when you pressed me, but I thought you would leave me.

'You see, I know what it's like to deceive someone you love. I've lied to you and I understand the turmoil it creates.' She turned to face me. 'Brian, I've known for a long time that you were hiding something. The letter that arrived before we came here, I saw the effect it had on you. When I woke up just now I thought I'd dreamed what you said on the yacht but I didn't did I?'

'No, you didn't'

'Tell me about her. Tell me about Madeleine.'

There was no other way to say it. 'She's my wife.'

174

'*Is?*'

I nodded.

She let out a long, ragged sigh. She had worked out a lot but not that, not that.

'I want to know everything,' she said.

'I was twenty-six,' I began. 'And I was stupid.'

'At least some things are constant.' There was a curl in her lips.

'I was on a ship bound for California. I had a contract to drill for oil in Long Beach, you know about that. It was packed with emigrating families and old couples, the professional cruisers. Also on board was a young lady from Alabama with her distinguished mother. I was bored. There was little to do except read or lean over the railings and watch the ship frothing up the sea. Some nights I played cards with a few off-duty sailors. Then, over dinner one night I met the young lady from Alabama.

' "Brian, meet my daughter, Madeleine Jacobs. She's been on the Grand European tour," her mother informed me. We talked about the countries she had visited. She was very pretty in a conventional way. Petite with short blonde hair cut in a flick across her face. Her eyes were quite arresting if they caught your gaze. But they didn't smile with the rest of her face. It's funny, I noticed that almost immediately, but it didn't register.

'Anyway, after the first time, dinner together became a regular thing. Mrs Jacobs organised it. She would ensure, half an hour beforehand, that I was with them. I might be out on the deck taking a stroll and they would bump into me, Mrs Jacobs holding her daughter like a priceless property. "Small world, isn't it Maddy?" she would titter. And then the gong would sound and in we'd go to eat.

'We got friendly. Our relationship grew through trying

to avoid her mother. There was a casino on board, and we'd hide down there. Madeleine loved the shady lights and smoky corners. And she was a good gambler. She won hundreds of dollars some nights and she would blow the money on lavish cocktails. I was still naive when it came to women. In many ways, she was more mature than me, even though I'd spent all my years since Cambridge in Sarawak, working hard and roughing it with the best and worst of them. I'd seen more but she understood more. She could read people like she read black jack. She seemed to know what was coming next. And for this, I looked up to her.

'We had a fun time together and when we arrived in America, we agreed to write to each other. I went to Long Beach, she went back to Alabama. The further apart we were, the closer we became. For eighteen months we exchanged letters and in that time I only saw her once. I had a week's leave and went to stay at her parents' house. Everything was very proper. We went dancing, went to the movies. On the last night, I kissed her. I got it into my head that we should be married. It wasn't a passionate thing, it simply felt like the next step to take.

'When I returned to California, I found out I was to be posted to Trinidad. I wrote to Madeleine and asked her to marry me and come live with me there. A proposal by letter. She accepted and her parents were elated. They thought she'd got a prize catch. There was a hasty but quiet wedding in New York. My mother and father didn't come; they thought I was mad. Marrying an *American*.

'There was no time for a honeymoon, but I thought life in Trinidad would be holiday enough. When our ship docked in Port of Spain, I felt I'd been washed up on the shores of paradise. A steel band was playing, a chance celebration to our arrival, palm trees lined the coast and miles of untouched white sand beckoned wherever we looked. It was perfect. But within weeks, our life together

176

started to fall apart. You see, Madeleine changed. She loathed Trinidad. She despised the people I worked with, saw them as "common roughnecks". The English are meant to be the snobs of this world, but I tell you, Americans are just as protective of their class – and just as bigoted. From day one she complained about the heat, about the food, about the natives. I was beginning to wonder what I had got myself into. She wasn't the woman I had known on the boat or the writer of those wonderful letters when we spent our months apart. She had become a whinger. When she married me, she knew what she was getting, but I believe she wanted to mould me into a different Brian Grover, a Brian Grover that would suit her purposes. She thought I was demeaning myself by doing the work I did and told me so straight. My work also kept me out of the house for long hours which she didn't like either.

'I thought it would all settle down. People acclimatize to new surroundings eventually, new couples learn to accept compromises. I did sympathise with her predicament. She was in an alien environment that demanded quite a bit of adapting to. Naturally, I was used to the life, but I was willing to help her. I wanted to show her the good side.

'Then I discovered her true colours. Behind my back she had posted home feature articles to her local newspaper in Alabama. I found out only by chance. The papers had sent over some copies and in the heat of fierce argument over some trivial matter she thrust the article into my face "This is what I think of you", she sneered. I read it. The article ridiculed the oilmen for their lack of refinement and belittled the Trinidadian way of life. It might have blown over eventually, but Madeleine deliberately left the piece lying around so that others would read it. As she saw it, it was her revenge for having to come and live in hell.

'Soon we were sleeping in separate beds. We became strangers. There was nothing to talk about, nothing to share. She wanted me to be someone else, I wanted her to be someone else. We were at an impasse. Then one day, six months later, I returned from work to find her standing in the lounge, suitcase by her feet, dressed up.

'"I'm going back home," she said. "If you come with me now, I will forgive you."

'Her forgive me! That was the depth of our misunderstanding. "I have a job, Madeleine."

'"Then, it's over, until you see sense."

'"Then it's over," I replied. and that was it. She returned to America and I stayed put.

'After a while, I asked her for a divorce but she refused. So I carried on as though it had never happened. I went back to Sarawak and joined up with Frank again. After a couple of years, I almost started to believe it too.'

I had run out of words. It was dark now, and cold. Sochi was quiet but the sea swishing up the beach sounded as though it was right at our feet. Listening to that sound, I thought: *In a hundred years, we will both be gone, and our problems and our arguments and our happiness and our heartbreak will all be nothing. But the sea will still be pounding that beach. Backwards and forwards with infinite regularity, as though nothing ever changes.*

Lena had kept her promise, saying nothing throughout my story. Now she asked: 'When you first met me, did you still love Madeleine?'

'No. The whole thing was a mistake. I came to Russia to forget it. I was a coward, I should have finished the matter properly. But as far as I was concerned when I met you, I was divorced in everything but name.'

She nodded her head, thinking it through.

'Lena, she means nothing to me. I mean nothing to her –'

'Then why does she write you these letters! Why does she track you down? Perhaps she loves you, Brian and you are hurting her.' She shook her head as if doing so would also shake away the thought.

'*No*. She-left-me.' The words came out a staccato growl. 'I wasn't gentlemanly enough, I didn't live up to the promise of my accent. It got so that she couldn't even bear to touch me!'

Lena ran a finger down my cheek. The few harsh words in her were spent. 'Then she was a very foolish woman,' she said.

'And I am a very foolish man.'

'It changes nothing,' Lena said. 'We are both guilty.' Then, 'Do you remember the promise you made on our first night in Grozny?'

'Cross my heart.'

'Yes. Now, you must take me back to England.'

'I'll have to go alone first Lena. Madeleine won't agree to a divorce without a fight. I couldn't bring you to London, the bride of a bigamist.'

Lena took my hand. 'How long?'

'I don't know, really. Not long, I hope.'

She gripped harder. 'Don't avoid my eyes. Tell me!'

'It could be some time. Up to a year.'

She let go. My palm felt cold and damp without her touch. She let out a long sigh then left the table, walked to the balcony railing and leant into the breeze. I was going to follow her but something in her movements told me she wanted time in private, time to mull over the implications of this twist in our lives.

'A year,' she said, turning to me finally. 'Then that is how it must be.'

And from that bleak acceptance, I formed a hope in my own mind. The lies now over, the secrets out, we could create something solid. Like a bone that has fractured and healed, and through healing become stronger.

Ivan came to the station to wave us off. We were leaning out of the carriage window when he passed me a small package wrapped in newspaper.

'It isn't much,' he said. 'Go on, open it.'

Inside was a perfect wooden model of the *Alba*. Only, it was no longer the *Alba*. Painted on the hull in Russian was the name *Angry Storm*.

'The big one's changed its name too,' said Ivan.

'It's beautiful,' I said. 'How did you do it so quickly?'

'With fast hands,' he replied.

The guardsman whistled and a plume of steam filled the platform. The train ground into motion. Ivan waved and as he disappeared from view he called out, 'Come back another time next year. I'll show you how to sail properly.'

'We will,' I called back.

Another time. Another false promise. We knew we would not return.

Part Three

INTO THE LIGHT

LONDON
October – November 1938

My head rattled against the glass as the bus changed gear. I peered through the smudged window and wondered why they were always dirty. A fat man sat beside me in a brown suit two sizes too small picking his nose surreptitiously.

As the bus lurched down Whitehall, the conductor swung from his pole at the back, yelling at cabs and pedestrians. At each stop he pirouetted on tiptoes, lifting his arms against the doorway to bar entry.

'Leremoffirsplleeease!'

He was an entertainment. I got the same bus, the number thirty, from Earl's Court to St Paul's every morning. He never missed a day, and he treated his passengers as a pub landlord might his regulars. A one man mission to lessen the load of commuterland misery.

To blot out the background noises, I pressed my nose against the window. I considered how I must look from the outside – like a ghost gazing at a world it was no longer connected to. A face from a passing bus, white oval, instantly forgettable. Just passing through.

At least, that's what I had planned. To pass through. But I was still here five years later, trudging to work in the sales department of an engineering company in Chancery Lane. And no Lena.

Raindrops pattered at the window in little waves. *Nyet*, they said. *Nyet, nyet, nyet*, . . . Then a white flash was followed by a deep rolling boom. Involuntarily passengers jumped. The conversations started again.

There would be war soon. No-one could know it for sure, but the feeling of it permeated everything. You could not switch on the radio or open a newspaper without hearing proclamations of impending upheaval. In March, Hitler's armies had moved into Austria, declaring it 'a province of the German Reich,' and since then the prospect of war over the Sudetenland had grown. The mood in London was both excited and fearful. The old, who had seen it all before, were bitter that the 'war to end all wars' had simply been a preliminary. The young, those with most to live for, they chattered until their eyes shone. This was history, this was adventure and it was happening *now*. Then there were the bigots, the know-it-alls with the loudest mouths, shouting about solutions to the present build-up of tension with a flourish of useless words. The thunder reminded them of the bombs they were hoping to hear.

If it weren't for the precious object in my pocket, it would have been unbearable.

I closed in on myself and counted down the stops. Five more, four more . . .

We make a formal arrangement to meet at her hotel. Her voice sounds clipped on the telephone.

At first she is civil, as though I never went to Russia, as though I had been away on some extended business trip. After the letters, I was ready for the worst.

'Brian,' she calls to me in the lobby, 'so good to see you.'

This is the woman who tracked me down, who threatened to tell the authorities. She greets me like an old friend, even kisses me coldly on both cheeks and I think, What does she want from me after all this time?

She picks a table by the log fire and orders drinks.

'It's best to get it straight out in the open. We both know why we're here.'

She doesn't seem to hear me, smiles the comment off with a flutter.

'I've come all the way from Alabama. I'm going to see a show, do some shopping. You may accompany me if you wish.'

'We're not here to make up, Madeleine. You damn well know that.'

'Oh Brian, baby Brian. You're so interesting when you're angry.' She sips her Martini.

'I want a divorce.'

Her eyes click shut for a moment as though she is processing the words for hidden meaning. There's nothing underneath – I couldn't be more explicit.

'You seem to have done things the wrong way round, baby.'

'Does she know?'

She flicks open her handbag. On the table next to us a middle-aged couple argue in hushed whispers. There are lines on the man's forehead. And he moves his head like a tortoise.

'I got you a present to remind you of home,' she said.

'Wherever you're thinking of, it's not my home.'

I open the neatly wrapped package. It is a maroon tie with thin yellow stripes woven diagonally across. At the bottom, in big letters is an insignia: ABF.

'Thank you so much, Madeleine.' I can't resist it. 'And what does the ABF stand for?'

'Alabama Banking Federation.' She leans forward. 'Daddy says there's a great job going just now. It would be perfect for you. A small opening but with your background and a few choice dinner invitations, you could be a manager within a few years.'

Her optimism is unbearable. I can't believe she's saying this. It's been seven years.

'For the last time, I don't want to work in a bank, Madeleine, and my home is not in Alabama!' I thump my fist on the table and the arguing couple look at me. The woman appears relieved at the distraction.

'You don't love me. You don't even like me. So why do you pretend?'

She won't answer.

'You'll give me the divorce eventually, Madeleine. And believe me, if you don't I'll –'

'You'll what? You can't threaten me. You and your slut. Bigamist.'

So she does know.

'Shall I shout it out?' She looks around the bar, then back at me. 'Shall I?'

'Why are you doing this?'

'Because I can,' she says.

In the end, the deal with Madeleine was a drawn-out affair, culminating in my handing over to her £2,500 which was the oil company annuity I'd received after leaving Trinidad. She'd used the bigamy charge as a bargaining tool to get the money.

I was divorced and I felt I'd climbed half the mountain, only to be felled by an avalanche of *nyets*. Again and again, the Russian Embassy in London refused me an entry visa. This time Talbot could not help. Along with most of the ministers he'd known, he had disappeared. I checked out his old address on The Strand. The entrance was boarded off, and nobody either side had heard of him. Thompson, my solicitor, knew nothing either.

I wrote to Lena to explain. She said she loved me and would wait. In desperation, I then took a job in Persia, staying there for months while I tried to cross the border into Russia. There was no way in. My record was filled with black marks. I wrote to Lena again. Again, she said she would wait. So, in 1936, I returned to London. While I waited and hoped, I could bask in the calm seas of a company whose employees' only aim in life was to secure their own little piece of authority. I could bide my time in dull backwaters of paper-shifting till new horizons beckoned. I could survive it. Things would look up. One day I would walk into the Soviet Embassy and they'd slap me on the back as though I were some almost-forgotten friend and say 'What took you so long? Of course you can come back Mr Grover, she's your wife after all.' And meanwhile we could still write to each other. And Ileana Petrovna, with her dark eyes never dimming in my memory, would wait.

Then the letters stopped.

'Chanceuuureee Lane!'

I grasped a leather strap and hauled myself past the snoring bulk beside me. It was seven o'clock and it was still raining. I stepped off the bus as it moved away and in one motion slammed my umbrella open. I took my normal route to the office. It was a short walk but it was also an opportunity to switch off. I pointed my umbrella into the wind and rain and watched my feet crash through puddles, negotiate curbs and swerve out of the way of oncoming legs. Like everyone else's along High Holborn they were on automatic pilot, guiding their owners inexorably to their destination.

It had been two years since the last letter. Two years I'd spent working alongside petty, small-talking, small-minded people who saw no further than an Easter break in a Highland Hunting Lodge playing at being aristocrats. Nigel and Alexander (never Alex, God forbid), Elliot and Jonathan treated me cautiously like some eccentric loner. They could not understand it, I should have been one of the team but I wouldn't play. And I could not tell them why. They would not have understood if I'd said I was living in a vacuum. I was still a relatively young man, an eligible bachelor with a wealthy background. There was fun to be had. But to me it was nothing. Dust on a table to be wiped away. I wanted more than they could conceive, but my outward appearance gave the impression of a man growing staid before his time. In many ways they were right. I withdrew from everyday life, became consumed with only one thought and that was how to get back to Lena. Her regular letters were my sustenance, my weekly visits to the Embassy the spur of hope that drove me on. But when Lena stopped writing and the Embassy told me flatly, 'Do not come back, you're not welcome,' I closed up completely. There was nothing left but a frustration which burned in my gut like a pool of acid.

But today was different. A cold wet, October day to everyone else, but for me, a day to savour.

I fed my hands into my pockets to check it was still there. I clicked my nail on the edge of the flap. It was gummed down hard. I would not open it until my head had been cleared of London's early morning mugginess. And that meant a deviation from my normal route. I passed the Old Square by Lincoln's Inn and splashed down Serle Street. There, a little café sat snugly between a shoe shop and a tailor's that nobody seemed to use any more. I'd been there a few times to while away the lunch hour, sitting by the window and watching the pigeons pecking other pigeons. The sign said *Maisies* though the lettering was hardly legible and was probably as old as the original owner. It was nothing special but it served a beautiful cup of tea to wash away the bitter taste of depression.

I went in, ordered a pot and took a table in the corner away from casual conversations. Above me, a clock chimed the half hour. I should have been in work by now. Today, it didn't matter. Nothing mattered until I'd read the contents of the letter. I placed it delicately on the table as though it might disappear at the slightest movement. The little Stalin stamp frowned at me and I smiled back. Whatever the message, it was still a message. It was her handwriting, her words. I would dissect every one for its meaning, pore over the pages until they were dog-eared.

My fingers shaking, I poured out a cup of tea. Physically, I was in an English café and Lena may be somewhere in Russia but now she was here with me in spirit. She could be sitting opposite. She might look tired and thin – was there grey under her eyes?

'Go on, open it,' she said.

The paper was poor quality and crumbled away under my nail.

My dearest Brian,
I am in Uren now. I was transferred two months ago. I give you the address in the hope that one of your letters gets through to me. I know you send them.

This is a terrible place. An industrial town surrounded by mile upon mile of flat farmland. There is no colour here. It is a place to work and produce, not to live. But that is not why it is terrible.

We were sheltered Brian. We thought things were improving

189

in Russia. We thought we'd seen the worst, but we had the good life – Moscow, Grozny, Sochi. I only realised how wrong we had been when I came out here. They needed extra nurses at the hospital and I wanted a change so I volunteered. I think my old employers wanted rid of me for a while anyway. I am not the model citizen. I thought, an old country town, that will be nice. But there are no farms and there is no country. All the food goes from the collective to the army and into the cities. They leave little when times are good but this year the harvest failed almost completely – the soil is overworked and so are the men who plough it – and what little is around is snatched away.

I am here to help patch up the mess. The patients in the ward are here because they are starving.

The tins are empty. There is nothing in the shops. There is no grain left to make bread. I have seen old women chew on cardboard as if it were a feast. They eat their food vouchers for dessert. I have seen children dipping their hands into glue pots. They come into the hospital because they can't get their hands out.

Fuel is running out. The coal goes to the furnaces to make more steel, to make more machines and more tanks. *Pravda* tells us to be vigilant and strong. These are trying times, it says, the mother nation must stand firm against foreign intervention. It does not say: 'Warning, this paper is not edible.'

There are organised groups now, going round the appartments to take your furniture while you are out. They say they are with the police and you cannot argue just in case they are telling the truth. They need the wood to burn, to keep warm. The neighbours say they sell it on the black market and get a good price.

But yesterday was the worst. It made me realise how much I wanted to get out. I saw a young woman, a mother with her baby wrapped under her arm. She was scrabbling around in the frozen earth for something, *anything* to eat. Her fingers were bleeding, but she kept going. She didn't know how to stop and no-one else had the strength or the inclination to stop her. I took her into the hospital, she was thanking me all the way there, but the admittance officer shook his head. I told him it was an emergency. 'They are all emergencies,' he replied. There was nothing he could do. I had to lead her back out. I was in my uniform and I had to push her into the freezing cold. She was screaming and it woke the baby up and it was crying and I just ran away. I have never done that before.

It is only October Brian, but it is already so very cold, and people know, they can tell instinctively, that it will be a harsh winter and we will yearn for days like this when there is no wind and the sun brings a little relief.

It is ten o'clock and I am starting night duty. I will be here till morning, alone with my friends.

I wonder what you are doing now. I want you. Even after all this time, I want you.

2 am

Most of them are asleep now which is a blessing. It is snowing outside. It is very solitary doing night duty. You have eight hours alone with your thoughts. My only company is a desk lamp and a line of men too weak to groan. I would love to see your smiling face now. I would love to look up from this piece of paper and see you striding down the ward. What would you bring me? I would ask for your arms around me, I would ask for a pair of gloves!

This letter will not get through. I know it in my heart. But I write all the same, for myself. Do something for yourself, Lena, I say so I will try. I curl up in the memories of the time we had together. They keep me warm, while outside everything is dead and hard as the concrete they keep churning out. But who can eat concrete?

Have you seen Talbot? He had to leave a couple of years back. He was very kind to me after you went but he could not help in the end. I still have the flowers he gave me on our wedding night. They are pressed in my special book, the one you gave me for our first Christmas, *Anna Karenina*. I have read it countless times and when I get to the last page, the flowers fall out and it reminds me of that night. And can you believe it, they still smell? They are fading, but they will be good for a few more years yet.

It is a long time since I heard from you but I cling to the belief that you still write. I imagine your letters read by some bitter, drunken clerk and chuckled over. I imagine a dustbin full of them waiting to be burnt in the back offices of a government building.

The other alternative I do not wish to think about. Perhaps you have given up? Perhaps it is better that way. Five years is a long time. If we saw each other maybe there would be nothing left. I know of friends, best friends who meet again after so long and they have nothing to link them. They sit in cafés and talk about old times, other people who they will never see again. They cannot look forward.

I'm in a black mood. I cannot cope with the patients. It's funny, as I get older I get less hardened. I remember my head nurse in training telling me to prepare myself for my first day on the ward. There were soldiers with their legs blown off, little babies whose faces had been cut by shrapnel but I was alright. I sailed through and everybody was impressed with my calmness. Then, they had a reason, they believed the suffering was worth it, they had something to fight for and perhaps die for. Not now. It is an endless, weary line of shrunken bodies with no meat on them, bulging ribs and cracked skin. And their eyes, Brian. Every time I walk down the space between the two rows of beds, I pray for them to be sleeping, or unconscious, and I know it is selfish but I can't help it because the eyes are unbearable. Those that are awake stare at me as they would a saviour. And I am, for I represent heat and food. But those eyes also say: 'I am the thousand people who are *not* here.' They feel *lucky*. Why should people about to die be grateful? I know the answer – they have their dignity. They won't die in the dirt and the gutter; they won't die in a frozen shack; they will die in hospital where the sick are meant to die. But I tell you there is no dignity in a five-month old baby, looking like an old man. There is no dignity in that.

I wanted to write something that would make you smile but I am not the person you knew, Brian. I am older, I am bleaker. I was never a coward, but now I want to run away completely. The incident with the young woman yesterday was only the trigger. I think I am beyond despair. Working in this hospital saps that soul. I will go back to Moscow soon, but I have seen too much here.

It is much worse than when you were last in Russia. The trials have shaken people to the core. I am not political, you know that, but I believe that people should have friends. Now, having friends is dangerous. They might snoop, they might say some- thing about you. You might laugh at the wrong joke. I can only talk to a letter I should not send.

Brian, please don't forget me. I can live without you, but I can't live without you thinking about me. You are in my thoughts all the time. Sometimes I am walking down the street and there is a face at the other end, in the crowd, slipping out of sight. I have run before, I have tried to catch up, but it is never you. I should know that by now.

It is no good. We must release each other. There, it is out, finally. It cannot be retracted. I want to be with you, now, this moment, but it is impossible. Thinking about it only makes it worse. It is like a slow death, not to accept the inevitable. Forever hoping, when there is none left.

You have done your best to return and the answer was no. I have done mine, God knows a thousand times, and the answer is always no. It seems now that God never meant us to be together. We should find peace in accepting his decisions.

I am your wife and you are my husband but you must live your life and I must live mine.

Cross your heart (and wish),

I love you,

Lena

FIELDS OF LIGHT

We must release each other.

I went over it five times, hoping the words might change.
I heard her voice saying them. Her lips were thin and
pale. She wanted to hold it in, I knew, but at the same
time realised it must come out eventually. There were no
tears in her eyes, just a coldness, a resignation. A slow
lingering death. She could not bear the waiting.

*God never meant us to be together. We should find peace
in accepting his decisions. I am your wife and you are my
husband but you must live your life and I must live mine.*

I don't know how long it was that I stared at those lines.
My eyes saw nothing but a blank white. I felt a pressure
in my chest, something uncoiling and rising up, spreading
into my arms and legs until I was consumed and helpless.
The pressure turned into a word and came out of me in a
shout. 'No!' My eyes focussed, the white dispersed, and I
looked up but there was no Lena. There was only the stares
of the other customers and a waiter's guiding hand pressing
at my back. 'I think you'd better leave, sir,' he said.
I staggered out of the café blind to the swelling ranks
of commuters and the cars swishing past. I couldn't go in
today, not now. I just wanted to go home, wherever that
really was, and stay there. All that I had done had
crumbled to nothing. It was out of my hands. I had waited
for events to turn my way as they always had in the past,
but this time the current had hardened into an unstoppable
force, propelling me in the wrong direction.
A car hooted behind me and I turned, leaping out of
the way. 'Bloody idiot!' a cabbie snarled. I pressed on up
to High Holborn, my head swimming with images of Lena
as she used to look: soft skin, silk-smooth except around
her eyes with her treasured smile lines. Lena pulling her
hair back, fiddling with a clip to put it in a bunch; Lena

in her cascade of flowers on our wedding night; Lena in her red dress in the box at the Bolshoi. The images held distinct and touchable so that I no longer saw the outside world. But each image would fade after a few seconds, super-imposed by my father in his armchair dismissing all my plans, my ambitions, with his slow-blink stare and then Madeleine in her drawing room, and me watching her with the sun streaming through the french windows, and a throbbing in my head '*Nyet, nyet, nyet, nyet.*'

I put my hands up to my ears to block it all out, my heart pounding and I felt sweat under my arms. I felt dizzy; I needed to sit. Across the pavement there was a ledge in the wall. I slumped gratefully against it, running my fingers along the mortar between the bricks, feeling reassurance in something hard and cold. As I looked up the street for my bus, my eye caught the curved glass of a shop front, one I must have walked past countless times on my way into work. A sign on the side said: 'This week's AIR specials – all 6d.' I walked over and peered through the glass. Rows of tin soldiers marched over fake felt hills, tanks negotiated a sandpit desert, jeeps chugged in indian file along a coarsely painted tarmac road, and above all this, hanging on a wire from the ceiling, was a beautiful model of a Fairy Swordfish banking in the air. It had been painted in minute detail, the product of hours of late night work, probably by the owner. A little tag on the wing tip bore the words 'NOT FOR SALE.' It dominated the display, the sheer grace of the thing eclipsing all else.

As I gazed at it, the rush-hour traffic fading irrelevantly behind me, I became aware of two tiny figures in the cockpit complete with goggles and flying leathers. One of them was looking out over the side and waving at a non-existant crowd of well-wishers. And as I stared, something clicked at the back of my brain and my stomach lurched with a sudden realization. 'Yes,' I whispered. I had the answer. I now knew what I had to do.

It was late afternoon by the time I reached Heston Aerodrome. Situated about twenty miles north west of London, it was a great flat stretch of fields criss-crossed with runways.

I signed up for a 'compressed' course in flight tuition. I was filling in my details in front of a bored desk clerk and was about to make polite conversation when he silently pointed his pen over his shoulder. In a handwritten sign stuck to the noticeboard was the message: 'NO CRASH COURSE JOKES PLEASE. CONTRARY TO YOUR OWN SENSE OF SELF-IMPORTANCE, YOU ARE NOT THE FIRST PERSON TO HAVE MADE THE UNFUNNY CONNECTION. Signed, by order, Irritated Admissions Officer.

I smiled and said, 'Fair enough.'

'You wouldn't believe how many ignore it . . . Do you have leathers?'

I looked at him, bemused.

'Flying leathers, gloves, jacket, goggles.'

'Er . . . no.'

'We can provide them, but they cost extra. You'll need them. It's cold up there.'

'How long will it take?' I asked.

'Until you are proficient and the instructor passes you. Some people a couple of weeks, others a couple of years. It depends.'

It would have to be a couple of weeks. The longer I left it, the worse the flying conditions would be.

'We can fit in your starter lesson tomorrow morning first thing if you want.'

'That soon!'

'You're lucky, someone cancelled only an hour ago. Cold feet.'

You're lucky. The words seemed appropriate again. This morning, my life had collapsed in on itself. Now, a few hours later, everything seemed possible. But to succeed, luck would have to play a massive part.

The clerk was right. It was cold, and we hadn't left the ground yet. It was eight in the morning and I'd been greeted on my arrival at the aerodrome by a hearty hand-shake from my personal instructor Ray Sedgely and a bitter wind sweeping down from the north.

'We won't be able to go up today, I'm afraid,' Ray said. 'Too dangerous. But perhaps it's better anyway. You can get to know the lovely lady before you give her a work out.' He smirked at me.

On the runway he said, 'I'm afraid she hasn't been taken inside. We were caught a bit offguard by the weather. You don't mind a wet behind do you?'

He had the calmness of a man who had been through this a thousand times before but didn't mind doing it all over again. He introduced me to the dilapidated first World War Gypsy Moth; a bi-plane which had seen better days. 'The most solid of them all,' he said.

When I climbed into the cockpit, I felt a sense of elation. Rain was lashing my face, within minutes my fingers were numb, but it felt real. Sitting there, the buckles digging into my legs, the wind howling under the wings, it felt achievable.

Steadily he explained each dial, how to read the alti-meter, the fundamentals of manouvring up and down, banking left and right; all the basics that would get me off the ground and with a little fortune keep me there.

The hour was up quickly. As we went back to the cafeteria for a drink Ray said to me: 'The most important thing of all, more than any technical detail, is to remember that a plane is like an untrained animal. It's willful. You must always remember who's boss. You must anticipate rather than react.'

I took lodgings in an anonymous guest house off the Holloway road and sent a quick note to my parents, telling them I'd moved, not that they'd notice. I wanted to become invisible. By now, their knowledge of the outside world extended as far as their privet hedge, and that was on one of their clear days. Nevertheless, I felt obliged.

From a secluded room at the back of the house, I put flesh to my plan. Every day for the next three weeks, I travelled up to Heston. I would sit in the front while Ray barked instructions from behind. By the end of the first week, I could do a figure of eight over the aerodrome, by the end of the second week I did my first nerve-racking solo flight, trying desperately to maintain a steady altitude. Ray assessed me from the ground and winced as I touched down like a rhino without a parachute. Two days later, I was taking written tests on navigation and air law and mechanics. And on the 23rd October 1938, I was awarded my pilot's license. 'No distinctions, no merits,' Ray said as we shook hands, 'just enough to keep you alive and stop you from killing anyone else.'

I thanked him for everything, privately vowing to send him a postcard when it was all over. His final words to me were, 'Go easy old man.' He looked a little worried.

From then on every night, and far into the small hours of the morning, I pored over the route I would follow. The guiding consideration of secrecy decided me to go via Stockholm. The obvious route was through Poland and Latvia, but both countries, I knew, would insist on knowing all about my business before letting me into their territory. So Sweden it would have to be.

There was a knock at the door. Probably my landlord again. He didn't like the hours I kept, thought I was up to no good. I opened it ready to tell him once again that I would appreciate a bit of peace.

But it wasn't my landlord.

Frank beamed at me, stepping straight into the room.

'So this is what you've come to? He glanced around at the papers and maps strewn across the floor, at my unmade bed. 'You've gone up in the world.'

I stared at him. He looked just the same. The red hair a little faded perhaps, a few more wrinkles around the eyes.

A million questions and greetings came to mind but in the end I settled for a rather pathetic 'Frank!'

He grabbed my shoulders with his great paws. 'Well you could try a hello, at least. Surely I deserve that?'

'If you refrain from crunching my bones, I might even find you a seat.' I cleared a space on the desk. 'Sorry about the mess. Been a bit busy lately.'

'I can see.' He put on a hurt face. 'Too busy to keep in touch?'

'I could say the same about you.'

'Took a while to track you down, nearly a full day getting your address out of your mother. But I did it.' Accusation lay at the back of his voice, but it was playful, a throwback to the verbal duels we'd had so many times in the past.

There was a pause.

Six years is a long time but the silence between friends who meet after losing touch seems longer. 'I think a drink is in order,' I said, grabbing my jacket, not waiting for agreement. For unless my friend had become someone completely different, acceptance of a drink would always be a constant in the complex equation of his personality.

At the pub on Seven Sisters road we bought each other rounds of bitter and relived old lives and caught up with new ones. Frank had returned to the States after Grozny. The situation had worsened after Lena and I had left. Open hostility became the norm, so he simply packed his bags one night and snuck away.

'Lily didn't really mind,' he said. 'There'd be many more like me. It was just a bit of fun for both of us.' He looked at me over his pint, a sadness in his eyes. 'Seems like it didn't work with you and Lena in the end either?'

I explained everything to him, right up to me leaving my job but no further. I wasn't sure I should tell anyone my plans, and I decided I wasn't going to until Frank said, 'Sometimes, you just have to give up. Sometimes it's best to let it go.'

I avoided his gaze. At the other end of the room an old man with a rolled up cigarette hanging from his mouth methodically potted a black on a rickety snooker table.

'Is that what you really think?' I asked.

'Yep,' he said, gulping down to the bottom of his glass.

I leaned forward. 'And has it made you happy?'

'Nope.'

All his relationships had been 'just a bit of fun,' and that was fine if it was all you wanted. I imagined us both in thirty years time, saying the same thing, quietly wishing we'd taken a different course in our lives but never quite admitting it to each other. I saw us both sitting there, in the same position, thirty years older, fingering our pints, and knew absolutely that I was making the right decision.

I thought it would be good to share my secret with him. So I said, 'Sometimes you've got to think "what the hell".'

'Well, that's what I mean,' he replied.

'No, you don't understand. Sometimes, you've got to risk everything.'

He perked up a little at this. 'What do you mean?'

'I've been taking flying lessons.'

'With you at the controls that probably *is* risking everything.'

I shook my head and smiled. 'I'm not doing it for the thrill,' I whispered. He looked puzzled.

'Work it out.'

I watched his contorted face relax, smooth out, then tense again into a look of horror as realisation dawned.

'Uhh-Uh,' he mumbled. Then, 'Ah, Christ man, you're not!'

I nodded.

'Tell me this is a wind-up Grover.'

'Not this time.'

'They'll shoot you down. And if they don't, they'll shoot you after you come down.'

'No, I worked it all out Frank. They won't see me – if I fly above the cloud. And once I'm in, I'll just ask to be arrested.'

'And they'll oblige.'

'I'll explain my case. They might listen.'

'Oh, they'll do that all right. Then they'll take you outside and line you up against the wall with all the other losers.'

I shrugged. 'If it happens, it happens.'

Frank's face reddened. 'How can you say that?'

'Very easily,' I said solemnly. 'For the last five years I've been dead anyway. At least this way, if it happens, I'll die knowing I did everything I could.'

'You're crazy. You – you're insane.'

'They mean the same thing, Frank.'

'Someone's minced your brain,' he spluttered.

'Feels good that way,' I replied. 'Fancy another beer?'

'Think I need one.'

When I returned, he was a little calmer. He eyed me slyly. 'There's just one thing I want to know.'

'Name it.'

'Does this mean I can have your room while you're away?'

I said goodbye to him that same night. I insisted that I didn't want him around because he'd only try to dissuade me, and made him promise not to tell anyone else. He agreed reluctantly to both demands. We shook on it as he cursed: 'Six years I don't see you, and when I do it's for two hours. Wish you well Grover boy, but you're cuckoo and you're also a maniac.'

'They mean the same thing too.'

I had £250 left in my pocket and a plane to buy. Through the air club, I met a few people who knew what was on the market. I wanted something new, easy to fly and with a long range. For that I was politely informed, I would not get much change out of a couple of grand.

I went round all the dealers, all the local aerodromes, becoming increasingly desperate to find something, *anything*, as long as it came with an engine and something resembling wings. Time was running short and winter was setting in. Then I chanced upon a dealer named Fellows, who operated near Hanworth. When he heard what I had to offer he grimaced, looked down his line of sparkling beauties, straight off the factory floor.

'I'm a bit out of your price range. Sorry,' he said. I thanked him for his trouble, and was about to leave, when he called out after me, 'Hold on. I might have something for you in the back here.' He took me through to a dark and dusty hangar, where dried-up pots of paint and oil canisters and dirty rags were strewn across the floor. There, in the centre of the room, half-covered by tarpaulin was what looked like a winged coffin on wheels.

'What was it you said you wanted it for?'

'Oh, just pottering about. Money's tight so – '

'Then this is your beauty,' the salesman declared. He pulled the tarpaulin back. 'Not much to look at, I'll admit, not the most stylish of planes, true, but it does its job. The trusty Klemm Swallow.'

It sat there in all its glory, covered in dirt, paint flaking from the fuselage and rust creeping around the engine casing. 'I've been meaning to get her souped up,' he explained, 'but *tempus fugit*, you know how it is.' Indeed I did.

I circled it, running my finger through the caked dust on the wings.

'But does it fly?'

'Does she fly?' Fellows bellowed, slapping the body like an old friend. The frame shook with the impact and I imagined the wood splintering under the canvas. 'She goes like a bomb, and keeps going until you tell her to stop. We'll take her out. Once you climb inside, you'll wonder why you ever bothered with automobiles.'

He pulled the shutters up with a rattle and we took the plane onto his landing strip. 'See that over there?' Fellows pointed to a low, grey building that ran down one side of the field. 'The Hanworth factory. That's where they make these lovely creatures. And I tell you, they're fifteen hundred quid straight off the production line.'

He spun the prop. It spluttered uncertainly to life, faltered and ran down again. 'Listen to that purr. Five cylinder, 80 hp Popjoys, top speed 75 mph.'

'What's it capacity?' I asked.

'Oh, you can tank her up. She's had quite a history this old bird. It will do seven hours at a time, if you push her.

That was perfect.

'I'll take her,' I said suddenly. He looked startled, but regained his composure. 'Two hundred seem reasonable?'

'One fifty.'

He grimaced. 'One eighty.'

'One sixty.'

'I could get more than that for scrap.'

'And you've got six wives and ten children to feed, I know, I know. I'll give you one seventy but that's it.'

I could see him ticking through the possibilities. Slowly, he nodded. 'Done.'

We shook on it and I showed him my papers. 'I presume cash is acceptable,' I said to him counting out the notes.

'Fine,' he said, and then grunted as though he wanted to add more. I looked up and held his gaze. 'I hope you don't mind me saying, but you seem in a bit of a hurry. What do you really want it for?'

'Let's just say, I'm going to visit an old friend.'

Over the next few days I read all I could lay my hands on about Air Navigation and weather conditions. The more I looked into it, the more I understood Ray's final look when I passed my test. He didn't know what I was going to do but, like Fellows, had sensed my urgency. Now, looking over the intricacies of the project, it became apparent that I was nowhere near qualified enough. It was one thing to do circuits around the aerodrome, quite another to navigate my coffin from one continental airport to another. I was no good to Lena if I ditched myself in the Channel a few hours after setting off. I would have to engage a professional pilot. He could take me as far as Stockholm. The rest, I would have to chance alone.

So I put an advert in one of the air periodicals and soon I had a partner, one Henry Mountjoy. He was experienced, lived for flying and was the proud owner of a moustache so huge he didn't really need a plane to take off. He agreed to accompany me for expenses only. I told him we were going over for a business trip, and that I wanted to polish my skills.

'Super, super, super,' he said.

Nice to know he was enthusiastic.

'Do a few whirls on the way, eh?'

'Well, I need to get straight there.'

'How about a few drives then?'

I was beginning to think he might not be such a sure bet, but I'd already offered him the job. He didn't wait for an answer, took my second's hesitation as a resounding affirmative.

'Super,' he said again. 'Can't wait.'

'*You'll kill yourself*', Frank had said. I might die, I thought now, but maybe not by my own hand.

On the 4th November 1938, just before dawn I met up with Henry Mountjoy at Heston. He had his head in the Swallow's engine when I arrived.

'Just caressing her arteries,' he said. He was wearing his goggles already, moustache wings tucked up behind the straps.

'How can you see what you're doing with those things on?'

'I can't,' he replied. 'But the way I look at it, one might as well get used to them.'

Within an hour we were ready to go. We packed our kit in the hold. All I had to my name was a spare shirt, a flask and a razor. It semed a paltry collection for my ultimate journey. Considering I was supposed to be on a business trip, I was surprised my partner didn't remark upon it.

In the changing rooms I donned my leathers and splashed my face with cold water to freshen up. I had aged. There were deep furrows on my brow, the odd wisp of grey above my ears. I wondered if she looked as weatherbeaten as me. She had gone through her own traumas, but I didn't know which was worse, waiting for someone who never returned or trying forever to return but finding your path always blocked.

We were given clearance to take off and Henry span the prop. The engine roared into life. For the trip over the Channel he would be sitting in the back cockpit with the main controls.

The runway sped underneath us until it was only a blur of grey. We soared over the outskirts of London, each little box house with its family still asleep, still safe in their dreams.

Conversation was nigh on impossible. Whenever I tried to say something to Henry he just looked non-plussed and mouthed, 'What?' I had hoped I could learn from him, but it was pointless in the Swallow for the engine drowned everything. So instead I concentrated on thinking about my solo trip from Stockholm. I would only be flying in a straight line after all. I would push on until the fuel guage dropped to empty. Then I would land wherever possible. The plane was dispensible, so if she got a few scratches it wouldn't matter. I tried to keep my thoughts on what would happen, how I would tackle events. But it was a void, I had no idea how I would be received. I would just have to ignore Ray's advice and react to problems if and when they arose.

We banked steeply to the left and the whole of Kent 4,000 feet below us tipped into view: a ribbon of the Rother winding through a patchwork of fields, flecks of white against slabs of green which moved if you looked hard enough. Sheep with no more worries than their next mouthful of grass.

I gripped the sides of the cockpit as the compass swung violently. I heard Henry's laugh above the din of the propellor. So communication *was* possible – if you had lungs the size of an elephant. I felt like a learner driver taking pole position at Monaco with all the engines revving behind him and Henry was the mechanic in the pits who'd loosened a wheel, 'just for fun mind you.' We headed south east, across the Channel passing over the long shingle beaches of the Folkestone to Dover coastline. Waves chopped on the surface of the sea. It looked windy down there. But it was windier up here, and a damn sight colder. Momentarily, I wished I weren't in this flimsy construction. I felt a sudden dash of nostalgia for my awful office job. but I buried myself in the cockpit, zipped my flying jacket as tight as it would go and thought of Lena and the sensation evaporated.

We'd been flying for about half an hour when we hit a thick patch of fog. It clung with dense cold. I turned to see how Henry was. He held a sandwich in one hand, a cup of coffee in another.

'Could have given me one,' I shouted.

Henry gulped down his last morsel. 'What?'

'I said, I wouldn't mine a bite myself.'

'Can't hear you,' he mouthed.

Suddenly there was silence. 'Bugger, I can now,' he said. The plane dipped nosewards and I felt my body leave my seat. 'What's happened?' I screamed.

'Engine's clogged up, must be the ice.'

We were losing altitude rapidly now, diving blind towards the sea. Henry tapped me on the shoulder, pointed his thumbs down. I knew what it meant.

Before we'd set off, he'd gone through different crisis scenarios. One, the worst case, was ditching in the sea if the engine stalled. The idea was to pick up speed, nose downwards, pumping the throttle at the same time. With luck the propeller might start again, with a little less luck the plane would glide down and we'd float on the water for days waiting to be picked up, with no luck at all we would be smashed to pieces before we even reached the French coast.

FIELDS OF LIGHT

We broke through the fog and the dark sea hurtled towards us like an infinite wall. The altimeter span as though someone were winding the dials on a clock. 1000ft, 900, 800. In 10 seconds, we'd be dead.

'Henry, pull back man! For Christ's sake!'

When I turned round, there was an intense smile on his face.

'What's done is done,' he cried and leaned back hard against his seat, ramming his feet against the elevator pedals and pumping the throttle for all his life. The Swallow jolted upwards as though a bomb had just exploded underneath it, and in the same motion the engine spluttered into life. 'Yes! Yes! Oh yes!' he whooped.

We drew level. The sea looked close enough to touch. I could see the crest of the waves frothing then slapping in on themslves. I realised that I'd held my breath for the last twenty seconds of my life and let it out in a harsh, relieved rasp. Although it was freezing, I felt as though I would boil. Sweat broke out on my forehead and froze almost instantly.

We climbed steadily for the next hour, did a wide circle round the radio mast at Cherbourg which was the conventional signal to show we were alright. As the night wore on it began to rain. Soon the rain turned to hail that battered into the fuselage like tiny bullets. A storm was brewing, my face was stinging and yet I felt happy to be alive.

I fumbled around my my bag for pen and paper. I wrote: 'How about an Irish coffee when we get to Hambourg?' and passed it over to Henry.

A minute later came the reply: 'How about a new plane?'

We sat in the airport lounge, our wet leathers squeaking when we moved. In time, whisky coffees were brought, topped with thick cream and crusted sugar. Nothing was said between us. We just silently raised our mugs to our lips and silently said a prayer of thanks. Henry for the excitement, me for still being here. Today Hambourg, in a few days Stockholm. Moscow, I hoped, very soon.

Later, after Henry had gone to bed, I watched the night through the windows and wondered what Lena would be doing now. The storm showed no signs of subsiding. The barman jolted every time gusts of wind slammed the panes of glass. My eyes felt heavy and sticky, but I didn't want to go to sleep just yet. So I sat there wanting to think about all the things I had and hadn't done in my life and the ridiculous thing I was about to do, until I was too tired even to hold my cup anymore.

I looked in the direction of Moscow and saw only impenetrable darkness.

OVER THE LINE
November 1938

The journey to Stockholm took four days in all and passed without incident. For most of the way Henry was content to scare me with the occasional hedge-hop. I was no fun for him. He wanted someone to share his excess supply of adrenalin. I wanted someone to get me to Sweden alive. He was insane, but he knew his stuff. The day after the storm subsided he spent the whole morning tweaking the engine and the Swallow had responded to his touch. A bit.

A bit was the best anybody could do.

The weather was kind to us now; clear skies and calm seas. For the first few hours the sun was in our faces, providing fleeting fingers of warmth against the steady onslaught of cold winds sweeping down from the North. We left German airspace at midday on 6th November and started our crossing of the Baltic. Far to the left was Denmark, its island shadows rising faintly from the silver sea; ahead of us in Sweden we would fly over countless lakes already freezing up as winter set in hard. But it was the world to my right, the grey distance to Moscow that stretched forever, that I concentrated on. It was nearly a month since she had written. What if they had read her letter before sending it on? What if she had just given up on me? She had said she was returning to Moscow but the way things were, people could be moved without notice, without choice. She could be anywhere. She could be dead.

The last thought I exorcised from my mind. Coulds and ifs and what abouts made no difference. If they were all you had to go on in life, nothing would move forward. And, whatever the outcome, however bleak the prospects, I knew I was going somewhere.

After Lena's letter I'd stopped thinking. The imperative to act had taken over and the possibility that I could make matters worse by flying into the Soviet Union had not entered my mind. But when we arrived in Stockholm I thought I should at least try to smooth over the not inconsiderable wrinkles in my plan.

I could go no further now until the weather changed. Low cloud was essential to cover my tracks. Any sighting of a strange plane would guarantee my being turned back before I crossed the border. The forecast was clear until the end of the week so I would have to use my time wisely. I spent the next few days ostensibly as a tourist. Each morning I would get up early, tell Henry I was off on a business meeting, go into the city centre and shop. On the first outing I bought a haversack, a new pair of pyjamas, a tooth brush and a shaving kit. All essentials – if I ever finally got to see my wife, I wanted her to recognise me, not be repulsed by some hairy stray in sweaty clothes. On the next, I accumulated presents for Lena, and barter for the rest of the population. Perfume, a couple of silk ties, hand-made chocolates and the best brandy money could buy short of bankruptcy. I returned to the hotel, arms bulging and piled them on to my bed. I was sorting them through when Henry entered the room. He let out a long whistle.

'You *have* been busy.' I was sure there was a glint in his eyes.

'Just presents for friends,' I explained, feeling the heat in my face.

'I don't know whether she'll be able to carry all that – with both of us flying that is.'

What was he getting at? Did he know I was going to leave without him? He couldn't. It was impossible. I was becoming paranoid, reading nuances into words that simply didn't exist.

'Don't worry,' I said after an unconvincing silence spent trying to rack my brains for a reply, 'most of them are going by post.'

He left the room soon after. I collapsed back on the bed and sighed. There was one item still to buy and I was glad I hadn't got it today – a set of luggage. When I sneaked away, I wanted to keep people off the scent for as long as possible. By leaving what looked like all my belongings in the room, it would appear, at least for a while, that I intended to come back.

As it was, Henry asked no more questions and made no comments. Looking back, I'm sure he was just making friendly conversation. I never got time to know him well, seeing him only as an essential inconvenience in my plans. He struck me as a bit of a loner. An obsessed one admittedly, but even lonely obsessives feel the need for company sometimes.

A further aspect of my plan that needed just a little brushing up was getting used to the Swallow. I had wanted to reach Stockholm so quickly that I had let Henry take the controls all the way. Before we left, all I had done was take it for a short spin over Heston aerodrome. Now I cursed my impatience. On the most vital leg of the journey, I would be trusting to luck.

So I took the Swallow up every day while the skies were

clear, practising manoeuvres. Every plane has a particular character. Henry and I had already learnt that she wasn't too partial to Northern weather. More troublesome, though, was the discovery that she refused to be rushed into anything. The Klemm Swallow was a pedal-operated model. The elevators and ailerons were all operated via low wooden poles at the feet – push down for lift, swing back to level out. The throttle was a little lever on the left wall of the cockpit. In theory, different combinations of the two meant you could make her do just about anything. In practice, she favoured Newton's first law of motion – once an object is moving, it wants to keep moving in that direction. The pedals were so heavy it was like trying to push a corpse, the throttle had a penchant for refusing to budge more than once every hour, and the flaps slept the whole way through. The first time I took her out of Stockholm, it was an hour before I could get her back to the landing strip, though I did get a beautiful sight-seeing tour of the city.

For once the forecasters were right. The skies of Stockholm remained dark but clear for over a week. Each day I filled my haversack full of kit and a thermos of hot coffee, stowing it in the Swallow's locker just in case. Every evening I topped up the fuel and oil tanks. When I could leave it would have to be an immediate departure; no hitches and no delays.

I went over to the window that morning, thick cloud stretched to the horizon over a city just creaking awake. It was drizzling but the rain fell near vertically. The odd car swished by on the main road leading into the centre, leaving yellow trails from their back lights, swirling in the darkness. The conditions were perfect.

My clothes seemed to go on by themselves. I was

checking my lists: fuel, oil, coffee, presents, gloves, luggage . . . I went over it again and again. When everything was packed I stood by the door and scanned the room. I felt sure something was wrong. But it was bare, I could see nothing incriminating. Just another hotel bedroom. I moved quickly down the corridor and slipped a note under Henry's door. The envelope contained thirty pounds and as many apologies but no explanations. And also one request – not to tell anyone about my disappearance. The money would be enough to cover the hotel bills and his passage home. I hoped he would understand.

I had just left the foyer when I stopped. With each step taken the feeling that something was wrong had grown. Now I felt sick. There *was* something. It lay on the fringes of my mind, nagging but not clear. I turned round and stared at the face of the building searching for my room, some trigger. Then it hit me. I'd left the place clean. I'd been so careful to hide the new luggage, tucked away at the back of the wardrobe, that I'd forgotten it myself. I rushed back upstairs, dragged it out and scattered it across the room.

There. Now it looked normal. I crept out again, and as I did so, saw Henry's door open. I hugged the wall as he wandered in an early-morning haze to the toilet. He walked straight over the envelope. While he was safe at work relieving himself I left.

There were few people around at the aerodrome so I reckoned it wouldn't be too difficult to slip away into the cloud without causing any commotion. I wheeled the Swallow out of the hangar, dipped my head in the engine to give it a final once over just to make sure, then angled her onto the runway.

I was in the cockpit ready to give myself contact when a man in blue overalls came running out of the control building waving his arms. I pretended not to notice him, flicked the ignition switch and jumped out to swing the prop.

He was shouting something, first in Swedish, which was impossible to understand even if I'd been able to hear it clearly, then in English; words carried on the air which left no doubt as to meaning. 'NO . . . Stop . . . STOP!'

He reached me, breathless and red-faced. It was Ake, a voluntary traffic controller who took his job very seriously. 'Mr Grover! Mr Grover!' He always repeated everything, as though people didn't understand him first time. More probably, they did not listen.

'You must not fly today. Must not. Didn't you see the sign?'

I hadn't looked, actually.

'Over there, I put it out first thing!'

I glanced at the control tower and saw nothing.

'Where?'

'It's in the window.'

And so it was, a small speck of white, almost invisible from 200 yards away.

'Ah, yes,' I said. 'What's the problem?'

'Bad weather. There are storms coming, big storms. No flying without radio. It is very dangerous.'

Unfortunately, though voluntary, he had the authority to ground me. Argument would receive a stony-faced silence. Persuasion and bowing to his sense of self-importance, however, might work. It usually did with officialdom.

I put on my humble, hard-done by look. 'I only want to do a figure of eight. Keep my hand in. I'm just getting used to her.'

'It's out of the question. No flying without radio.'

'I'll be up and down within ten minutes, I promise.'

There was a long pause. He looked over the shoulder the way people do when they're about to agree to something they shouldn't. There was nobody there.

'Please.'

Nothing.

'*Please.*'

Perhaps it was the repetition of the word that tipped it my way, I don't know, but he nodded solemnly. 'Alright. Five minutes. *Five* minutes.'

'Heard you the first time,' I said and smiled. I swung the prop. For once the engine started first time. I jumped into the cockpit and slipped on my goggles and ear muffs, immediately encased in a new world of muffled sound and vibration.

Ake still didn't get the message. As the plane trundled down the tarmac, I looked back. The last I saw of him, he was standing chest out, overalls flapping in the slip-stream of the Swallow. One hand held aloft, fingers splayed. *Five* fingers splayed.

Rubber burned runway. I eased the throttle to full power, pushing against the dead-weight pedals as the Swallow reached take-off speed. I felt the freedom, the freedom that all pilots know when the wheels leave the earth. You feel suddenly that gravity is tainting. It restricts expression. In a plane, the normal world of squabbling bosses and money worries and guilty consciences disappears. The clutch of worry loosens its grip the higher you go. Soon there is nothing else except you and your plane and the air, somehow holding you up.

My back slammed against the cockpit seat as I accelerated. The nose pointed straight for the cloud. At five hundred feet, a side wind picked up and the plane wobbled. I adjusted to level out and overcompensated. She wasn't being as stubborn as usual. Or maybe I was just inexperienced and nervous. I decided on the former.

We climbed, the Swallow and I, and the world grew insignificant. At 1,000 feet I entered cloud and it seemed I wasn't flying at all. There was no perspective. Everything was a dusty white. At any moment I expected a rock or a hill to loom out of the haze and hammer into me. Flying blind, even when you know there is nothing in front of you for miles, is a terrifying experience. On more than one occasion I swerved objects only as solid as my imagination. When I reached 2,500 feet the cloud thinned into a transparent skin. The cockpit filled with pale yellow light and then I burst through, the sun smacking the fuselage so brightly I had to shield my eyes.

I was in the cloud country. The land above the land. The place you dream about as a child. In the land above the land you can walk on air, pluck strands of floss from the white sponge, dive into it knowing it will bounce you back up. It stretched beyond the horizon without breaking, so solid I wanted to touch down, step out and take a stroll. When I looked up I saw the real sky, a pure blue canvas between earth and space. The moon and sun in the same picture, the crescent and the orb.

At 10,000 feet I levelled out, checked my watch, 8.10 am, and set about charting my route. I had been unable to get hold of any aviation maps for the Soviet Union. That would have aroused suspicion more than anything else, so I had to make do with an old school map of Russia bought in a second-hand bookshop on Charing Cross Road. A more detailed chart would have been quite useless anyway. Up here, there were no landmarks to go by. The only way to determine my direction was to draw a straight line between Stockholm and Moscow. The angle between it and the meridian gave my compass bearing. Stick to that and hope for the best. I couldn't allow for drift because there were no instruments to tell me the velocity of the wind.

Once I'd calculated that, there was nothing more to do but sit back, concentrate on the dials and wait. But my mind wandered. Henry would have read his note by now. He'd be sitting on the side of the bed, packing his things.

He'd be cursing a lost opportunity, but if I'd taken him, or rather he'd taken me, he'd have made plans for sky-diving the Kremlin or making a sortie into the Arctic. He'd be glum – the way home was by boat and to a man like Henry that was purgatory. I chuckled, picturing Ake. He would be radioing other airfields to see where his 'figure-of-eight' beginner had got to. He'd be feeling important – Ake Kristensen at the centre of an inter-national incident. But he'd be sweating. Naughty boy for believing me. He knew now what he could do with his five fingers.

The cloud scudded by, the sun lay still in the sky, the needles on the dials remained constant. And the cold crept in. Insidious, creeping cold. I didn't notice it at first. My flying jacket and cap and five layers of vests and shirts kept it out. But slowly my fingers numbed, the joints stiffening. At 10,000 feet once something is cold, it stays that way. It was futile but I concentrated on finding ways to get warm. I stuck hands under legs but the buckles from my gloves jabbed into me causing more discomfort than before. I stamped my feet on the floor of the cockpit. A timid effort. In films people always stamp their feet to get the circulation going but the simple truth is, it just wastes energy. If you're in Arctic conditions, nothing gets the circulation going like finding somewhere warm. I had only a few places to choose from. Lean slightly against the left side of the cockpit, lean slightly against the right. Or just stay in the middle and imagine myself on a beach in Trinidad sucking the juice out of ripe mangoes as the sun beat down. Whichever way, bits would be dropping off me soon, frozen and useless.

I pulled out the Thermos from under the seat and savoured a cup of steaming coffee. The heat of the liquid blew into my face as I drank. Within seconds the coffee would be tepid. I gulped it down, my chest constricting in protest at the change in temperature. I checked the time. Ten-thirty. It could count as early elevenses.

Two minutes later I looked at my watch again. And then again. Shivering, I watched the second hand moving, the gap between each click an eternity. I was sure that when I stared at it, the hand hesitated before moving on, but when I looked away it hurriedly caught up with itself.

Aches crept up my arms. My lips chapped into craters and the desire to lick them better grew incessantly until I could no longer bear it. My tongue darted out against central command's strictest orders, and regretted it. The wind froze the spittle almost immediately – a blunt razor criss-crossing my face.

I put my head down and watched the seconds again. This time I challenged myself to count as high as possible between each movement of the hand. 'Onetwothree forfisisevehaynintenele – '

'Onetothefufifsiseveghaynitelvutwelthirtinfor – '

I wanted to reach fifteen. Fifteen was the magic number to get to. Then I could stop the game and think of something else. I must have tried twenty times until even my brain was numb.

I looked up and my neck creaked with the effort. Not even three hours into the flight and I was waiting for it to end. I thought of a time when I was a young child out for a walk with my parents. It couldn't have been more than two miles around the copse and back but it felt like a trek into the wilderness with no return. Mother gripped my hand and dragged me stumbling behind her. They grumbled amongst themselves in grown-up speak while my mind slowly became consumed with one thing. I needed the toilet, desperately. I wanted to go home, I wanted to go *home* that's all. But I couldn't say 'wee' or 'toilet' in

front of Mother. Father would be furious, he would roar
at me like a great lion. I counted each blade of grass that
passed, worshipped each corner that turned us towards
home. By the time the house came into view I was about
to explode. The sight of it was too much. I felt the release,
and with all my effort stopped it. A tiny patch of wet
appeared on my shorts.

'Mother?'

'What is it dear?'

'I need – '

'?'

'I need to go behind a bush.'

Mother's face dropped.

'Brian! We're nearly home. Be a gentleman.'

'But I have to.' Already I was edging towards an inviting
tree. The trickle was coming back. I turned and ran and
pulled down my shorts. Father pounded after me.

'Don't you dare, boy!' he shouted but there was nothing
I could do. It streamed out in a long luxurious release.
All the while Father harangued me, clipping my ear and
smacking me with the flat of his hand. 'A real man can
control himself. You should be *ashamed* boy. We'll send
you out in the wilds, is that what you want? To become
a *savage*?'

Normally, I would have crumbled under his fury, but the
sensation of despatching with my ballast was so over-
whelmingly delicious that nothing else mattered. Mother
refused to speak to me until we got inside, Father went on
one of his long diatribes, occasionally shoving his face into
mine, his wiry moustache scraping my skin, and asking me
questions about a man called Friday that I did not understand. But I was happy. The awful waiting was over . . .

No more clock-watching, I told myself now. You can't
dissect the journey into fragments of seconds and expect
it to go quicker.

I tried to keep alert, doing crosswords in my head, playing imaginary chess against an imaginary opponent. But each time within a few minutes the construct would collapse into nothing. The cold was really beginning to worry me now. I had expected to be uncomfortable but the temperature was well below zero and the chill-factor from the wind made it dangerous.

There was nothing I could do. If I descended I might gain a few degrees, but the chances of the engine being heard from the ground increased dramatically. Where I should really be flying was below the cloud layer where the heat was trapped in, and that was out of the question.

An hour passed. I checked my map and tried to work out my position. The Baltic was behind me now, so too Latvia. I calculated the speed of the plane, the time I had been flying and drew a dot just past Karsava.

I was in Russian airspace. For a while I felt renewed energy at the thought. I was half way there. I had crossed the border that had kept me out for five years. Then the small reality of my cramped cockpit closed in and I was running on reserves again.

I felt dizzy, my head flopping from fatigue.

I blacked out.

You are blindfolded in a house where all the shutters have been drawn. You are at the bottom of a staircase. Up there, in an attic somewhere, you know a window has been opened. An opportunity. Laboriously, you climb the stairs, one foot in front of the other. You reach the first landing; you reach the second; you reach the top and you know the door is ajar. Your hands flex in front of you. Through the door is something you need very badly. Through the door is your dream, waiting for you to grab it. The fresh wind tickles your nose, dispersing the acrid air. You scent victory at last. Where's the handle? If you can only touch that handle. You are inches away. You reach out, you feel the coolness of the brass before you touch it. You think this time.

Then the door slams hard and you recoil. Then you are downstairs in a house where all the shutters have been drawn. You are at the bottom of a staircase . . .

Time contracts to a point where it can be plucked, a glassy pebble, from the sand. It can be hurled high, can be watched as it dips in an arc towards the sea.

Brighton promenade on a cool spring morning. Madeleine is going back to New York tomorrow. I will not see her again. I can hear her breathing in, short little gasps. She says she will stay there with her uncle for a while. He's in the antiques business. She says she is interested in old things. They retain their value. Perhaps, eventually, she will set up there.

The boat leaves from Southampton. She does not want me to see her off, she says. I wasn't going to offer.

The solicitors are happy, I am relieved but Madeleine lost.

The cheque is folded in her purse. Neatly tucked away for another day. When I gave it to her she grimaced. The end of her control. It is a pay-off for her silence. It is real life come home. She doesn't want to say goodbye to her hold over me, but spite wears you down and she is exhausted of it. She won't tell.

We take coffee at a table outside an empty café. Not much business before the Easter rush. It rained earlier and everything is damp. Madeleine lights a cigarette and flicks ash into a damp saucer. The smell lingers then is whisked away by a rare breeze from the sea. Her expression is damp too, the hardness has gone. We are poles apart, but I want to say something that will dry her up. That would make it easier.

FIELDS OF LIGHT

It is 1936, I haven't seen Lena for two years. Madeleine wants just a bit of me, something to hold onto but we both know it is gone and we both feel sorry for ourselves and perhaps, despite the bitterness, we both feel sorry for each other.

We watch the gulls wheeling and diving by the West Pier. It hasn't opened yet. The covers are down on the ice-cream kiosks, the deck chairs are folded away, the carousel ground to a halt months ago.

'Why did we come down here?' Madeleine says.

'You were the one who insisted.'

'I didn't.'

I let it go. It is pointless arguing. 'Neutral ground, I suppose. To give you the cheque.'

She stubs out her cigarette and grinds it into the ash paste. 'I hope you never get there, Brian,' she says. 'You screwed up my life. I hope you do as good a job on yours.'

I see her again, as if for the first time, and I realise there were two Madeleines. The sharp, young woman with the razor wit, and the dulled, older woman with razors but no wit to sharpen them by.

'You left me,' I say. The words pop from my lips. Pop, pop, pop. They pop the guilt. I married twice. I broke the law. So? 'You wouldn't give me a divorce, we couldn't live together. I did nothing wrong.'

It is enough. She's had too much of my life. I don't want to hate her. She hates me, she loves me. (Pick the petals, which will it be?) Neither. She only loved what she wanted me to be.

I get up. I leave. She doesn't follow.

There is a boy on the shingle bank now. He has appeared from nowhere. He picks up a pebble and chucks it out to sea. It spins as it flies and I seem to be seeing it from close-up. I am flying behind it, following the parabola, heading nose down, accelerating into the hard skin of water. The pebble smacks the sea and I just have time to see tiny bubbles popping on the surface before I plunge in, arms tight behind my back. There is rope around my hands. Someone is pulling the other end. I am yanked around to witness the receding surface. Deeper and deeper I go, arms bound and stretched behind me. The light fades and the cold comes. All around me, a black cold that seeps into the pores of my skin. The light fades until I cannot see.

'And this is how it ends.'

Madeleine's voice. A hiss in my head.

I was sucked back into the present by a cough from the engine.

I jerked awake with a rush of fear. The sun was sinking below the clouds, leaving the day to die and me alone. The light tapered into blackness, the sky a sheet of tar, pricked through with stars shepherded by an incandescent moon.

Icy tentacles slipped down the crack between my jacket and chest. I thought about tightening my scarf, but there was no response from my body. Then I thought about turning to look forward. No response.

I became aware of a pressure at my neck. Slowly, my reasoning clicked into gear. An arm. My left arm. It was angled behind my back like a contortionist. Through the corner of my eyes I saw my right arm stretched out in front of me, holding the joystick, rigid. I sat there like a corpse, scared to do anything. A novel way to die. Two miles up, a preserved pilot with gangrenous limbs, maddeningly sentient to the last. The perfect punishment, devised by a creative lesser demon from the lower levels of hell. I wanted to laugh but feared my lungs would snap.

How far had I gone? How long had I been out? How had the plane stayed level? I knew the answer to the last

225

question. The bird wanted to keep moving in the same direction. Nothing could alter her path, other than a determined thunderstorm or a particularly solid mountain.

I forced my neck to move first, straining it left then right then up and around, getting the circulation going. Next my arms. Gingerly, I shifted my weight to release the dead one. It flopped out, swinging pathetically by my side. My other arm was no better. It took all my effort to prise it away. The leather was stuck to the metal, frozen hard. I concentrated on working the blood back into my limbs and regretted it. As feeling came back so did pain – a deadly ache that no amount of rubbing and cajoling could diminish. I shook my legs, using only the muscles at the top, until they too decided to come back to me.

Complete again, I checked my watch. Couldn't be right. I checked it a second time. 2 pm it insisted. My watch would not be told. My stomach contracted in panic. I had to go down. Had to go down *now*. I fumbled in my jacket and pulled out the compass. The glass was cracked, the fluid seeping out in a frozen film. Boys' Own stuff, navigation by stars or the position of the moon. But it was never on a crippled plane thousands of feet up in the air with nothing to eat, a body that didn't work, crumpled clothes soaked through with sweat that solidified the instant it escaped your skin and a compass that would have preferred to stay on a school geography desk.

'Damn!'

It was the first word I'd uttered in several hours, but I couldn't hear it. With the roar of the engine and the wind blasting my face and my ears bunged up behind a mass of fur, I had to rely on the rough numbness of my lips rubbing together to know that I had spoken. My mouth was hard, brittle like china.

My brain wasn't working. It had co-operated begrudgingly in sending broken signals to the rest of my body but now it felt rubbery from the blackout. A thought entered my head from some unseen space, tweaked my senses, then fled. To check the altimeter, to tap its face, was a mountain climb. It was a long path between the acceptance that something must be done and the realization of it. The messages travelled slowly through my body. *What height am I*. Six foot two. *What* height *am I*? Look at the dials. My eyes rolled down slowly from the hypnotic sky to the control panel. Too many dials. *Middle top*. I leaned forward and my spine felt it would pop. Like the compass, the glass was opaque with frost. I peered through it, willing a glimpse of the needle. A solid, horizontal line of white underneath the sparkling grey. It read zero.

Great, so I've landed. I can relax now. Bloody great. I looked along the wings. They were covered in sheet-ice at least an inch thick and the tips were vibrating violently.

What woke you up?

Think . . . Quick man!

Coughing.

Where from?

From the engine.

So . . .

Fuel.

Clap. Clap.

I rubbed the dial, achingly slow, five fingers becoming one. A clumsy animal learning a new trick. I could see nothing.

Then an image formed in my mind. A steaming hot coffee at Maisies café. Hands curled round it, bringing the cup to lips. Liquid scorching the back of the throat. A sharp pain in the chest fading to a warm glow.

Thermos. The connection was vague. But it was there somewhere. I just had to find the thread and pull the elements together.

Coffee
> hot chest
>> thermos
>>> fuel.

I closed my eyes and welcomed the absence of clutter. See it as an equation. What does coffee equal if thermos is container and fuel is life?

No good.

Think of opposites.

Ice, cold. Coffee, warm.

The solution solidified in my mind, and I willed it to stay there.

I fumbled underneath the seat for my bag and cursed the straps as I tried to pull it open. They wouldn't budge so I yanked them and the flask tumbled to the floor. Leaning over, pain shooting through my legs, I retrieved it. Five minutes later I had the cap off and then wondered what I had intended in the first place.

'Ah, yes,' I said to no-one and poured the coffee over the fuel gauge. For a few seconds the ice slid away in a cloud of steam to reveal the needle hovering in the red zone. The tank was almost empty.

On cue, the engine spluttered again. The propellor juddered, missed a beat. Down to the last few dregs, the sludge that should never be used. The Swallow shook in protest, then accepted. It could only be minutes before it happened again.

The cloud country, now a mushy brown like well-trodden snow, merged into the sky, as if on the horizon a painter had smoothed over the dividing line with a flat knife. It was time to leave; to leave before it turned on me.

From a reserve section of my memory, the place where the really important information was stored and sealed with double locks, I plucked out the procedure that Ray had drummed into me. 'Most important of all before you land, even if you're just going up for a figure of eight – check everything works.' He'd said that to me on my final day before the test. 'It must become second nature, or one day you'll regret it.'

I did the aileron pedals first – feet forward, up; feet back, level. The plane responded wearily. Then I came to the tail fin. Left, the plane crabbed right, straightened out, just as it should.

Then it kept turning. I pushed the joystick left but it wouldn't go. I pushed all my weight behind it, but its will was stronger than mine. The plane continued to turn right in a slow circle. I checked the wings. One of the flaps was stuck. I looked over my shoulder, shuffled round to see better, then along the fuselage to the tail. The rudder was jammed full out to the right. Frozen.

Angrily, I hammered the joystick, relishing the groans of the pain that it caused.

Something snapped.

Get a grip.

Compensate, push the right flap up, level out then throttle down. The whine of the engine lowered in pitch. The nose dipped and I felt my back pressing slightly against the seat.

But the plane, my trusty Klemm Swallow that had taken me so far, was still turning to the right. Like a horse that refuses at the final fence, it had had enough.

I looked down the wing again. The flap stayed put. The whole machine was freezing up.

Slowly, the Swallow descended in long circles, the tumble of clouds looming closer with each rotation. This was not how it was meant to be. Spiralling pathetically over God-knows-where in a shaky plane with only a few cups of petrol left in the tank. This was not my vision. I would glide smoothly into the outskirts of Moscow, find a clear area and land. I would stride purposefully from my machine, and to anyone who challenged me I would declare, 'I've come for my wife. Take me to the police.'

I grimaced at the thought now. How grandiose your plans when you're cooped up in the safety of your home toasting your toes against the fire. You don't think of fingers so numb you want to snap them off simply to stop the pain, or the aching claustrophobia, the agonizing cramp of sitting in a cockpit for endless hours with only your conscience for company. You don't consider the mental toll of trying to concentrate for such a long time, trying to stave off the overpowering wish to sleep – the little voice, so sweet, so reassuring, that says 'It's OK, steal a little nap, I'll look after you while you're gone,' and the words between the lines, unsaid, 'You might sleep forever, if I get it wrong.' Your head nodding, invisible fingers tugging at your eyelids – *just close them* – and the jerk of fear when you come to again. No, in your dreams it is easier than that; it is a trail into a golden sunset, a fanfare greeting your landing. A loved one, tears streaming down her face, leaping into your arms.

The wheels of the Swallow sliced through the first wisps of cloud and I realised there was something I should have done before I set off. I unbuttoned a shirt pocket and brought out the silver case with Lena's portrait in it. I opened it up and kissed it. Through the hole in the top I had threaded a ribbon and tied it to the rim of the windshield. She would be with me on the way down. And after that, she would be with me soon.

The cloud enveloped me. It was like diving into a trampoline that gave no resistance. It looked so thick but felt of nothing. This was the world I had entered on the way up, a world bent on confusing you. In the earth of the cloud-country there was no direction. Just an endless expanse of cloying white.

Over the Line, November 1938

I focussed on the picture of Lena. For minutes I saw nothing else, felt nothing else but the vibration of the engine, taking me down smoothly to what I prayed would be a flat stretch of land.

The tone of the engine changed. It coughed, then screamed, a jarring cry. Then it went silent.

It was the silence of death. It is what all pilots dread. The shudder through the fuselage, then the jerky deceleration of the propeller. Then nothing. A ton of metal and canvas and glue and wood, held up only by the insufficient pressure of air.

The Swallow tilted to the right. I gripped the joystick like a lifeline. But as the world swirled around the cockpit it felt like a straw.

My head jerked back with a snap, blood rushing to my cheeks, eyeballs slamming into the back of their sockets, and then I was nothing and nowhere.

A long way. She's coming towards me. The mist clears as she walks. She is wearing a smart navy suit that makes her look like an upturned triangle. Her hair, sharp blonde, swings in a slow arc as she shakes her head. Her mouth opens, and I know instantly she is shouting, though there is no sound. It's a delay. She is so far away. Then her voice hits me in a wave.

'IT'S YOUR FAULT, IT'S YOUR FAULT. STUPID, SELFISH, IDIOT! YOU DESERVE IT, YOU HEAR THAT? YOU DESERVE IT.'

I recognise the voice. It is Madeleine's. And now she is laughing. It echoes like a fog-horn far out at sea. 'DOWN YOU GO, DOWN YOU GO.'

There is movement behind her. A rustling sound, the hem of a dress scraping the ground.

'I told you Brian.' It is my mother. 'What did I tell you?'

'Ne –' I say.

FIELDS OF LIGHT

She nods. 'That's it? Come on, the rest.'

'DOWN, DOWWWNN.'

'Never . . .' But the rest refuses to come out and play.

My mother shakes her head, a reproving look in her eyes. 'I give you one piece of advice. One piece. In all these years, and you can't remember it. Never mind your friend Mr Talbot. There is only one motto:

'NEVER MARRY A WOMAN WITHOUT MONEY.

'And what did you do? You married Madeleine. Then you married Ileana. You married TWO women without money. At the same time. I give up. You rushed into this frightful escapade without a thought. You can't salvage your soul by crashing into Moscow. That would be most, how should one put it . . . ineffective. Now,' she claps her hands and I am tiny, a young boy again. 'That's better. We're going to play a little game. Madeleine over the other side, Lena, my dear don't be shy.'

And she comes out, a girl of about seven with brown eyes the size of globes and wavy hair that spirals down both shoulders. She is wearing a simple white blouse with buttons missing on the sleeves. She creeps out from behind Mother who places a firm hand at her back and pushes her into position.

Mother is the teacher, Mother is the instructress. 'Close in everybody,' she orders. They link hands around me, lean out and start to dance, leaping to the right in rhythm. '1,2,3 . . . 1,2,3,' Mother barks. 'Remember the words everyone?'

And they spin around me, Madeleine gleeful, Mother dispassionate, Lena bewildered. What is this game?

When a man has lost his bottle,

Give him a length of rope.

Show him how to pull, then throttle,

Sit back and watch him choke.

Mother says this in a sing song voice, but there is no tune behind it. And then they all join in, three faces swinging into me on the word choke. I look down at my feet. I'm on a revolving platform. It's going in the opposite direction to the dancers, their faces merge in streaks as I spin around and around.

   'Choke,' they scream 'choke, choke, chokechokechoke-choke –'

My eyes snapped open. I was vertical in the air. The Klemm was screaming. I felt my cheeks trying to hide inside my head. There was a crash to my right and I caught a glimpse of sheet ice flying off the wing, slicing into the side of the plane. Wood splintered on impact sending shards of debris tumbling in the slipstream. The Swallow veered violently, air trapped inside the fuselage.

   Choke? Flood the engine, prize out the last drops.

   I was still in cloud, with no bearings except down. I forced myself against gravity, reached for the throttle. My hand shook in triple image as I stretched, swiped at the handle, slammed it back then forward, back then forward.

   'Come on. Come *on* . . .'

   Nothing. Only the wind howling.

   Then the cloud broke and it didn't seem to matter any more . . .

If this is death, then that's fine. Let the light suck me in, let me be a part of it, it is beautiful. The rush underneath, by my side and above, white and blue. Where does the light come from? I thought the sun had gone down. Now it's above me, smiling, a burning disc. I could hold onto it. It will help me. I like it, so it must like me too.

   This is the light of the perfect dream, stretching infinitely. I can hold it all. It lets me.

   'It's the most reliable craft you'll ever have the pleasure

of flying in.' The salesman smiles as I hand over the bundle of five pound bills. 'Built for comfort, built for safety. She'll never let you down.'

Then why am I going to crash? She'll never let me down. She never let me down. (Use your feet.) She won't even know. She was beautiful. This is beautiful. Let it go, let it suck you in.

(Must clear the forests, glide over the tops of trees. Like funeral pyres. All for me.)

Go into the light. Fields and fields of light. It is warm there. Every colour is there. Count the colours. Red and green and violet, yellow and pink and orangeanindigoand-silversilversilver –

(The elevator, the pedals, use your feet to push the pedals, to raise the elevator to slow your fall.)

Time stretches and snaps and moulds itself. It is time to wipe away the ifs. Time enough.

To say to Ivan, 'We won't take the boat out. It looks a little rough.'

To take you home with me instead of leaving you there. I sort out the papers in Moscow, then we make my parents smile when we walk through the door. They welcome you as another daughter. They do.

To say on the banks of the Moskva, 'I hardly know you, but I won't go.' To not slip over when you run away. To catch up and grab you and tell you the truth, so you know everything and you can be my judge.

But best of all:

To say politely to Madeleine and her mother, 'That is very kind of you but I have a prior engagement, perhaps we can eat together another day.' And then, simply turn my back and watch the gulls balancing on the rails.

But the time for that is always past. I am sorry Lena, I am so sorry.

MOSCOW
November 1938 – January 1939

She was there in front of me when I opened my eyes. I greeted her with a smile. The miniature swung on its ribbon, tiny movements back and forward. The glass on the front of the locket was cracked. My chin was resting on the fuel gauge. There was a red smear on the panelling. Blood seeped from a gash in my scalp, freezing almost immediately upon contact with the air.

Carefully, I lifted my body upright, waiting for the stabbing pain. None came. I flexed my fingers. They responded to my commands. I leaned back in the cockpit, took in the surroundings. I was in a stubble field that went on forever. It was packed down with snow that shimmered in the low sun. There was a hedgerow about half a mile away. It cast long shadows towards me. Within the pool of darkness were tiny sparkling hillocks that caught the sun. Beyond the hedgerow was another field, then another, smooth and untouched since the first snow had fallen. I wanted to go there, where the colours bounced from the hard ground so clearly they were touchable. The light was energy, I wanted it wrapped around me like a veil, to be drawn into it and accepted. I could walk in a straight line across the fields, could walk until I no longer felt the pain in my limbs, keep going until I fell face down, into the light, and forgot.

I blacked out again. Like a hand calmly smothering my face. I knew it was happening but did not care, being too weak and too confused.

Next I heard Russian voices, the sound of feet, lots of little feet.

'Uncle, Uncle! Wake up!'

I felt fingers poke my cheek, tug at my eyelids. I was happy where I was. It had been a nice dream where the light was warm and welcoming. With consciousness came the cold and the pain and the questions. I opened my eyes and saw a young girl with rosy cheeks.

'Take me up in your plane,' she said.

I undid my safety strap and stood up in the cockpit. For a moment I swayed on my feet. Instinctively, the girl held out her hand to steady me. She was wearing a goatskin coat and a cap to match, fur gloves and tall leather boots. She was smiling. There was a crowd of children behind her, all in similar uniform, and it seemed she was their representative.

'Well?' she said.

'I can't. She crashed.' The Russian was a little creaky, but they didn't seem to notice. 'Perhaps tomorrow we'll get her fixed and I'll take you up then.'

At this there was a mêlée of voices crying, 'And me, me too, and me . . .'

I clambered out of the plane.

'Where'd you fly from?' a little boy asked.

'England.'

They all laughed. This silly man comes out of the sky in a plane like this and says he comes from England.

'Didn't your parents tell you it was bad to lie?' the girl asked.

'Stalin says it's wicked,' another voice piped up.

'I'm not lying.' They all giggled again.

I went over to check the damage at the back of the plane and the pack of children followed me. The tail had sheered off to one side. Further back two wheel tracks trailed off into the snow. I followed them unsteadily until they stopped. A few hundred yards behind that was the forest I must have passed over on the way down.

'What's your name?' I asked the girl.

'Petra,' she said proudly.

'And yours?' This to a sallow-looking boy who stood slightly apart from the crowd.

'Traktor,' he mumbled.

'Speak up!' one of the others shouted. And then they all started jeering him. 'Traktor, Traktor, Traktor.'

'Quiet, quiet,' I shouted, as much for my own head as for the little boy's blushes. 'Where are the grown-ups?'

'They're coming. Over there, see!'

Two men had appeared at the edge of the field. One was carrying a gun.

'They can't run as fast as us. They told us, "Come back," but we just kept going.' Petra peered up at me quizzically and said, 'Are you a criminal?'

That was debatable. I smiled at her and waited for the men to arrive, praying they weren't trigger happy.

They approached and the group of children parted to let them through. One of the men gave me a shaky smile. They stopped a few yards from me, warily.

I had prepared a little speech for this moment, but now it seemed faintly ridiculous. But there seemed no other way to put it.

'My name is Brian Grover. I have flown from England to meet my wife Ileana Petrovna because I have not seen

237

her for five years. I know I have broken your laws but no offence is meant. You can arrest me and I won't struggle.'

There was quite a long silence then one of them said with a tickle in his voice, 'You're mad.'

'I'm desperate,' I replied.

The other one said accusingly, 'You're not English, you're Russian!'

'I assure you I'm English.'

They weren't convinced.

The man with the gun motioned to the other who frisked me head to foot.

'Come with us,' he said.

'Where am I?'

'Glukhovo Collective.'

The two men shushed the children away as they milled round me, but they took no notice. We trudged away from the plane.

When we reached the beginning of the lane that led to Glukhovo, I turned round to look at the scene one final time. The evening had faded into night within minutes, leaving only the faint outline of the forest and the luminous glow of the ice-packed fields. I stood there for a while, breathing in the silence, and wondered where the light came from, how it seemed to come out of the snow. Then I realised my knees were buckling underneath me, that I should move to stop from falling, so I followed the men and the rest of the group down the lane. Everyone fired questions at me and I tried to answer, but the effort was finally too much, my words disappearing in a fog of freezing breath.

That evening I was introduced to the entire population of the Glukhovo Collective. For them, I was an eccentric curiosity that broke for a while the endless drudgery of their lives.

After an interview with the head man, in which I explained my story and urged him to contact the KGB immediately, I was posted with an old couple who had a mattress and a spare room. I would be leaving for Moscow tomorrow the boss said. I didn't know whether to be elated or petrified. In the end I decided that it made perfect sense to be both.

'This is her, here.' I held out the miniature photo of Lena for the old woman, Ludmilla, to look at.

'Beautiful,' she said, 'so beautiful.' She stroked the silver frame lovingly and for a second I wasn't sure if she was referring to my wife. But then she said in an earnest voice, 'You've done the right thing by her.'

'You're one of the few people who believe my story.'

'It doesn't do to trust foreigners,' she said. 'Not in public anyway. She stared into the log fire as it spat on the damp wood. Her eyes rested on the flames and I felt she was remembering days when she was young and happy.

'You did all this?' she asked, then turned to her husband and cackled. 'My sloth of a man. Look at him. Asleep and it's only nine. There is excitement in this village for the first time in a decade and he snores in tribute! Cah! He can't even be bothered to get up in the morning and pull turnips for me. And cross an ocean? For *me*. I'm an old woman with mousy hair. He'd rather have a heart attack. At least then he'd get a sniff of more vodka.'

As if hearing the word through his slumber, her husband sat bolt upright in his seat. 'We must celebrate, young man. I have one bottle left.' His knees cracked as he rose and staggered to the kitchen.

'You always have one bottle left,' Ludmilla called after him, but she smiled as she said it. 'I love him really. When he's able to complete his sentences without vomiting, he's quite a friend.'

We drank, crouched around the fire, and later Ludmilla

brought in a pot of thick broth full of vegetables and chunks of beef. I asked if her food was always this good. Seeing the question behind the compliment, she replied:

'If you smile at the right people, the right people smile back at you. Remember that and you might be lucky.'

As I drifted off to sleep that night in a spare room cluttered with farming tools, I thought of her words and hoped that she was right.

It had taken me eight hours to fly alone from Stockholm to Gluckovo. It took four policeman – Agan, Slava, Vitya, Arkady – and a regulation Soviet truck two days to go the one hundred miles to Moscow.

They came for me the next morning. The sun was not yet up when Ludmilla gently tapped my face to wake me. The room was crusted in shadows.

'They are here,' she said simply and thrust a bundle of damp cloths in my hand. 'Chicken,' she explained. 'You will be hungry, and so will they. You can share it on your way. They will like that.' She paused, her eyes searching the spaces around me, never directly looking at me, as though the room had been empty too long but was now filled by the wrong person. 'They are good people, I know them. The young ones especially, tell them stories, make them smile. You will be alright.' Then she whispered, 'But watch Agan, he is bitter and small-minded. Do not make conversation with him, he will twist what you say.' She spoke as though from experience.

I dressed quickly, splashed cold water into my eyes from a tub Ludmilla had supplied the night before. Voices and the sound of feet stamping on packed ice filtered through the walls. I gathered my belongings, stuffed the chicken in the sack and went to meet them.

They were in line like a firing squad. Their green uniforms were crumpled, the brass buttons dull from too little polishing. One stood slightly forward from the others. I presumed he was in command. He had decorations draped over his chest and the sure look of someone who knows he is unassailable and likes others to know it too. His face was pinched, as though all the juice had trickled down into his stomach which was full and firm and jutted out like an expectant mother. He had to be Agan. The others simply looked forlorn and bleary-eyed from getting up so early. They had travelled a few miles from the nearest town, probably knew nothing of their task until a few hours ago. I suspected they had spent last night drinking the greyness away.

They looked like actors from some second-rate theatre troupe. I almost giggled. But I held it in. People were watching. As I walked up to the lorry I became aware that the whole collective had turned out to see me carted off. They stood straight and rigid, hands by their sides, only their eyes moving. There was no sound except the first calls of birds in the woods and my feet clicking on the hard ground.

Agan gripped my wrists and slapped handcuffs on. 'Hurry,' he said, 'there is a long journey.'

'You don't need to do that, really,' I said. 'I'm not going anywhere.'

'You're not escaping either,' Agan replied and shoved me into the back of the lorry. He slammed the doors and darkness enveloped us.

My last memory of Glukhovo is of Petra, the little girl who had popped her head over the cockpit. She was there when I left, when I was bundled into the back. I caught a glimpse of her face as I fell forward onto the floor of the van. She didn't look frightened and she didn't look sad. She was just fascinated, watching events with the detached eyes of the innocent.

At first there was silence, Agan and the driver in front surveying the road for potholes, myself sandwiched between the two youngest officers. We left Glukhovo behind. The cold made progress slow going. Great piles of snow were piled up on either side of the road like model mountains. It was a fantasy land that I had forgotten. A land of gnarled ice sculptures that cascaded rainbows at all angles as the sun came up. I concentrated on the scenery. It looked uninhabitable but at regular intervals along the way the horizon would clear to reveal farm complexes like the one I had just left. Great grey buildings of corrugated iron, centres of frenetic activity where tonnes of grain were offloaded into waiting trucks. But out in the fields, swathes of flat land that had been turned over to agriculture, tractors and ploughs and combines lay stranded like cattle that had never been called home. Determination and decay, it seemed, had reached an uneasy equilibrium.

We had travelled about twenty miles when Agan asked me suddenly, 'Do you think you are clever?'

'I'm sorry?'

'Some kind of a hero?'

'I just want to see my wife.'

He ignored me. 'You are not a hero. *They* are the heroes.' He pointed vaguely to the fields but I knew what he meant. I would have to watch him. A sentimental Stalinist. He lapped it up, he fed from it without questioning. 'If you knew where you were going now, you would shit yourself in fear.' He turned round, eagerness in his eyes. 'Do you know where you're going?'

'I hope it's Moscow,' I said politely.

'Oh yes, we're taking you there, but not to meet your pretty little wife. You're going to hell. You're going to *Lubyanka*.'

'But that's what I want.'

He paused, smiling at what he thought was bravado. Slowly, he shook his head. 'Nobody wants to go to *Lubyanka*.'

We reached Moscow on the second day. The night before we had stayed in a tavern at Staritza. It had been requisitioned by the army many years before and was now stripped bare of its character, the lights and the paintings pilfered over the years to leave only bare tables and uncomfortable chairs. I had made friends with Vitya and Slava, as Ludmilla predicted. We played billiards in the games room with ball-bearings from a lorry while Agan sat in the corner over a bottle of cognac. He had ended up being a man to pity rather than fear, a man who, Vitya confided in me, everyone mocked behind his back. They had laughed as I tried to play with my cuffs on, my cue slipping everywhere. They reached five hundred while I was trying to make twenty. I asked for a re-match without the cuffs.

'Agan, what do you say?' Slava shouted above the din of drinking soldiers.

He grunted, 'The man gave us a chicken and he wants favours back,' and turned away from us.

'It's worth another bottle of whatever you want,' I tried.

He threw the key to Slava without looking up.

'He loves lemon vodka,' Vitya told me. 'It's the only thing he smiles about.'

I obliged but it was a false bargain. I lost the next game five hundred to forty.

Now the van was weaving through Moscow's Bulvar Ring, past churches and factories side by side, and crowds milling their way to work.

'Not long now for the hero,' Agan said as the van pulled up, two wheels on the kerb.

'Take no notice of him,' Vitya whispered, 'you'll be

243

fine. Be polite, tell them your story and I'm sure they'll let you go.'

I shook my head, resigned to the fact that I would never get through to some people. 'I don't want to be freed. I want my wife back.'

Through the front windscreen I could see the *Lubyanka* building. It resembled a massive cake. Layer upon layer of tiny windows separated by lines of yellowing crenellated bricks that stuck out like piped cream. I knew the inside was not so sweet. For half an hour I was left with Vitya while the others went inside to bring news of their cargo. We sat in silence, listening to trucks steaming down the road, footsteps tapping by, the general hum of a city going about its business. For the first time, the nerves began to bite. Without realizing it, I started shivering, though it was warm in the van. Vitya lay a hand on my shoulder. 'Slow down, breath deep. Everything is fine.'

I couldn't sort out my feelings. Lena was so close, probably pressing her uniform right now, ready for her night-shift. She had no idea I was here. I had achieved my aim. To be brought before the KGB and plead my case. But what if they thought I was a lunatic? What if they dismissed my story? Violation of their sovereign territory was potentially a capital crime. They could throw me away in some cell and let me rot. They could execute me without a squeak from the outside world. The Embassy might never be contacted. I could be lying at the bottom of the Baltic right now, for all they knew. And if they exiled me, how would Lena be treated? What had I unleashed?

A sharp taste filled my mouth. I wanted to be sick and told Vitya so. He edged away, then ruffled in his pockets and brought out a paper bag.

'Almonds. Suck on one. The feeling will pass.'

I did. Bile rose in my throat. I forced it back and the queasiness subsided a little.

'What have I done?' I said quietly. 'I've been a fool, a terrible fool.'

'Sometimes, there is no other option,' he whispered back. 'Sometimes the fool plays an ace.'

The back doors opened and I gulped in fresh air. I stumbled out into the arms of a burly guard. While Agan oversaw the exchange of handcuffs, I said goodbye to my three unlikely friends. 'Good luck,' Arkady mumbled under his breath so Agan would not hear and I smiled at him so Agan would not see.

I was marched past Diaghalev's Monument, a forbidding black statue of another Soviet hero gone to the ground, then under the black marble entrance and up to a set of glass double doors. Here, my papers were handed to an armed sentry who demanded that each of us in turn whisper our names in his ear before he would let us pass. It didn't matter that the guard who was taking me probably drank with the sentry after work. Orders were there to be obeyed.

This procedure happened three times, each set of doors sturdier than before. The guard I was cuffed to said nothing, looked at no-one.

Eventually we came to a lift. I was pushed forward into a separate compartment where I was shut in alone; there was an eye-hole in the door through which I was observed. The lift creaked to a halt at the seventh floor. We entered a deserted corridor, carpeted edge to edge. Silence reigned. We took a turn right and it led to a dead end. The guard knocked at the door and we waited. For a long time nothing happened. I avoided his eyes, stared at the wall and tried to compose myself. Then a voice cried: 'Enter.'

I was led into what looked like the rest room of a Victorian gentleman's club. It was huge, with wood panelled walls decorated with imposing portraits of Lenin and

Stalin. There were a few conspicuous spaces where the wood was lighter – pictures that had been taken down as the subjects became less than persons. In the centre of the room, flat on a polished slatted floor was a priceless Kashan rug. On top of the rug was a twelve-man mahogany dining table. At the dining table sat twelve men. And before each of the twelve men was a telephone.

I hovered by the door, unsure what my next move should be. All the men wore black suits, white shirts and black ties, except for the man at the centre. His clothing was grey. I presumed it was deliberate, a ploy to make him stand out. The chair he sat in was different too. An old pre-revolution piece with a high back and carved arms. Their faces were lit from below by concealed lamps. There were no windows in the room.

The man in the centre spoke: 'Step forward.'

I did so.

'Take a chair. Any one will do. Though I suggest you pick the one opposite me.'

I obliged, and as I sat I got a closer look at his features. His hair was lank, thinning at the top, his eyes were small beads held in by tight lids, but it was his chin that was most noticeable. It jutted out a full two inches from the rest of his face. It was so prominent in the eerie light that I felt a strange compulsion to reach out and touch it just to make sure it was real.

He went straight to the point. 'Why have you flown into Soviet territory without permission?'

'I haven't seen my wife for five years. I tried everything to get back here but was refused a visa each time. It was a last resort.' I pulled out an envelope full of official letters from the Soviet Embassy in London that proved my case and realised suddenly that I was still wearing my flying jacket. It was all I had brought with me, but it seemed inappropriate somehow. I hadn't shaved since leaving

Ludmilla's either, had only had time for a quick rinse in cold water. I wondered what this man saw before him. A mad tramp? Or perhaps something more sinister.

He gave the documents a cursory glance and passed them down the line. They were unimportant, not what he wanted.

He learned forward. 'Tell me, Mr . . .'

'Grover.'

'. . . Mr Grover. What did you notice during your flight?'

'Not very much. I flew over cloud the whole way.'

He nodded. It was a fact that could be verified, and probably already had been. 'Let me put it another way. What were you looking for?'

'My wife.'

'It is a long way from Stockholm to Moscow. What did you do to pass the time?'

'Nothing. I blacked out.'

There was a collective murmur from the others, glances exchanged. They discussed me in snatched whispers as though I wasn't there.

'Pardon?' the man in the grey suit said.

'I was delirious for most of the way. From the cold.'

'How convenient.'

I couldn't answer that comment. I didn't understand the meaning.

'And your friend. Did he not try to revive you?'

'Sorry?'

'I think you heard me Mr Grover.'

'Nobody revived me. I flew alone.'

Without a word, he got up and left the room. The other men stared at me, a line of impassive eyes, questions in their expressions but nothing coming out of their mouths.

He returned a few minutes later a different man.

This time he introduced himself. 'My name is Feodorov

and these are my assistants. You brought another man in with you from Stockholm, did you not?'

'No, sir,' I replied.

'It's no good you saying "No sir," to me. This isn't a dressing down in a public school. I have it in black and white in the next room.'

'That's not true. If you want proof, you have only to ask at Stockholm airport.'

Feodorov smiled. 'We did. They said you arrived with a man named Henry Mountjoy.'

'That is true.'

'And now he cannot be found.'

'I left him money to go home.' He made me feel like I was lying. *Where was Henry*? He must have left immediately. Surely, if they checked out my story, they would see all the facts tallied.

'And you also left clothes all over your room. To make the authorities believe you were returning.'

I nodded.

'You brought this man Mountjoy into Russia to spy on us. What is your position?'

'Do I look like a spy?' I said desperately.

Feodorov leaned back in his armchair and swept a hand through his thinning hair.

'If you looked like a spy, you wouldn't be one.' His eyes were unnerving, designed for discomfort. I felt he knew things about me that even I didn't know: what my first words were, whether I snored in my sleep, perhaps what I would be doing in five years time. Maybe he knew the last all too well.

'You are in very serious trouble,' he said and rapped the table with his knuckles.

On cue, the guard appeared and escorted me to the lower depths of *Lubyanka* where all my personal belongings were taken off me and listed. I was given a pair of grey overalls to change into and shown to a shower room. The water went on automatically as I entered. It was freezing and smelled strongly of disinfectant.

Later, like a dog on a leash, I was led down brightly lit corridors, all painted off-white, and passed door after door, all closed. Left then right, then a U-turn then a T-junction. It may have been a disorientation process to unnerve me further, as if it were needed. Eventually we reached the jails. I was designated to a cell and left in it to stew.

Save for an iron bed, a tiny washbasin and a bare bulb hanging from the ceiling, the room was devoid of features. I stared into the white walls, trying to find consoling memories but they had deserted me.

The next day before breakfast, a new face appeared at the door. A blond man with centre parting and a slightly raffish look.

He strode in offering his hand and speaking at the same time, 'Sorry to barge in so early. The name's Maclean, from the embassy.'

'Good to see a friendly face.'

His smile lasted a quarter of a second. Everything about him said, this is a formality, let's get it over with. 'How've they been treating you?'

'They think I'm a spy.'

'That doesn't answer my question.'

'Is this another interrogation?'

'Play the game man. I'm here to help.'

'Then inform them, diplomatically of course, that I'm not a spy and you want action at the highest level taken on my behalf as soon as possible.'

'It doesn't work like that. You broke their laws. We can plead your case but we can't order.'

'I see.'

'Actually, I'm not sure you do.' He perched on the bed, looking distinctly out of place. 'I should warn you, they can do what they like with you. If they want to make you a spy, they will.'

'But it's obvious. They just have to check out my story.'

The expression on his face changed and it sent fear through me. He felt pity. 'You should know by now that truth doesn't matter here,' he said.

'I came to see Lena,' I said feebly.

'I know. You've caused quite a splash.' He pulled out a pile of papers from his briefcase and threw them on the bed. '*The Times, Telegraph, Mail* . . . They love a story. A good old British hero. One in the eye for the commies, just in time for Christmas.'

They'd dug up a photo of me in all my finery at my graduation, mortar board slightly askew, broad smile, eyes that anticipated nothing but a life of adventure. Well, I'd achieved that but to what end? I looked so much younger. I looked innocent.

'How did they get hold of the story?'

'That little air traffic controller chap you tricked in Stockholm. A local reporter prised the story out of him, so I'm told. And once it starts, it *starts*.'

His eyes shifted away from mine then. 'You've landed yourself in a bit of a pickle, haven't you?'

I stared at the photo. They must have got it from my Mother's paltry collection.

'We're doing all we can.' He was up again, close to the door now, eager to leave. 'Our boys will liaise with the relevant authorites. We'll keep you informed of developments.'

Doing all we can. Liaise with the relevant authorities. Officialspeak. This was just a social call, really. The Embassy doing the decent thing. If only I had had tea and biscuits we could have talked about cricket or rugger.

'You'll get a few months here, perhaps a fine. Most likely a fine, they need the currency.'

'But what about my *wife*?'

'I'm not sure on that score, Grover. She really isn't any of our business.'

Maclean shook my hand vigorously and knocked on the door for the guard. 'Cheer up,' he said with false good humour. 'It's my job to paint the worst picture. Just in case,' he assured me. 'You'll probably be home in no time. Your wife is a different matter. That will be very difficult.'

I couldn't look at him. I'd been home for five years and to me, it had been no better than this cell. There was a pause, as Maclean hovered, then the cell door clicked behind him. My hope had been sucked out with his final words. For when a man from an Embassy says something is difficult, what he means is it is impossible.

Time broke down in a blur of polishing floors, shaving at my basin, and doing sit ups against the iron bed. They kept the lights on all the time, a bare bulb in the middle of the room. I slept fitfully, got up, walked to the basin, stared in the mirror, lay down, closed my eyes, counted to a thousand then started again. Soon, I was judging the passing of each day by the length of stubble on my chin. One day, as the food was brought in, a bowl of green liquid and a damp roll, I asked the guard for a book to read.

'What kind?'

'Anything, I just need something to do.' An unwise reply. He returned with a farming manual. Fertilization, machine maintenance, grain storage. Official advice from ill-advised officials. I read it anyway.

Every few days I was taken up to the eleventh floor. I'd been isolated from the other prisoners but I could guess what happened to them. Sometimes, on the way up to my interrogation, I heard muffled shouts. The rooms were sound-proofed but that didn't stop the thuds and the bumps, the vibrations of an inanimate object meeting a nearly inanimate object, drifting into the corridors.

The men who questioned me only hinted at physical harm. They were content to wear me down mentally. One officer would play the friend, offering coffee and mouth-watering snacks. He would invite me to a table in a warmly lit corner of the room. There would be a soothing picture of horses grazing in lush meadows on the wall. Sometimes I would play a game of cards with him and he would jokingly say, 'If you win, you're free,' and proceed to deal me the best hand. It was to soften me up, to make the little man feel grateful. Then in would come Feodorov, always the enemy. He would stick his jaw in my face, spit rapid fire accusations at me, twist my answers as he had on the first day, and wait for me to break, to confess to something which did not exist. To begin with I knew it was all a game. It was a process that had to observed. 'I have told you everything,' I would say. 'I know nothing more. All I want is to see my wife.'

'We have evidence to the contrary,' he would say. 'You work for British Intelligence. We have a report from an operative in London. He saw your name in their files.'

'It's impossible. You know that's not true, so why do you say it?'

'I ask the questions,' he would shout, 'you answer!' Then softly, 'Is that all right with you, Mr Grover?'

And I would have to bite back the frustration, play humble. 'I'm sorry.'

'That is not an answer Grover.'

'Yes, of course it is alright.'

'That's better. Now . . .'

And it would go on and on and on, his voice nibbling

away at my strength. All questions about Lena were met with blunt rebuttals.

I held fast to my story and they held fast to their lies.

Feodorov was in his favourite armchair. There was a grey folder on his desk. It said BG1027. He bent the corner back with his thumb nail and released it with a click. I was not asked to sit.

We were alone. I had lost count of the times I'd been up here but each time there'd always been more than one face.

'There has been a new development,' he said. Click, click.

My heart thumped at the words. At last, they believed me. They had finally admitted I was telling the truth. I sighed, and I shouldn't have. Feodorov took it as a sign of capitulation.

He looked at me sharply. 'Well you may sigh, Grover. Your wife has been brought in. She told us some interesting stories.'

'Where is she?'

'Don't interrupt me, Grover, it's rude. Now, you tell me, then I'll tell you.'

'Tell you what?'

He ran his finger along the mahogany desk and inspected it. He shook his head at it. 'We need a better class of inmate. Perhaps you could polish it next time. I hear you're good at that.' He paused. 'Tell me what Ileana told us.'

'I don't understand.'

'Negligence is no defence, even in English law, isn't that right?'

'I don't know what you want me to say.'

'I don't "want" you to say anything. I want you to tell the truth. Once, finally, for all time. Then perhaps we can make a little progress and see what can be done with you. That Maclean might be junior but he knows his stuff. He has – how do you English quaintly put it? – "saved your bacon" many times. Somebody up there must like you, you're still in Hotel Lubyanka. But we, we grinders here down below, we don't. We don't like you at all. So – the truth.'

I opened my mouth, hesitated – was it worth it? – and went through the same story yet again. Feodorov started to tap his fingers after about the second sentence and his eyes glazed over; he was bored too. About half way through, he waved a hand. 'Enough. Your darling little Lena has confessed everything. You wrote to her saying you wanted revenge for the way you were pushed out of this country before. You were going to apply for citizenship here then work on the wells again. Sabotage was your aim.'

'With respect,' I said, though my voice held none at all, 'I have never heard anything so ridiculous in my life.'

'Well, it's up to you. You have twenty-four hours to tell me. Go away and think about it, think of *her*. My office is always open.'

I made to leave, but as soon as my back was turned he screamed, 'Here! Now!'

Slowly I returned to my position, wondering what could be next.

'You think you have it worked out don't you, Grover. Your story tallies, you've covered your tracks.'

'There are no tracks to cover.'

'No?' We all have a past we'd rather forget.'

'Dig away.'

'Oh we have, we have.' He opened the folder now and slid a large, grainy photograph across the desk. I caught my breath. It was me. In a long trench coat, scarf around the lower half of my face. I was handing a package to another man outside the door of an indistinguishable block of flats. He looked vaguely familiar and very nervous.

'Do you know this man?' Feodorov asked.

It must have been when we delivered the documents for Talbot. But there were thousands of them. I couldn't single out a name or a time or a date.

'No,' I stumbled, 'well, I must have met him at some point but I've no idea who he is.'

'An acquaintance of Stephen Talbot. You know *him*, surely.'

'I knew him, but I haven't seen him for years.' What was this?

'He left the country two years ago.'

I shrugged. 'And?'

'And, in his absence, he was found guilty of currency speculation. This gentleman, here,' he stabbed the photo with his forefinger, 'received five years as his accomplice. Does that interest you?'

Nausea washed through me, settling in my stomach. Talbot. Currency speculation? How could he do this? I'd considered him a friend. He'd got me a job in the Caucasus, got Lena to Grozny, he'd always been there . . . I'd owed him a lot and I'd been grateful. I'd told him so, many times. I thought of the night of our wedding, the feast he laid on. I'd thanked him for all the times he'd helped us out and Lena called him our guardian angel. He'd smiled an embarrassed smile and said, 'You'd do the same for me in times of need.' And now I realised I already had.

'You were in league with him.'

'No.'

'You helped exchange millions of roubles for dollars. You acted as his go-between.'

'That's not true.'

'Then how do you explain this photograph?'

'He hired us as runners. He set up contracts between your government and British businesses. We delivered documents, proposals, that's all.'

Slowly, Feodorov shook his head. 'You didn't notice some packages were fatter than others? You didn't notice how many "documents" you were handling? You expect me to believe that?'

'He knew everybody. He dined with your ministers for God's sake. Important people. Who was I to question what he was up to? I'm not a detective. I came here to work on the oil rigs. Talbot said if we helped him, he'd set us up with a representative of *Soyuz* and that's what happened.'

'A favour for a favour.'

'Yes . . . No, not in the way you mean.'

'You obviously did him a big favour. He arranged your wife's transfer did he not?'

'Yes.'

'And you didn't wonder why he was so good to you?'

'He was a friend. We were grateful.'

'So it seems.' Feodorov smiled slyly. 'And is he a friend now?'

'What do you think?'

I'd been used. We all had. Frank, Lena, me, probably everyone who'd been in contact with the man. After all the things I'd done that were wrong, to be found guilty for something of which I had no knowledge was a cruel irony.

When the guards came this time they grabbed my arms and pushed them behind my back. 'You're going to jail for a very long time,' Feodorov said as I was hauled out of the room.

That night, no meal came and when I called for something to drink the guards looked past me as though I wasn't there.

Moscow, November 1938 – January 1939

We are by a river on a hot July day. We dip our feet in the water, feeling the current rushing between our toes. The remnants of a picnic are scattered around us – half-eaten sandwiches and a tub of wilting salad. We sit for hours as the sun sinks behind the trees, casting cool shadows over heat-flushed skin. There is nothing to say. Words are unimportant. Bliss needs no elaboration.

I roll over, the grass scrunching under my weight, and rest my chin on her shoulder. She flops back, arms above her head, and stretches. Soon she is asleep. I watch her. Her eyelids flutter in response to some dream and at that moment I know it has all been worthwhile. We are together, finally. Everything else is irrelevant.

Later we walk down river, hand in hand, and discuss our past as though for the first time. It seems like a great adventure now, a dusty newsreel from decades back.

This is the future I want.

The future I want is for us to grow old together with no regrets, for us to walk together slowly hand in hand and for the river to slow with us . . .

What seemed like weeks passed and nothing happened. I wasn't called up again, no-one came to see me. I began to think they'd forgotten me. Though I knew it couldn't be true I fantasised that my file had been lost in some dusty pile, that Feodorov had been moved on, that perhaps I would be left to rot here forever. I stared at the white ceiling for hours with only my thoughts and my conscience for company. Sometimes the silence was interrupted by the tap of footsteps down the corridor. Sometimes there was nothing but the sound of my heart pumping blood pointlessly through my body.

Maclean came a couple of days before Christmas. He wasn't happy with me.

'You didn't mention Talbot. How are we meant to help you if you don't tell us what's going on?'

'I didn't *know* what was going on. Feodorov showed me a photo and said "There you are handing over illegal currency. Do you plead guilty or guilty?" I didn't know what he was going on about. It was five years ago, anyway.'

'I should be at home now,' Maclean said. 'I haven't been back for eight months. I was looking forward to a nice Christmas with my friends and then you crash land on my bloody head and they tell me I have to stay over and deal with the case. And now I find out not only are you a romantic idiot, you're also a petty thief stealing from the great Soviet state.'

'Sorry for making you do your job,' I said and immediately regretted it. He was pompous and he was arrogant but he was the only friend I had. In a softer voice, I said, 'Really, I didn't knowingly do it.'

'Well, guilty or not, luck might be on your side. You've become an international incident. The papers are clamouring for your release. And that puts pressure on the boys upstairs. If His Majesty's Government doesn't do anything, it makes them look bad. If the Soviets are lenient with you, it might make them look good in the eyes of the outside world.'

'Last time you said you were doing everything in your power.'

'Well, we are.'

'You implied that it wouldn't amount to very much. You said you didn't have much influence over events.

'You've got a lot to learn about propaganda and diplomacy, Grover. "Doing everything possible' can mean anything from coming round for a chat and making you feel better to threatening sanctions unless we secure your immediate release. It all depends how important you are. I think you'll find things start moving quite quickly from now on.'

Sure enough I was summoned to Feodorov's office the next day. He looked disappointed. There was a document on his desk. He shoved it across to me. 'Sign it.'

I hesitated. 'What am I signing?'

'It is your indictment. You're going to trial. You must sign to show you understand the charges.'

I read it through. A summary of the evidence against me. Illegal violation of sovereign territory, flying over forbidden frontier zones and damage to a field belonging to Glukhovo Soviet Collective. A smile crept across my lips.

'The charges for spying and racketeering have been dropped, Grover, but rest assured I will be pressing for the maximum sentence. You have two defence solictors to choose from, both top men. Pick one.'

The names meant nothing to me so I chose the first on the list, a Mr Komodov. Feodorov grunted and filled in the necessary form. I waited for him to excuse me, but nothing was said. So I asked him if I could leave. He looked up at me, hatred in his eyes, and said, 'You'll never see your wife again.'

I had misjudged Maclean. He was still a junior, so that might account for his persistence. He really had done all that was possible. Clearly, if Feodorov was disappointed, that could only be good. I could put my case before a judge, plead guilty with mitigating circumstances. I had a chance. And if Feodorov had been wrong about me going to jail for a very long time, which now seemed to be the case, then he might also be wrong about Lena. If there was pressure from all sides to see a diplomatic resolution to the problems I'd caused then maybe they'd let Lena come with me too. After all, as Maclean had said, it would be a massive propaganda coup. Bolsheviks have a heart too. What use was a scared, unhappy nurse to them? And what harm could it do?

For the first time in months, a smile crossed my lips.

The trial date was set for New Year's Eve. I had a week of waiting and wondering to get through. Komodov came to visit me on Boxing Day. He bought me a box of Belgian Chocolates. 'You can spend the day getting fat like everyone else in England,' he told me. They must have cost him a fortune and I thanked him profusely. I had nothing to give back except problems.

He sat down beside me on the bed, which shuddered under our combined weight, and brought out his folder. The situation, he explained, was simple. Since I was pleading guilty, his job was to try for as light a sentence as possible. The rest, he said, was dependent on how good the judges were feeling on that particular day.

I asked him if he knew anything about Lena. He had done his homework. As far as he knew, she *had* been brought in, and been given the heavy treatment. Nothing physical, but they had tried to crush her mentally.

'They don't like the mix,' Komodov said simply. 'She is fine Russian stock, you are tainting her. There are some outside of this room who will do everything to keep you apart.'

'Do *you* believe it is wrong?'

Komodov stood up and said stiffly, 'I am a solicitor not a philosopher.'

'I'm sorry. Stupid question.' Even by asking it, I could jeopardise his career. It just took one guard, one official to overhear and elaborate. Even bringing the chocolates had been risky.

I wanted him on my side. I also wanted desperately to find a Russian in power on my side.

Maclean and Komodov were waiting for me on the steps of Moscow City Court as I was bundled out of the police van. It was my first taste of fresh air in seven weeks and it was sweet. Handcuffed to a grim-faced guard I shuffled through the snow.

'How do I look?'

Maclean gave me an embarrassed smile. 'You'll do.'

The trial had been moved forward a couple of hours at the last minute, giving me scant time to prepare myself. Under my leather flying coat was the shirt I had flown in, still crumpled, still sticky. They'd boxed my clothes away in the prisoner's personal effects room and they'd lain there all this time. I'd managed to reclaim one of the silk ties I'd bought in Stockholm but it was stuck around my neck like an afterthought.

'I'm a mess.'

'Heroes can look like rogues,' Maclean said. 'The world's press is in there. You can't lose.'

Komodov gave him a sharp look and stepped in, a reassuring hand on my arm. He was not given to such sentimental predictions. 'Soviet judges don't go by appearances. If you're late, however, you really won't look good, so let's move.'

Like the town hall in Grozny, this court was a beautiful throwback to pre-Revolution days. The central hall had a floor of polished marble that echoed each footstep high into the arched ceiling.

I had been expecting almost a secret trial but when I was led into the courtroom, there was an expectant hush. The gallery was seething with reporters, photographers and embassy officials. Maclean had told me that Lena and I were becoming news items but this was incredible. I felt suddenly sure that it was going to be alright. Not even the might of the Soviet authorities could ignore this presence.

The handcuffs were taken off and I made my way to the dock, Komodov by my side at all times. The bench was deserted, and for a while I stood there not really knowing what to do. I looked around, smiled at some of the correspondents. One photographer sneaked a quick shot and was immediately escorted out of the court by a couple of burly security guards.

Then a bell rang announcing the arrival of the judges, one woman and two men. Everyone stood as they filed into their places at the bench. Komodov whispered. 'The woman is the head judge here. She is renowned for her fairness. Make the most of your story, it might sway her.'

She sat in the centre, her well-groomed assistants beside her, and motioned for the court to do likewise. When the charges were read out there was a muted cheer from the gallery. This was the first official sign that I was no longer considered a spy. The judge cast a weary eye upwards and said in a deliberate voice, 'I will have no rowdiness in this court, if you please. This is a serious case and will be dealt with as such. Any person who participates in premature celebrations is both foolish,' she cast a glance at a correspondent who had bellowed particularly loudly, 'and in danger of being extricated from this court. I hope that is understood.' Then she turned to me.

'Brian Grover, you have been informed of and understand the charges brought against you. How do you plead?'

'Guilty, your honour.'

She chuckled. 'There is no need to call me that. This is not England.' Her associates smiled. 'Just answer the questions simply.'

'My apologies.'

'They are not needed either.'

To this I just shrugged my shoulders, which seemed to amuse the court, though I have no idea why.

She continued, 'There are no witnesses to be called in this case, either for the defence or the prosecution so this should not take up much of our time. You took off from Stockholm aerodrome on the morning of 14th November 1938, and landed at Glukhovo at 3.00 pm the same day. Correct?'

I cleared my throat. 'That is correct.'

'You immediately asked to be arrested and taken to Moscow.'

'Yes.'

For the next quarter of an hour the questions followed almost exactly the ones I had first been asked by Feodorov and his team. The judge, as Komodov had said, seemed fair in her questioning, interrogating for facts, not nuances of meaning that might be twisted out of my answers. However, when she was finished she gave way to her two assistants who were keener to unearth the real motivation behind my actions.

'You say you came back to be with your wife.'

'She is all I care about now.'

'If that is the case, then why did you leave in the first place?' The prosecution counsel's eyes were eager. He was aiming for the jugular and had found it.

The question took me aback. I hadn't prepared for it. Frantically I searched for a plausible answer. If I mentioned Madeleine, no amount of soul-wringing explanation would persuade them. If I said that I felt I was being hounded out of Grozny, was unhappy at my situation in Moscow, then the trial would take on a political tilt, something which had to be avoided at all costs.

'Well?'

I became aware of the whole court watching me, waiting

263

on my answer. My heart thumped in a hollow cage – *say-something, say-something* it whispered.

'I . . . I heard that my old employers might be taking on staff again, for exploration work in Iran. It was only a rumour on the grapevine, but I thought I should follow it up. I told Lena I had to return to London –'

'So you were prepared to abandon your wife, the woman you say now you would die for, in order to make money? What sort of a romantic are you?'

The twisting had started in earnest. How could I get him off my back?

'We arranged for her to follow me later when her exit visa was processed. I thought it would be a formality, since we were married . . . But the visa never came. And I was not allowed back into the country.'

'And is that unreasonable?' the prosecutor asked. 'You decide you can find better work elsewhere, perhaps taking trade secrets with you?'

'It wasn't like that . . .' I was floundering for words. I looked in desperation at Komodov, who stood up immediately.

'If I may intervene, I think we are straying from the point. Mr Grover has admitted all charges, he freely gave himself up. His motives are clear for all to see.'

The judge nodded, and said to the prosecutor, 'I think your line of questioning has gone far enough. Do you have any more queries?'

The prosecutor, put in his place by her stare, shook his head.

'Defence. Your mitigation.'

Komodov stepped forward, addressing the court as a whole rather than just the judge. He had told me his speech would be short. 'They don't like us to go on,' he had said.

'The Soviet Government prides itself on its security.

The guarding of our frontiers against the intrusion of spies from foreign countries is of paramount importance, and rightly so. My client, Brian Montague Grover, was ingenious and resolute in his deception, and he broke one of our sacred laws. Clearly, as he himself confesses, he is guilty. But an examination of his case reveals no political motives. On the contrary, he came at great personal risk and expense to draw attention to his domestic affairs. He chanced everything for his dear wife who he hasn't seen for five years. He knew the dangers and was prepared to face them. While the Soviet State may frown upon frivolous attachments between foreigners and Russian women, so much more do they respect and approve the genuine devotion of a committed couple. Here is a young man who became dissatisfied with capitalism, who entered the Soviet Union to engage in work that aided the First Five Year Plan. His record was exemplary.'

He paused and turned in a graceful sweep to address the judge directly. 'In summation, he must know that the Soviet frontier cannot be violated with impunity, but nevertheless has a right to expect a just verdict from a Proletarian Court.'

The judges acknowledged the end of his speech then retired to consider their verdict. Komodov and I were taken to a bare antechamber where we sat down on a hard wooden bench and stared in silence at the walls.

There was nothing left now but to wait. I was quite sure Komodov was in no mood to speak. He hadn't been pleased with the way I'd answered some of the questions. I tried to put on a brave face and thanked him for his excellent final speech.

When he looked at me his eyes were dull. 'I've had a lot of practice. This was not a difficult case. I defended in the show trials.'

'Who?'

'It doesn't matter who. They were all nobodies by the time they were dragged before the prosecutors. You'll know how it ended.' He looked suddenly forlorn. His life had been devoted to defending clients who were condemned before they even knew they were going to be charged. The Great Purge was over but not for him. It had stayed with him, a memory that could never be shaken off. I found myself consoling him, rather than he me.

'The cards were stacked against you. You could have done no more.'

'I could,' he said fiercely but under his breath so no-one could hear. 'I could have told the truth.'

'And found yourself in the dock.'

He sighed. 'You are right, of course. There is only so much anyone can do. But you did more. That is why there are so many hounds out there, baying for your story.'

'They may be helping me. World opinion. Extra pressure.'

'Don't count on it.'

There was a rap on the door and we jumped up.

'We'll soon see if you're right.'

I gripped the dock as the judge stood up to deliver her verdict.

'After careful consideration, the court finds you guilty on all counts . . . However, the reasons behind the crime cannot be overlooked. We consider it an established fact that the defendant is sincerely in love with a Soviet woman. Their love has passed the test of time and demanding separation and is therefore to be respected. For this reason, and this reason alone you will not be sentenced to imprisonment as would normally be the case. You are fined £60 sterling, your plane is to be confiscated and you are exiled from the Soviet Union for five years. You have four days in which to lodge an appeal if you so wish, during which time you will be required to stay in Lubyanka jail. That is all.'

With her final words, the court erupted in a riot of cheering and applause. Dazed, I looked around at the public gallery, the photographers were shaking their fists at me in salute, the embassy officials were shaking hands on good work done. Even Maclean was smiling. *Didn't they understand*?

I turned to Komodov, who had his head sunk low. He alone knew.

'They won't let me see her! I want to appeal, Komodov. I have to!'

'I would advise strongly against it.'

'But –'

He shook his head. 'You're a free man, Brian. That is a great concession. I am sorry, but you must accept it.'

The courtroom smudged as tears filled my eyes. The cheers became hollow cries, the smiles distorted into diabolical sneers. As the press pack closed in, firing questions, security guards manhandled me down the steps. After that I remember only vague images. The blackness of the van, the iron smell of old blood as my face pressed against the hard floor, then nothing at all.

I woke up to the light of the bare bulb in my cell room and the harsh clanking of steel against steel. At first I forgot where I was, forgot I had been to trial. Then it came back, the clean sharp facts. I would stay here for a while until they sorted out the paperwork and processed the payment of my fine. Then I would be free to go. It had come to nothing. I'd nearly killed myself for precisely nothing. I would return home to nothing except reporters desperate for my story and parents desperate to play it down. And in five years, when the term of my exile had elapsed I could try again. If Lena were still alive, if she hadn't been quietly imprisoned on some trumped-up charge when the fuss had died down. They had her marked now. She was on the list. Liaison with a criminal foreigner, marriage to an abortionist on the run. She wouldn't last long.

I wondered if she knew I'd even managed to get here, that she'd been questioned by the same man as me, that after five years she'd been less than a corridor away from me. My antics wouldn't have been reported in *Isvestia* or *Pravda*. And Feodorov wouldn't have told her. He'd let her worries fester out of spite. Why was she being brought in after all this time? she'd be asking and she might guess the answer, but she wouldn't know for sure. And that was the worst feeling of all. Perhaps now she'd never know. We'd have to feed off our memories, the few months out of the years we'd known each other when we'd truly been left alone to be ourselves. We'd have to believe that they were enough.

The cell door opened and a guard barked 'Dress, Mr Grover.' He threw my clothes on the bed. They were clean and newly pressed.

'But I'm not leaving until tomorrow?' I said.

His face remained impassive. 'Dress please,' he said again.

We walked along the corridor I had gone down so many times before. I was joined by another guard. They pressed in on either side. I stared down at the floor and watched my feet moving forwards. Each step seemed to take an interminably long time. I asked where I was going but was met with silence. Soon I was in a part of the building I'd never seen before. Door after door passed by, each decorated with a brass number placed neatly in exactly the same place. Occasionally someone would shuffle out of a room clutching a sheaf of papers and sneak a quick glance at me as they went about their business. Not just another prisoner. The Englishman, the madman. Our eyes would meet and there would be an instantaneous shift in their expression, a sharp momentary interest smothered immediately by the realisation that any interest at all might be frowned upon.

We walked for five minutes and I thought of the thousands of people employed in this place, each with their own room, their own desk, and their own typewriters, all filling out forms in triplicate, paper decisions that changed individuals' lives forever. This was the heart of the machine. Where the sticky-tape to catch the flies was painstakingly manufactured. Somewhere in here, all my applications for visas had been scrutinised, assessed and rejected.

We stopped. One of the guards turned and knocked at the door in one swift movement which suggested he, at least, knew exactly where he was.

The room was large. A hazy light streamed in from two barred windows casting faint shadows over a thick rug which covered most of the floor. The floor itself was marble, meticulously polished. At the far end of the room was an ornate ebony fireplace and mantelpiece, on top of which stood various antique statues and ornaments. But for the obligatory picture of Lenin casting his eye over the proceedings, the place looked more like a lounge in an exclusive private members' club.

Before me was a mahogany desk, inlaid with brown leather, and the back of someone who must be extremely powerful. At first there was silence and I was not sure what to do. Then I heard a rustle of paper and Laurenti Beria swivelled round in his chair. He smiled immediately. A wide affable smile.

The second most powerful man in the Soviet Union had

aged. There were bags under his eyes, and the hair on his head had receded, though it was still putting up a struggle. What little remained was going grey.

'So Mr Grover, a reunion.' His handshake was firm. 'Please, sit down.' He gestured at a chair. I took it gratefully, my legs weak with anticipation.

Beria looked down at a grey file lying on the desk. He doodled a circle on a spare piece of paper and delicately filled it in. Without lifting his head he said:

'You may wonder what you're doing here.'

I nodded, and felt suddenly stupid because obviously he wasn't looking at me. It didn't seem to matter that he got no answer for he carried on. 'It's quite simple really. I wanted to see in person the Mr Grover who violated our international borders with the aid of a second-rate map, a cheap compass and a rusty-engined light aircraft.'

Now he leaned back and the leather chair squeaked with the movement. 'The very same man I handed an envelope to, how long ago was it, six years? You're a remarkable man, Brian. I don't forget men like you, I make it my business to know all about them.'

I wanted to say to him, 'I don't doubt it.' I certainly thought it but the use of my first name put me off-balance. The seeming sincerity in his voice made my pride swell. He had created a bond between us in a few seconds without me even realising it, without me wanting it. Languidly tapping his pen against his knuckles, he stared right at me, his dark eyes searching mine.

'You've caused us a bit of trouble, Brian.'

There it was. The crunch. And now the punishment. Nobody gets off easily here. Komodov was right. To walk away free was a great concession. Now I'd done something to make them change their minds.

'And if I may say so,' he continued, 'your attitude has surprised us all.'

He could tell I was waiting on every word he said. He was enjoying it, this 'hero' cowering before him, every muscle in my body rigid.

'Do you think you are a brave man, Mr Grover?' He paused, just long enough for me to open my mouth in response, then continued, 'Or a foolish one?' Each word was clipped now, the syllables precisely pronounced.

He was leaving it open to me. It was time to make my final plea.

'With respect, your Excellency, I think it is neither foolish nor brave to want to live with my wife. I have to live with Ileana. Nothing else matters.'

It seemed so simple to me, so obvious. But I wasn't sure that Beria could see it.

'I like it Brian,' he said. 'But do you really think we should allow our people to be contaminated by Western values? What would happen to this great nation of ours that we have rebuilt with such toil, such diligence? Should we let it crumble into dust through greedy hopes and self-seeking actions?'

I had gone too far. By stating plainly what I thought, I had put him on the defensive. I wanted to tell him that I loved my time in Russia, had learned much from its people, had spent some of the best years of my life here and never regretted it once. But now it would seem fickle, as if I was only saying it to flatter him.

Then he started laughing. 'Do I live up to expectations? Good little speech eh?' He learned fowards, switching to serious mode in an instant. 'You think your words might sway whatever decision it is I am about to make. Do you think you have that power? I must applaud your belief in the power of the individual, however naive. But individuals are such malleable beings. Cluttered with emotions and personal want. Facts, plans, logic, consequences, they are the only things to believe in. The truth is, cases like yours need careful consideration. *Collective* consideration. They must be discussed at the highest levels and weighed up until a course of action is agreed upon.' He nodded at the ceiling, raising his eyebrows in respect for some higher deity. 'If you see what I mean.'

'I think so.'

'I'm sure you do. I have spoken to Ileana myself.'

'You've seen her! How is she?'

'I have spoken to Ileana,' he repeated calmly, 'and she is fine. She's a good woman, a credit to herself and her country. You needn't worry about anything Feodorov said. It's all a ploy to get at the truth. She was brought in for routine questioning and released. It may surprise you to hear but we are good to the goodies, and nasty to the nasties.' He smiled, that quick snap at the corners of the mouth that never held, and I remembered him shaking my hand on the podium. The thin gesture, the dead eyes.

'I remember your heroics at Grozny. You did us a good turn, so . . .' He paused, savouring the moment of truth. Then he drew back from it. 'You seem to be straight people, both of you.' At this, he giggled.

He was going to let me see her, I knew that now. He might have said it in a roundabout way, but that's what he meant. We could leave together, start our life again. I wondered what the expression on her face would be when she saw me, what words would come out first after five long years and then I imagined us in silence, a warm silence as I wrapped my arms around her and hugged her for hours and hours.

Beria leaned forward until his face was only a few inches from mine. His breath smelt sweet.

'You have three days to leave the country. Together.'

I closed my eyes. 'Thank you,' I said.

When I opened them, he was looking at his watch. 'I have twenty minutes before my next meeting. Would you care for a vodka? A little celebration. I don't get a lot of time when I'm not meant to be doing anything. Seems as good a reason as any to drink to, don't you think? The sublimest drink must be accompanied by the sublimest music.' He put on Prokofiev's first symphony, the Classical and poured me a hefty measure. We sipped together as the sound of violins and shrill flutes cascaded around the room.

It was beautiful but bizarre sitting in that room, soaking in the music and the vodka, knowing that the fight was over, eager to leave but aware that to do so might be taken wrongly. We chatted for a while, him asking questions, me answering. He wanted to know about my parents, about my work on the oil fields and did I have any brothers and sisters? And what were they like? All the time I talked I waited for him to turn, for me to trap myself with some careless word, fearing his notorious changes of mood.

The last chord ended abruptly as Beria downed the remnants of his drink, timing our meeting to the last drop. He stood up and took an envelope from the file. 'Inside here is the rest of your life. Her exit visa, enough roubles to get you both to England and her address. She should be there now. Get off at Yaroslavsky station, a pleasant ramble for two miles and you find yourself in Bolshevo. She doesn't know you're in Russia. After all the trouble we've been to, don't give her a heart attack. Take it.'

I reached out, and he whisked it away from my hand.

What? I thought.

'Before you go I have one more question. Where do you intend to make your home?'

'In England. Why?'

He shook his head slowly. 'Don't live in England. It's not safe.'

'What do you mean?'

'War. It will happen soon. Your country will be attacked and I fear she will be overpowered.' There was no flippancy this time, no idle chatter. He meant every word he said. 'Take your wife somewhere far away where you can enjoy your life together in peace.'

He handed me the envelope again and this time let me take it.

We shook hands. As I was at the door, about to leave, he said, 'Hurry home. I might change my mind.'

I grabbed my belongings from the release office, waving my papers like a man who'd just won a lottery. I ran through the sets of double doors, my haversack banging against my back, and out into the streets of Moscow.

It was pitch black outside and snowing violently. No cars passed, no people walked by me as I made my way to the station. A biting wind blew into my face, whipped snow like dust from the untrodden pavements. Under a street lamp I stopped, collar up and back to the onslaught, to rip open the envelope Beria had given me. I pulled out the address. The words were scrawled in an almost illegible handwriting. I held it away from me to see it in stronger light, made out the word Bolshevo. I headed towards the station. The last train was running just past midnight. I looked at my watch – 11.58 – and ran until my lungs felt they would explode.

The train was leaving as I got there. I followed it all the way up the platform, gauging its speed, and leapt onto the footrail under a door on the second last carriage. Angling myself to the side, I swung it open and collapsed into the nearest seat. For a few moments I just sat there, catching my breath, wheezing like an old man. I leaned against the window, watched the white-capped trees flitting by faster and faster as the train picked up speed, and prayed to God that I could find Lena's house. It was an area I didn't know well.

Half an hour later, I stepped onto Yaroslavsky platform. Thick dark clouds loomed overhead, the moon hidden behind them. Beyond the confines of the station buildings there was no light to guide me, only the faint outlines of a track leading into open countryside. This was the outermost edge of Moscow, where the suburb dissolved into an endless expanse of flat land. Two miles Beria had told me. A pleasant ramble, Beria had told me. Who said the Russians had no sense of humour?

The weather was getting worse. I pulled my cap tight around my ears, bent my head into the wind and ploughed on. The further I went, the deeper the drifts got until I found myself wading knee-deep in the darkness. Beria had also said something else, and it began to plague me. *I might change my mind*. The man had enjoyed playing me along. Would he do it again?

It's not worth thinking about, just keep moving. If I didn't I would freeze. Lena would walk into Yaroslavsky tomorrow morning to be greeted by the frozen corpse of a husband she hadn't seen for five years.

Ice formed a crust on my nose. The track climbed the only hill for miles around. A hundred times I slipped and fell. Soon I was on all fours, crawling to get to the top. When I finally did, I sank down in the drifts, my head lolling from side to side. I wanted to stay there. The last of my energy had drained away. Words from Lena's letter kept coming back. *God never meant us to be together*.

I became aware of a yellow dot swaying in the distance, down at the bottom of the hill, no more than a few hundred yards. At first I thought it was someone walking with a lamp. Then I realised the dot was moving because my head was. With all my will I held it still, and stared harder.

There were squares on the horizon, deeper black than the background. Solid things. Houses. It must be Bolshevo.

With renewed strength I picked myself up, and slipped down the slope towards the light. I fell on my backside half way down, my leather coat catching as I tumbled. I ripped it away. The track levelled off, the light became brighter. As I got closer, I saw it came from the first building in the group. I looked for a street sign but it could have been anywhere, covered under the drifts. I stumbled up to the old oak door.

And hesitated. My hand hovered over the knocker. The light had come from an oil lamp in the window, a diffuse glow through faded curtains. I went over to it, peered inside, but could make nothing out. I had to knock. This was the only place that showed any sign of life. Everyone knew everyone in these sorts of places. They might know where she lived, if not they could direct me to her street.

Make yourself presentable, you don't want to kill them with fright. I pulled off my cap and patted down my hair. Next I stuffed my gloves in my pockets and rubbed my face. Coarse stubble like sandpaper grated my skin. Nothing I could do about that. I rehearsed my line – Sorry to bother you so late but I'm looking for Ileana Petrovna. I got lost in the snow, but I know she lives somewhere round here. Can you help me? Probably I'd get a slammed door in the face, but there was nothing to lose.

I lifted the knocker, rapped it three times. I waited, stamped my feet (though I knew it would do no good), was reaching for it again, when I heard the shuffle of feet behind the door. A scraping as the latch chain was put on.

The door creaked open. A thin head-scarfed face peeked out, covered in shadow. I opened my mouth to speak, then saw the mole on her cheek. The face peered forward, the lips moved, frightened, 'Yes?'

Silence. Then a whisper. 'Brian . . . no, it can't be.

Brian!' She yanked at the latch, ripped it from its hold. The door swung open and snowflakes danced into her house. We stared at each other like strangers, me outside, her in, the line between us blurring as the winds blew more and more snow into the hall. She was thin and frail, her hair tied back harshly, a darkness under her eyes. But it was Lena.

Five years older. Five years more beautiful.

*

The ship's horn sounded as we entered Harwich harbour.

'Looks like we stopped the traffic.'

'There are so many of them!' Lena cried. 'Why are they here?'

'You're royalty now. I should have brought you a diamond tiara in Hambourg. You'll be the talk of the society columns.'

'Brian, I'm scared.'

I squeezed her hand. 'Relax,' I said. 'Enjoy it while it lasts.'

We smiled and we smiled again as questions were fired at us from every angle. A perfect New Year story. Someone threw confetti as we descended the steps of the great liner. Cheering crowds strained against a thin line of policemen. There must have been over a thousand people jostling for position, some with flowers, some with WELCOME HOME banners, most just there to greet us. Lena slipped her arm around my back and rested her head on my shoulder. She held me urgently, bewildered but excited.

'Brian?' There was a tremor in her voice but it was gone the moment it appeared. She stared at the rows of out-stretched hands not sure what to do. I turned her face away from them and kissed her.

'It'll be alright,' I whispered in her ear.

'Where's Frank? He said he'd be here.'

We searched the sea of faces. 'There!' she squealed and pointed. 'There he is!' He was right at the back, pushing his way through. As we got closer, he saw we were watching him. He lifted a banner above his head.

YOU LOST YOUR BET. YOU OWE ME

'What does it say? What does it say?' Lena asked.

Before I could answer, there was a loud pop above us. We turned to see the captain of the ship frantically shaking a huge bottle of champagne. It shot up in a frothy fountain and cascaded all over us.

Lena shrieked, then licked her lips. 'Tastes good.'

'As good as in the Metropol?' I shouted.

'Better.'

I picked her up and swung her round as the champagne drenched us head to toe. The cameras clicked, bulbs popped and the world watched us spin.

We became freeze-frames, dancers caught in a flash of light.

EPILOGUE

SOUTH AFRICA
1992

It crept up gently in her sleep. For many weeks she had been frail, though still just as headstrong. The body winds down even if the spirit won't accept it. She refused her food, told me to stop fussing. I think she knew.

We lay together on the night she died, her head on my chest. It was dry and hot and still. We talked in snatched whispers as though the silence itself were listening. She told me my heart sounded as loud as an ox and just for a while it seemed we were back in her little house in Grozny discovering miraculous lands in the shadows on the ceiling. She said, given it all again, she would not change a thing, that she had seen more than most people could ever have wished. The words came hoarse out of her mouth, like crumpled paper. And then she looked up at me and said, 'Thank you'. The smile was still there, but it was transformed. There was a dignity in it, a confidence that came with acceptance of the inevitable. I buried my head in her neck. I didn't want her to see me crying.

And then she changed everything. 'You could at least have shaved,' she said.

'I'm sorry.'

'Too late for that now,' she rasped and then her chest started to heave in a terrible way. I drew back to give her space. Her hand gripped mine with ferocious strength and her eyes sparkled. Suddenly I realised she was laughing.

'Get back here. I'm not finished yet,' she ordered. I tightened the sheets around us and curled my arms behind her shoulders. She peered at me with an eagle eye. 'Will you remember me?' she asked.

'Don't say things like that.' I turned away. 'I won't need to remember you. You'll still be here.'

'But *will* you?'

'Lena, how could I not?'

She shuffled under the blankets, rearranging her body with difficulty until her head was back on my chest. In a quiet, wicked voice she said, 'Alright Mr Grover,' and bit my nipple with all her might. I yelped. 'You'll remember me now,' she said.

Soon after she turned onto her back. 'I need to sleep. Stay with me, please?' I nodded, smiling silently as her eyes closed. Outside, cicadas clicked in the grass, the earth contracted as the night deepened. I thought again of the time we returned to England. I took her to the old house in Monmouth where I'd lived as a child. We went there in late January, one blustery afternoon. I wanted to show her round the grounds, the little pond where the tadpoles had hatched, the tunnel through the copse. We walked across the green where I had stroked diamonds from blades of grass and I told her more about Miss Roberts. She thought it a very peculiar institution, having a governess, very English. She laughed at my nostalgia and pointedly explained to me, 'There is no past. There is only ever now. But ours will be a good now.'

I grabbed her hand and started running. She stumbled behind me, laughing and slipping on patches of frost.

'What are you doing?' she cried.

'I want you to see something,' I called back between breaths.

We reached the grove and I was struck once again, after all that time, by the stillness of the place. It was untouched, wilder than when I had played in it as a child. Ferns spilled out over the old pathway, branches broken in autumn gales hung limply from lopsided tree trunks. It had been left for so long that it had become its own little world. Whatever went on outside, it stopped at the beginning of the tunnel.

It was hard work fighting our way through but I wanted to show her. I had almost given up hope of finding it when we came to a clearing and there, to the left surrounded by long wisps of dark green grass was the tree stump.

'Come on.' I beckoned to Lena and she looked at me as though I was mad. She caught up, fidgeting as I stared at the stump. It had rotted away inside, each year line slowly weathered until it crumbled into a brown sludgy pile in the middle. But on the outside great swathes of moss had grown into the bark and at the base a small patch of snowdrops had broken through the soil.

'Why do you show me this?' Lena asked.

I told her about my tantrum over Alex murdering the tree and about how upset Miss Roberts had been. I told her how in my imagination I had envisaged the tree in all its majesty, then opened my eyes and seen the stump again. 'There is a past,' I said, 'but it changes each time you go back to look at it.'

The grandfather clock in the hallway chimed four and I woke up with a jolt. The temperature had plummeted the way it does on clear nights about to turn into morning. When I breathed there was mist in the air. Lena was lying in the same position, her head still resting lightly on my chest, but she was no longer breathing.

FIELDS OF LIGHT

That was three years ago to the day. Right now, I'm holding the miniature of Lena in its silver case. It is engraved deep around the sides, intricate little swirls on each corner. The grooves are filled with an accumulation of dirt older even than me. Specks of dust, skin, grease — pressed into the metal until they have become a part of the case itself. Fragments of lives long gone, of those who haved touched it for the briefest moment. I turn it in my hand, release the catch. It clicks open with the tiniest of squeaks. I touch the paper. The portrait is fading and the edges are crinkled brown under the frame. It is tiny, a wash of watercolour no more than thirty deft strokes, but the likeness is there. Her hair is a rusty brown with a few wisps blowing away from her head. I remember the first time I felt her hair, the first time I pressed my face against it. I remember the strands brushing my cheeks as we made love. I remember the crease at the corner of her mouth, the mole at the back of her neck, the small dimple just above her chin.

An opened case on a table in a drawing room. So it ends there? A small object, insignificant to the disinterested, worth a few pounds at auction maybe. What'll you bid? To the interested party it is priceless. It was passed down from mother to daughter on Lena's side of the family and I should, in turn, pass it on to our children when I die. But I would like to put it somewhere, bury it by the cut-down tree in Monmouth so that one day, much later, it will be found again, scraped from the soil with its hinges snapped and its metal gone black.

An artefact, with a different story to tell.

Perhaps I should make one last journey.